P9-DVO-225

The
Umbrella
Mender

A NOVEL

Christine Fischer Guy

A Buckrider Book

© Christine Fischer Guy, 2014

No part of this publication may be reproduced, stored in a retrieval system
or transmitted, in any form or by any means, without the prior written
consent of the publisher or a license from the Canadian Copyright
Licensing Agency (Access Copyright). For an Access Copyright license,
visit www.accesscopyright.ca or call toll free to 1-800-893-5777.

Buckrider Books in an imprint of Wolsak and Wynn Publishers.

Cover images: istock
Cover and interior design: Marijke Friesen
Author photograph: Diana Renelli, drenelli.com
Typeset in Adobe Caslon
Printed by Ball Media, Brantford, Canada

The publisher gratefully acknowledges the support of the Canada Council
for the Arts, the Ontario Arts Council and the Canada Book Fund.

Buckrider Books
280 James Street North
Hamilton, ON
Canada L8R 2L3

Library and Archives Canada Cataloguing in Publication

Fischer Guy, Christine, author
The umbrella mender / Christine Fischer Guy.

ISBN 978-1-894987-90-5 (pbk.)

I. Title.

PS8611.I78U43 2014   C813'.6   C2014-904077-6

For Drew, with love

mush-faker *n.* (also **mush-fakir**)

An itinerant umbrella repairer, a tinker.

···

1899: 'J. Flynt,' IV.395 *Tramping with Tramps.*
Mush-fakir, an umbrella mender. The umbrellas he
collects are frequently not returned.

– *Oxford English Dictionary*

PROLOGUE

Cochrane, Ontario, June 1952

SHE HAD STOPPED CRYING OUT. Over the course of many hours, she had learned to let the contractions catch and overtake her, to stop trying to outrun them. She was naked and sweating, reclined on the damp earth of the silo floor. Between pulses of her heart that shushed like the ocean in her ears, she could hear the river.

The pressure of the child, hard and unyielding, gave her the impression that she was giving birth to all the babies in all the places of the world. She saw her shadow: she was voluptuous and perched on the brink of creation, a sketch on a cave wall, a sculpture anointed with the oil of a million million fingertips in a remote clifftop shrine. Then she laughed, delirious with the pain and the solitude, the fragile echo glancing off the walls and spiralling up and out into the night.

Even though Hazel had seen this many times before, even if she knew the mushroom dampness of a baby's head as it appeared between a mother's thighs, the pain of crowning was exquisite. Her hands curled into fists and her fingernails cut into her palms. With the next contraction she bent forward instinctively and the baby's head emerged. In the next wave, the twin mountains of the shoulders. She slipped her hands under the baby's tiny arms and lifted, straight up, as if her daughter should be launched into the sky, toward the stars, back to heaven.

She held the baby at arm's length but couldn't bring her into focus: she could distinguish the ends of her from the beginnings of the night, the way she pulled her knees toward her chest, the oblong shape of her head, the spastic movements of her arms. But she couldn't fix on her daughter's face. She sat until her nurse's brain urged its wisdom: her blood pressure was spiking. What she needed was rest and a cool cloth. But just then the baby's voice broke the silence in that small stone enclosure. She tucked the child into the crook of her arm and reached into her bag for the clamp and scissors she'd brought, and used them on the cord without fuss. She knew how to do this. Then she leaned against the wall and let her head rest.

The rim of the roofless silo described the night sky. The baby suckled until she slept. Hazel laid herself and her daughter on the blanket and was drifting into sleep when her body twitched as if to stop her rolling off the edge of the earth. What her brain had forgotten, her body could not. She crawled toward the crude low opening, moved the suitcase and the wooden box away. The humid air smelled of manure and algae and fresh-cut hay. Her knees buckled when she pushed herself up to standing. She collapsed against the wall and slid to a squat, barely feeling the scrape of stones as they tore minute openings into her skin. One more contraction and there was so much blood, a flood of it, on the ground between her feet. She flicked her tongue over dry lips and wished that the water had not run out hours earlier.

There was cricket song and stars and night sky and tall grass and a baby, her baby, inside the silo behind her. She walked unsteadily toward a cold firepit a few feet away and picked up a charred stick. She pressed it against the cool wall of the silo and, with the blue light of the moon illuminating her progress, she drew.

ONE

Cambridge, Ontario, April 2010

MUCH IS UNDECIDED. THE DOCTORS talk over me, debating the possibility that I'll speak again. I feel more fluent now than I ever was. Colours are radiant and I am one with the intricate weave of the curtains and the soft nubs of cotton on the blankets and the currents of air sweeping out into the hallway. I am perfect and whole. I am everywhere.

There is a sound I recognize without effort. A name. My name. It sets down boundaries and calls me back. Hazel. I am Hazel. I shrink and miraculously fit back inside the single small body that is somewhat worse for wear in a bed that is not mine in a hospital room that is stripped of every comfort and every untidy incidental beauty. There is a startling rush of memory like breath and the habit of thought returns, fluid as a well-trained muscle.

"Jude is here. You remember your grandniece, don't you?" The nurse repeats your name in her singsong voice as though I could leave you behind so easily and I want to slap her. Nurses make the worst patients and even if I haven't practiced in almost six decades it seems a lasting condition. Back then I couldn't always follow the rules to the satisfaction of my superiors either and as I was only in my twenties you couldn't say it was the cantankerous reaction of an old lady to a brain incident.

I can't argue. The stroke has seen to that. But I can move my hands and I can blink and I can hear you, Jude. Food still tastes good and if someone would bring me a glass of wine I would drink it down and hold it out for more.

My mind starts down a known pathway. He is there as always. For the first time in all the years since, I'm charged with the certainty that more time wouldn't have bought greater happiness. We couldn't have expected more of each other. It would be untrue to say that I never raged against the injustice of it all, that I never wished that things could have been different, that I never tried to close myself against the million natural shocks that repeated exposure brought. But these were momentary lapses in faith and nothing more. Even in the depths of my misery I never tried to bargain away the fact of his existence and will not do so now. It could have gone no other way.

I wouldn't fault you for thinking that this act of self-forgiveness is an expected after-effect of what I've been through. You might blame my advancing years and the vagaries of memory but I assure you that I'm of sound mind. Each prick of conscience is as sharp now as it ever was. But offered the chance I would make the same decisions, endure every anxiety, walk every path in the same steps to ensure the accident of my acquaintance with him. There is no delusion in this line of thinking and I haven't come to it in haste. Sixty years is long enough.

I told no one about him, as though my tongue was a blunt object jailed in my skull. And now it is.

WE WERE GOOD COMPANY FOR ONE another at the lake, Jude, weren't we? You'd arrive on two wheels, cold with the sting of the spring wind. I'd leave my boots at the back door as if I'd just gone in for a moment and watch from the window as you set your bike down and surveyed the piles of dirt and garden tools. You'd call "Hello, Aunt Hazel" as though there was only a single generation between us.

Until this spring when I asked my sister about her granddaughter I'd met you only twice. I told her I was getting on in years and needed help with the yard. That was mostly true. Your mother left one day without so much as a note and you were in a hard place. Maybe there was something I could give you that you'd never had and I'd never given to anyone else.

The first time you visited I let you explore the place on your own so you'd see that it was big enough for one old woman and a couple of cats. Not you. It was never going to be an arrangement like that. I watched you pause at the old wood box and examine my tubes of paint and see the lake through the back windows. You shuddered when you noticed the falcon in his weathering shed but you didn't ask about him then.

We went into the front yard and I handed you a shovel. There's a carving above my front door and your eye found it even though the gash in the wood had healed itself long ago. On cruel days I've judged my work as the predictable result of a Swiss Army knife flung open on impulse but in truth I'd found the right tool and I was methodical. My strokes aren't feather smooth because I'm no expert with a blade.

The light through the window has gone amber and you are still here. If we were at the lake and not in this hospital we would put away our garden tools and go inside for tea before it was too dark for you to cycle back home. In all the hours we passed together I never told you about him. I suppose I thought I would always have the chance.

No matter. You are here now. The clunking and arid and unvaried syllable that comes out of my mouth can't hope to match the pleasing clarity of the voice in my mind but in time I believe this will change.

I want to ask if you've fed him and flown him. When you leave the hospital, where do you go?

TWO

Moose Factory, Ontario, June 1951

THEY HAD ANOTHER HOUR OF LIGHT if they were lucky. Lachlan
stood beside her and squinted upstream as if by force of will alone
the HBC *Mercer* could be made to appear on the horizon. The
hospital dock dipped with the irregular rhythm of every impatient
shift of his weight. It wasn't the first time the survey boat was late,
but that wasn't it: he was not, by nature, an impatient man. The
restlessness Hazel knew well, and it was born of a genuine appetite
for the work they'd both come here to do. The boat they waited for
carried more than a dozen Inuit patients, every one of them with
disease-clouded lungs, from Great Whale and a few posts further
north.

Yesterday she'd stood at his office door and watched him lift one
spectral x-ray film after another to the light box, saw him shake his

head in disbelief, heard the repeated catch in his throat. The swaths of gauzy clouds on this lot of chest films, flown in from Great Whale for him to examine, seemed to choke the air out of his own lungs. The rate of tuberculosis infection was worse than he had expected, worse than he'd seen in any other Inuit community, and she knew that this reality would cast doubt on all of his preparations. Even now he'd be recalculating dosages, recounting beds and rewriting requisitions, an endless series of minute adjustments to the running tally in his head. Only the boat's arrival would slow this constant computation, and then only temporarily. His agitation came off him like smoke.

Hazel had done everything she could do. Extra beds were ready, the kitchen was preparing broth and bread, a dispensary inventory waited on his desk. She was beginning to wonder whether she should check in with Cook when she heard the boat. There it was at the bend in the channel, skimming the north shore of Sawpit Island, mainsail down. The light wind was a hand run the wrong way against the surface of the water and the sound of the boat's hull skipping across it was a drum roll. She checked her watch. Nine forty-five. It would easily be ten-thirty by the time they were settled in the wards.

"How many children this time?"

"Four for certain, three others for a closer look. With any luck we'll be sending those home tomorrow." Lachlan slid his hand through uncombed auburn hair that was weeks beyond a haircut. "We've got to have better equipment. Three blurry films is three too many."

She could make out movement at the bow and along the side, black-haired shapes of varying sizes lined against the railing and leaning toward shore. Curiosity was fine, better than reluctance by a long shot and easier to deal with.

The boat cut the engine and the grinding mechanical chug stopped. Lachlan set his clipboard down and caught the rope that Henry threw, then wound it around the post nearest him. He moved with surgical elegance and tied the knot as though he was a career deckhand, not a tuberculosis specialist from southern Ontario and chief of staff in the new hospital behind them. He was utterly without pretense, as though there was nothing unusual about the way he was disregarding the social hierarchy by performing this simple labour. Not a single doctor she'd worked with before Lachlan Davies would have dreamed of doing the work of a deckhand. But she wouldn't have followed any of them to a remote northern outpost, either.

Hazel stood near the gangplank and held out her hand. A young woman stepped forward first. Oil-black braids snaked down her white wool parka and she wore several southern dresses under it, layered for warmth.

"*Aye,*" she said. Her calloused grip of Hazel's hand was firm. "*Nakurmiik.*"

"She says thank you," Lachlan said, unnecessarily. Hazel knew she had much to learn of the Inuit language, but these were words she'd understood for months. He motioned for the woman to stand aside so the others could disembark. "Check them as they come off the boat. See if any need help getting up the hill."

The back door to the hospital was less than a hundred feet from the dock, but by the skeletal touch of her fingers, Hazel knew that the next patient wouldn't make it on her own. She was a sparrow of a woman, no more than eighty pounds. Her skin was bloodless and translucent as tissue paper and her cheeks were hollow and flushed with the fire of the disease. In her two years of TB nursing Hazel had only seen a handful of patients as far gone. They'd do what they could.

The woman's knees gave out as her feet touched the dock. Hazel caught her under the arms and leaned against the railing for support. Henry stepped deftly around the other patients on the boat and gathered the woman into his arms. He was no taller than Hazel was, and ordinarily she would have insisted that she could carry her own weight, but she let him do this.

The woman's head lolled and her dark eyes were fixed, staring. Her delicate arms hung from their sockets. Nothing of the struggle for life remained in her emaciated body. Lachlan pressed two fingers to the side of her neck and swore under his breath.

"Get her to a stretcher, Henry. Now." He took one long-legged stride up the ramp for every two of Henry's and yanked the hospital door open. "Oxygen, stat! Where are you people?"

The door slammed behind them. The rest of the patients on the boat shuffled into a nervous, crooked line in front of Hazel. She picked up the clipboard and began to check her list against the government identification discs that hung on leather cords around their necks. Charlie Wilcox, pale with seasickness as always but uncharacteristically dishevelled, made his unsteady way off the boat. "Nineteen by my count, Doctor Wilcox. Your list says twenty?"

"Yes, twenty. Count again."

Still nineteen, and only six children. The deck of the *Mercer*, a forty-five-foot Peterhead on loan to Indian Health Services from the Hudson's Bay Company for the summer x-ray survey of the northern communities, was small enough to take in with a glance, and the hold was empty. She scanned the deck again. There, in the pile of canvas pooled around the base of the mast, the slightest twitch. Aha. She stepped on board. The canvas was motionless now; the vibration of her steps on the deck must have done it. No matter, now that she knew where the child was hiding. She crouched beside the mast and lifted a corner of the sail.

The child appeared by degrees, the fringed shape of the mukluk, the smooth tan of the leather legging, the eggshell white of the wool parka. Her need for comfort was clear and urgent and Hazel reached out instinctively, but the child shrank from her. Hazel sat back on her heels. She'd still not even glimpsed her face; the girl faced the mast and clung to it. Hazel let the sail settle around the two of them, closed her eyes and listened to the uneven rattle of the girl's breathing. The fact that she wouldn't make eye contact left Hazel with few options. Her grasp of Inuktitut was stronger every day but couldn't be considered anything more than fledgling, wholly inadequate for negotiation, and she refused to add to the trauma of the trip by taking the sick child off the boat by force.

A lullaby she'd heard Cree women singing to their children came into her head just then, and she began to hum it. The rattle of the girl's breath quieted for a few bars, then resumed. If only she'd thought to pocket some raisins or candy before leaving the hospital. It had worked before. She backed out and replaced the canvas.

"Is the child's mother here, Doctor Wilcox?"

Charlie thumbed through the papers he was carrying. Before he could answer, Lachlan strode back down the ramp. Hazel couldn't read his expression. Had he been able to revive the old woman? He faced the group of new patients. "*Kinnaup paninga?*"

The woman nearest Lachlan frowned and spoke at rapid pace. Anyone could have deduced what she was saying by the keening rhythm of the words. The girl's mother had been left behind. It was not uncommon in this situation. Sympathetic murmurs moved through the group.

"Your vocabulary has improved," Charlie said. It wasn't a compliment.

Lachlan blinked. "Not by nearly enough, but now I know that this child's mother isn't in the group. Can you tell me anything else about her?"

"Of course I can. I was checking my notes to be sure I had the right child." His curly hair seemed to stand on end and his blue-green eyes had gone flinty. It was common knowledge that Charlie had also applied for chief of staff when the hospital opened, and he'd never really been able to let it go. Why he'd agreed to come as a staff physician was a mystery. "Her mother was absent. Dead. Who knows. Just missing and no time to waste searching for her. It was a job persuading the father to let her come with us."

"When you say persuade, what you mean is ...?"

A familiar chasm opened between them. Charlie's shoulders stiffened and Lachlan's head tilted aggressively toward him. Hazel was not optimistic that they'd be able to sidestep their differences. The hours they'd been keeping were long and she knew, now, what the edge in Lachlan's voice meant. She'd known it from the minute she'd taken the old woman's hand in her own, but the Inuit elder hadn't even made it inside the hospital. It was their first loss. Even if he'd expected it, Lachlan would be counting it as a personal failure. It wasn't so much that his perfect record was broken as the unalterable fact of a death on his watch. She'd never known him to accept it easily.

"I mean that I did what was necessary, Davies, as you would have. The x-ray said what it said. You read it yourself and judged her in need of treatment, and that is why I brought her back. You know as well as I do that this is a war. We can, at least, agree on that." The ends of his words had become clipped, staccato like gunfire. "Extraordinary times, extraordinary measures."

The height difference between the men was something she rarely noticed, and though Lachlan was a full head taller he would not normally have emphasized it. But now he took a step closer to Charlie so that the shorter man was forced to look up at him. The men had a slim build in common, but where Charlie's height made him trim, Lachlan was a sapling reaching for sunlight. "Families aren't to be casualties, Wilcox. We have discussed this, have we not?"

"The hospital is over capacity, as you are no doubt aware," Charlie said, backing up the slope until they were eye to eye again.

"Would you have me bring the healthy population, too? Where, exactly, would you like me to put them?"

The group of patients behind the doctors had fallen mute, watchful; the edge in the men's voices was independent of language. The familiarity of the scene didn't make it easier for Hazel to stomach. These people had made a long journey and were not only ill but exhausted. Both men knew that there was work to be done, sick to be healed, a country to be rid of disease. The cure had been a long time coming and now they held it in their hands. This grappling for power was an indulgence they couldn't afford.

She cleared her throat and nodded toward the boat. "Gentlemen." Before either could react, the woman who had come off the boat first stepped between them and back onto the deck of the *Mercer*. She ducked her head under the sail and then lifted it over her body. Hazel strained to hear what she said, but there was no further sound until the woman worked her way free of the canvas, holding the child's hand. They walked together past the doctors and stood with the others.

For several moments, no one moved. The water lapped the shore like a second heartbeat. Hazel became aware of the slow, rhythmic thud of the boat's hull against the dock and wondered who would break the silence. If she'd been a betting woman, she'd have laid her money on Lachlan: of the two, he was likeliest to back away from conflict first, if only to clear away the detritus of untidy emotions. Henry pushed up the sleeves of his plaid work shirt and dropped a pair of rubber mooring buoys over the side of the boat.

Lachlan slid his wire-framed glasses from his face, closed his eyes and massaged his temples. His struggle with the volley of his conflicting emotions was brief, betrayed only by a twitch of an eyebrow. When he put his glasses back on, the tension was gone.

"Well then, Doctor Wilcox, miles to go before we sleep. Shall we?" If she hadn't known them both so well she might have assumed he was having a pleasant conversation with an old friend. He waited for the other man. Charlie frowned and hesitated a moment, then picked up his bags. "We should have a look at those x-rays you sent."

Lachlan turned to her. "Nurse MacPherson, take the women and children and get Joseph to help with the men. Check for anything obvious and let them settle in. We'll start proper exams first thing tomorrow morning."

He and Charlie led the way up the ramp behind the hospital. The sun had set and the only sound from the new patients was the loose rattle of their coughing. Most knew they were sick and wanted help. Success in persuading them to board the white medics' boat depended on that; Henry Echum's presence on the *Mercer* was no real consolation where the culture gap was concerned. His mother tongue was Cree and he knew only a smattering of Inuktitut, only slightly more than Lachlan did. The hospital's only Inuit orderly wouldn't go out on the survey boat no matter what Lachlan said. Hazel had chalked up Joseph's refusal to a fear of water, but after the old woman's death, she began to consider another possibility.

She reached into her pocket for paper handkerchiefs, miming the way to cough into them before handing them around. They were only steps from the hospital, but the journey from Great Whale had been long. They shuffled up the ramp as though chained together at the ankles.

"The new streptomycins are working." Lachlan's voice had become uncharacteristically shrill. There was colour in Charlie's cheeks again and he was nodding slowly. "But we have to get to them sooner. We need two boats, not just one. I'll draft the request tonight."

Hazel watched Lachlan and wished that she could share what he felt, wished that somehow the past six months of proximity to him and distance from the familiar might have awakened the kind of zeal she wanted to find here, twelve nautical miles south of James Bay, doing this kind of work. A year of nursing in Toronto had been long enough for her to know that she had no desire to spend her career wiping noses and weighing babies. She'd been a TB nurse at Mountain Sanatorium in Hamilton for a year when Lachlan announced he was going north to open a new hospital in early 1951. Good nurses were needed, he'd said. Why wouldn't she have gone? The five hundred miles separating Moose Factory Indian Hospital from the tuberculosis wards at Mountain San might as well have been a galaxy. The rates of infection were the highest anyone had seen. That the new medicine was untried on the native population made the prospect more appealing, not less. They'd be the vanguard, armed with the new cure for a disease that had dogged mankind and confounded healers from the beginning of time. They were going to save them all.

IT WAS UNLIKELY THAT CHARLIE had tried to impart even the most basic facts about their illness or where they were being taken. The language of treatment was the best they could offer the new patients; their bodies would heal with or without an intellectual grasp of the disease's workings. She'd heard him advance this philosophy often enough. Making themselves understood in the time they had to get the sick on board was at best a lost cause and at worst a waste of precious resources when they had none to spare.

As he passed Hazel at the back door to the hospital, one of the Inuit men covered his eyes with a visor carved from antler. Snow goggles. A slit for each eye bisected its smooth surface. It struck her as a logical response to the overlit interior, which made a snow-blind contrast to the soothing dark they were coming from. He'd have seen the survey boat coming into his community from a long way off, then. The *Mercer* had been visiting Inuit settlements for a few summers by then; he would have watched some of his loved ones leave on it. He must have had a sense he'd be on board this time and gone home to pack a few things. There was no other explanation for the presence of such a precious belonging in mid-summer.

Once they'd been found to be sick, Charlie granted no returns to the community, not to change clothes, pack a bag or make preparations for those staying behind. He simply did not have the manpower, his argument went, to allow such a thing, and in any case they were all familiar with the resistance white medics encountered from time to time. What if, after diagnosis, the patient went home to collect his belongings and never came back? What then? It was vital that they take all of the sick to Moose Factory for treatment, and if even one went missing, he'd be responsible for allowing a confirmed case to return to the community to infect others. That wasn't something he could live with.

Hazel had heard his justifications often enough and turned the problem over and over in her mind. With or without an explanation the Inuit could understand, the sick needed to be brought to Moose Factory. That was the bald truth of it. It was the reason that cultural sensitivity had taken a back seat, even with Lachlan Davies at the helm of the campaign. The disease could wipe out entire communities, already had in some places. Charlie's logic was hard to refute, and if it had been her own call, she wasn't sure she could have made a different decision. After watching them come from the boats with only the clothes they stood in, motherless children among them, she'd examined it from every angle. With more time, more hands to do the work and a dedicated translator, they might have been able to allow new patients to put their affairs in order, pack a few things. But they had all the resources they could get. It wasn't ideal, but it was the best they could do.

The carving on the snow goggles was remarkable. By then she had a pair of her own, a gift she'd been given in the small hours of the night by a young Inuit man who thought he wouldn't last until dawn. Hers were smooth and serviceable, but the ones this man wore were adorned with a delicate spiderweb tracery and were the obvious mate to the parka the man wore. In six months she'd seen a great number of parkas made from a variety of skins, but this was the first she'd seen made of ptarmigan. Dozens of the small bird's plumed skins were quilted together. The man's hands were partially hidden by the feathers on the sleeves. He must have felt her stare. Henry caught up with her and nudged her across the threshold.

With no goggles of their own, the rest of the group rubbed their eyes and squinted against the glare as they made their way down the short staircase to the main hall. Some of their faces were rigid masks; they were saucer-eyed, slack-jawed impersonations of the people they'd been. Many were laid bare with exhaustion and gave over to every shock, their tears silent or barely repressed. Conversation dwindled to almost nothing beyond the soothing murmurs of the women to the children that walked beside them.

Early in her stay on Moose Factory Island she had felt a dull ache in her chest at this spectacle, knowing that most of them wouldn't see their communities again for years, if at all, but by June she hadn't felt that for months. She wasn't hardened to their suffering, but she had learned how to channel the emotion into scientific curiosity by watching Lachlan. She'd begun to notice patient types – the introverts, the extroverts, the worriers – and had found some success, and satisfaction, in locating the rehabilitative activity that would settle or draw them out. She'd also been around long enough to watch the drugs do their healing work. She told herself that this parade of unhappiness was expected as they settled into hospital routines. If she could see it as temporary, if she could resist being drawn into their sorrow, she'd be better able to help them adjust.

The lights dimmed as they made their way along the hall and up the stairs to the TB wards. Hazel would ask the aides and orderlies to distribute flannel gowns and put boots and coats into outside storage. Tub and sponge baths could wait until morning. Tonight they could have broth, bread and as much tea as they wanted. She'd make them as comfortable as she could.

Earlier that day, she and the matron worked out the patient master list. It made sense to keep patients from the same community together for emotional reasons, and they did that wherever possible, but it was also important to place new arrivals with existing patients. Language lessons had begun a couple of months earlier. The most basic translation from a countryman was superior to the makeshift sign language the hospital staff concocted to supplement their own imperfect attempts at Inuktitut.

The double doors to the maternity ward banged open. "Finally made it, did they?" A fresh spray of tawny curls cascaded from the loose coil at the back of Ruth's head. The hospital's nurse-midwife fell in step with her. "We're going to need more beds."

"Done," Hazel said. They'd become fast friends when she arrived in January. Ruth was as solid in character as in build; Hazel found that she could depend on her to speak her mind and know her work. "Before I went out to the dock."

"Where'd you put them? Last I checked, the ward was full."

"We rearranged things a bit to squeeze a few more in. Only a few in the hall this time."

"You can't be thinking of keeping them all here." Ruth counted heads. "Mountain doesn't have room?"

"They're close to capacity, but they'll take some in a few days. These people have to rest before going further south, anyway. And so do you." There were dark shadows below Ruth's green eyes. Hazel had heard Ruth's familiar step on the stairs just after dawn, and by the time Hazel went to the kitchen for coffee, Ruth was already gone. "Why don't you go. There are enough of us here and these people are exhausted. I expect them to fall into their beds. We'll deal with details in the morning."

"Ach, I'm alright, Captain." Ruth's freckled hand tapped out a melody on her thigh. Hazel had watched her bake a dozen loaves of bread at midnight in this adrenal state. "Pair of lovely girls, big healthy ones, this morning. One with the cord twice around the neck. There were a few moments there. But they're all resting comfortably now and the mum is happy."

"Good. Let's get these people into bed, then." There was no sign of Lachlan. Hazel assumed he was on the ward already and expecting her to be there, too.

SHE HAD ALMOST FINISHED SETTLING the children. A few nurse's aides worked with her, rubbing backs, offering sips of milk or apple juice, smoothing blankets. Three toddlers shared the crib in front of her. Two of the three were curled like cats against each other, asleep, but the third was the girl she'd found clinging to the mast of the *Mercer*. She lay quietly on her back, body rigid and eyes staring as if she was afraid to close them. There had been no time to talk with Charlie about the scene of her departure from Great Whale, but it was easy to guess what had happened. Hazel checked her watch. She'd already spent nearly half an hour with her; she should go to the dispensary now. She tried the lullaby again and wondered if she had the right tune.

There was a shout. Agonized and shrill, it moved unimpeded through the quiet hospital corridors. The girl's eyelids, which had only moments earlier given over to her fatigue, sprang open. She looked up at Hazel from the crib with a dark, serious stare. The last half-hour of soothing was undone. Hazel patted the girl's hand and pulled the blanket up to her chin. Now she did have to go.

As the reality of their situation sunk in, protests of this kind weren't unexpected, particularly among the men, but they were unusual this early in the stay. Fatigue, disorientation and the added malaise brought on by a long journey in cramped quarters usually sapped a patient's energy for all but critical functions. Tomorrow morning, after a good night's sleep and breakfast, staff would be on alert for something like this. But to see it on the night of arrival, this late in the evening? It was without precedent in her six months here. As she hurried along the corridors, she checked her mental catalogue of the men who'd come in tonight for likely candidates. There were a few possibilities. Whatever the source, this needed to be brought under control before the commotion spread like a virus to the other wards. The protocol required all hands on deck, everyone who could be spared. Lachlan would expect her.

She rounded the corner and opened the door to the men's ward. There was a popping sound like rifle shot. Broken glass chimed as it hit the bare floor. Whoever was responsible would need close monitoring: if he was resisting this early and this violently, they might need to put him on suicide watch.

Joseph emerged from the room she'd just passed. Without a word, the broad-shouldered Inuit orderly fell into step beside her. The line of his mouth was thin and flat. They'd both been through this before.

"Have you seen Doctor Davies?"

He nodded. "He's in there." His high cheekbones seemed more pronounced since he'd shaved the moustache he'd been trying to grow. The door to the next room was partially closed, but she glimpsed the back of Lachlan's white coat. No one was talking. Joseph stopped and faced her, all business. "Stay here. I will check first."

She opened her mouth to protest and the door swung fully open. A metal water pitcher soared through it, hit the opposite wall and clanged to the floor. Joseph turned and walked into the room. She stayed where she was.

Besides Henry, who knew – or claimed to know – very little of the Inuit language and rarely entered the hospital anyway, Joseph Weeltaltuk was the hospital's only translator. He'd been an orderly since his recovery a year ago. It wasn't uncommon for former patients to stay on as staff after the long convalescence that healing demanded, the hospital having become home and family, but she'd wondered if he'd lost his family in the Belcher Islands to disease before being brought here, if that was why he stayed. His community had been particularly hard hit. Before this group of patients, his had suffered the highest infection rate of any community they'd surveyed, eight sick out of every ten. Lachlan wrote about it for one of the medical journals.

There was murmuring inside the room in the rounded, gentle syllables of Inuktitut. She could easily distinguish Joseph's voice from the other man's by its evenness. He never raised his voice. He didn't have to. At six feet he was an imposing silhouette in any doorway, and he'd have been an asset on a football field.

The other voices had softened. Wood scraped against bare floor and bedsprings complained. She inched closer to the room. Two beds, one pushed against the other, were still blocking the doorway. Glass crunched underfoot.

"Now," Lachlan said. "Tell him we can talk now that he's calm."

Joseph spoke in soothing tones. A taut thread of sorrow ran through the other man's reply. "He says he sleeps in his *tupiq* with his wife. Not in this hot box with men that are not his kin."

Lachlan sighed. "Not here, I'm afraid. It's against hospital regulations. You know why. Explain it to him."

Joseph spoke long enough to make Hazel wonder what else he might be telling the man. For some time, there was no response. Had she missed something? She inched closer.

"Tomorrow," Lachlan offered. "Tell him that he can see her tomorrow during visiting hours."

There was another silence. "This man does not want to visit his wife. I will only anger him if I tell him that," Joseph said, finally, enunciating with a controlled, parental pace that told her how vexed he was. "He is calm now. We must leave."

She stayed in the hall while the beds were rolled back into place. The ward was quiet and dim again except for a stray cough here or there. Was there anything for her to contribute? She'd already sent the other orderlies away. Lachlan switched off the light as he left the room and didn't seem surprised to see her standing there.

"Wise decision. I assume you heard everything?" Joseph walked past them to the supply closet down the hall and then back again, carrying a broom and dustpan. He didn't make eye contact and his expression was difficult to interpret.

"Enough of it." Lachlan started down the hall. She had to hurry to keep pace with him. "What's his name?"

The words were out of her mouth before she'd properly thought it through. Of course he didn't yet know the man's name. Other matters had been more pressing. In his sharp, annoyed glance, she also read self-criticism. "Time for all of that tomorrow. I have other patients to attend to."

In the soft grey light of early morning, only the stray shard of glass on the floor and the cardboard in the window told of the night's explosive grief. None of the new patients in the room seemed fit to throw a chair through the window, and she might have described several of them as weak, even docile. When she entered the room, their conversation stopped. It was a space designed for four beds that now held seven, three against each wall and one in the centre, headboard against the window. She assumed that this was the reason for the funk in the room, and that the baths today would take care of it. Now that they were sharing bedside tables, the sputum cups also needed labelling, and she made a mental note to remind one of the aides to do it. She moved with care between the beds to give the streptomycin shots, bracing for the unhappy patient to object the way he had the night before. She finished the left side of the room without incident and realized that she'd underestimated the value of stoicism among the new patients. A needle's sting was nothing.

She recorded the doses in their charts and tried to remember whether she'd heard Joseph use the angry man's name last night. New patients were identified by tag number in the first couple of days, and none of the new charts she'd seen so far listed anything more than that. She could be looking at him and not know it.

The snow goggles lay on the table beside the next bed, and the man's pale-feathered parka lay under it. Of course. This was the source of the rich odour. She was surprised he'd been allowed to keep it with him. She lifted his chart from the nail at the end of the bed. In the top right corner, *Suujuq* was scrawled in Lachlan's loose, looping hand. He'd already been there, and it was barely seven. She wasn't surprised. Even before she'd asked about it last night, he'd probably planned to make early rounds.

She lifted the man's sleeve and found what she'd been looking for in an angry pink scratch that ran from his forearm just below the wrist to the centre of his palm. So he'd been the one. There seemed no trace of rage left in him now. She daubed his shoulder, gave the injection and set the needle back on the tray. On impulse, she picked up his hand. She'd been treating Inuit men in this hospital for six months and on the surface this hand was much like the others, sun-dark and wind-tough, scarred by hunting and skinning and hauling and building. But this hand had also ranged over the surface of a pair of snow goggles with a carving tool, seeking beauty. The delicate line it found changed them utterly. She picked up his other hand and brought it to meet the first, as if she was checking for swelling. There must be something that marked these hands as capable of such artistry, some unusual physical feature or occupational callus.

When she reached for a fresh ball of cotton and dampened it with alcohol, he pulled his injured hand away with a jerk and tucked it under his opposite arm. "Come now," she said. She held her hand out and waited the way a schoolteacher waits for a disobedient student. "Let me fix it up for you. Won't take a minute."

"Don't." The voice belonged to a man, but Suujuq's mouth hadn't moved. She dropped her hand and he turned to face the wall. The voice came again, the single one-word command. Joseph stood in the doorway, arms folded over his broad chest. "You are only embarrassing him. It will heal without your help."

Of course it would. It was a surface wound that wouldn't have warranted a moment's attention out on the ice, in the bush or, ordinarily, here in the hospital.

If Lachlan understood his effect on a room he didn't show it, but, at his side for rounds, Hazel knew it well. That he radiated a specific energy was obvious from the first time she met him. If she stayed close, learned what he had to teach and kept working hard, surely she'd begin to feel it herself. Surely the work would claim her the way it had claimed him.

He had recently begun speaking to her as an equal, or as much an equal as a nurse could be to a doctor, which she sensed had not gone unnoticed among the other nursing staff. There were conversations that seemed to end abruptly as she rounded corners, for instance, the kind of behaviour that indicated guilt, envy or deception. She wasn't sure which it was. Lachlan was demanding but fair and never condescending or inconsiderate to any of the nurses, but even from her own perspective she was being favoured, if greater responsibility and more work could be considered preferential treatment. That day, for instance, she'd arrived well before the start of her shift, and, seeing her in the hallway, he'd invited her to join him for rounds. But if any jealousies existed, they'd been concealed.

As for Lachlan's intentions, she wasn't naive. There was a limit to what she could expect. Nurses weren't groomed to become doctors, not even in a northern outpost, nor did she detect even a flicker of chemistry between them. He was just that absorbed in his work, and she was always there. She saw the beginnings and ends of shifts as guidelines, and then went back to the nurses' residence to read anything she could lay her hands on about the treatment of the disease. She'd begun, even in her own modest estimation, to hold her own in a conversation with him.

"We're flying blind here, Nurse MacPherson," Lachlan said, as he breezed along the hallway to the women's ward. She hurried to keep up. "The disease shows itself differently in these people. Its entry point doesn't matter. Once the bacteria enters the bloodstream, the disease moves without resistance. We're seeing it everywhere in the body. These people seem to have no natural immunity. That being the case, how can we assume that the streptomycin will have the same effect it has in the Caucasian population? We're nearing the maximum dosage period in that new group from the Belchers, and they're still not cured. Some of the new arrivals are worse off." He stopped and patted his coat pocket for a pen, leaned against the wall and wrote in the file. "There are no studies. We're it. But we have no choice if we're talking cure. And we are. No turning back." He closed the file and started walking again.

Until that point she'd assumed that the conversation was one-sided, as it so often was, and that if he wanted anything from her it was attentive listening. But now he seemed to be waiting for a response. Her mouth dried, and the back of her neck beaded with cold sweat. She swallowed. "I'm sure you're right." Her voice was a tense, maddening squeak. Now she was flying blind. She'd been studying all she could, but was it enough? She hoped she wouldn't embarrass herself or disappoint him. "We have to use any means we can, and watch them carefully."

"Exactly," he said, nodding. The pace of his speech kept time with his accelerated stride. "We cut our own path. It's the only way."

The overnight lights went off, though the rising sun had made them redundant more than an hour earlier. The women's ward was a hive of early morning activity. Sally Cheechoo bustled from hall to bedside, balancing trays of eggs and hot cereal. "Good morning, Doctor Davies and Nurse MacPherson," she sang. "They've had their pills."

"Good, good. Everybody in good spirits this morning?" It was not an idle question. Lachlan genuinely desired that his patients maintain an optimistic outlook; he'd told Hazel more than once that emotional upsets caused increased respiration, upsetting digestive and metabolic processes, and he'd written passionately on the subject in an article she'd just read in *Canadian Nurse*. From the time they entered the san, he felt that they needed to know they'd recover and be useful in their communities again.

"Oh-uh-yeah," Sally said. Hazel loved the lilt of Cree-inflected English. "Morning is always good as long as I bring coffee!"

"Let them have as much as they like, then." He stopped in the doorway to the first room and waited for Hazel to enter first.

Hair that hung straight or braided past their shoulders was a telltale sign of a new patient. Those who had been in the hospital awhile wore southern styles, cut to chin length and set to dry on curlers, then combed out and tied with bright bows, the work of a nurse's aide trying to fill the long hours of their convalescence and assuage their boredom as well as her own.

Hazel stopped at the sink and rolled up her sleeves. Lachlan continued to the centre of the room, still talking. She should have called to him, but she was curious. How far had his train of thought taken him? Would he notice that she was no longer at his side? She'd almost finished scrubbing when he appeared at her elbow.

"You might have said something."

"It seemed rude to interrupt."

Their exchange would have been more grist for the rumour mill if any of the aides had been in the room to overhear it. Hazel was aware that such a conversation, so lacking in the kind of deference nurses were normally expected to show doctors, would have been an anomaly in any of the other hospitals she'd worked in, and, in some places, a flirtation with dismissal for insubordination. But Lachlan gave no indication that he thought it was unusual, and, carried away on the subject of rehabilitation, it probably didn't occur to him. She dried her hands, reached for their gowns and held his out for him. He waved it away.

"I won't bother. I'm only here a few minutes."

It wasn't the first time he'd ignored the hygiene rules for a TB ward, and with the recommendations changing every few months anyway it was pointless to push it. She slipped her arms into her gown and tied the sash. Lachlan scanned the room and fished a wrinkled cloth mask from his coat pocket, tying it loosely to his face as he made for the bed closest to the window. All eyes in the room followed him.

The woman in the bed had arrived on the *Mercer* from Great Whale, and she was now the eldest of the Inuit women on the ward. Whether she was serene or resigned was unclear. She lay unmoving in the centre of the bed, her arms at her sides, not looking at him. Lachlan lifted her chart off the nail at the end of the bed.

"Aye, Annie. *Chimo. Qanuippiit?* Did you sleep well? I trust the bed is comfortable. They gave you the best seat in the house, you know. The sunsets out that window are spectacular, aren't they?" He tried to catch her eye and spoke as if she could understand every word. The warm smile behind the mask showed itself in his eyes. He seemed to expect charm to carry the conversation, but when Annie lifted her chin an inch and fixed him in her gaze, she didn't blink and the line of her mouth was flat. The erosion of Lachlan's confidence was slight, but Hazel saw it in the wane of his smiling eyes. He cleared his throat. "Let's see if we can't get someone to help us out. Nurse MacPherson?"

What the old woman had conveyed in that simple gesture seemed clear enough, but Hazel did what he asked. Finding a translator in this room wasn't difficult. Some of the younger women were enthusiastic about the language lessons and they'd already absorbed smatterings of English. Of them all, Caroline was keenest. She'd been here since before Hazel arrived and was recovering well, always a willing participant in any activity brought to the ward. She had an ear for languages and spoke the English words she knew with only a trace of an accent. She swung her legs over the side of her bed.

"Easy now, Caroline." She'd picked up more English since Hazel had last spoken to her, obviously. "No rush." She was wearing a garish pink cardigan over her flannel gown that Hazel was sure she hadn't seen before. The shipment of clothing they'd been expecting from the Lion's Club in Toronto must have arrived. She read Caroline's chart and nodded to Lachlan. "You've been practicing your English?"

"Yes, ma'am. Every day."

"Good." Hazel paced herself to make sure the young woman could follow. "You can help Doctor Davies. Come sit here and tell her what the doctor is saying."

Lachlan moved to the far side of the bed and slid an x-ray film from the manila envelope he'd been carrying with him. He lifted it to the window and then took it down again.

"Where's that film we took yesterday?"

"Which one?"

"The normal one. Has the patient been discharged yet?"

"This morning. But I doubt they've put the file away yet." She exchanged a glance with him, trying to guess at his motivation. "I'll go get it."

She heard Lachlan tell Caroline a knock-knock joke as she was going out the door, heard her girlish laughter. The film was where she expected to find it at the nurses' station, and she assumed he wanted to show it to give Annie hope. That she was here and accepting treatment wasn't enough; Lachlan wanted more than acquiescence. If she understood the goal of treatment, she'd take a more active role in her recovery. Caroline was still smiling when Hazel walked back into the room, but Annie's expression hadn't changed. Lachlan was writing in her chart.

"Hold it against the window for me, would you?" He picked up the other film. "This is the picture that Doctor Wilcox took on the boat, Annie." He glanced at Caroline and waited. She sat straighter in the chair beside Annie's bed and said a few words. "This is a picture of your lungs from the inside. Can you see the clouds there?" He pointed to the cumulus masses on the film and waited. Annie's nod was barely perceptible. "These are disease clouds. They make you cough and struggle for breath." He paused when Caroline frowned. "They make it hard to breathe. But we have good medicine. See this picture?" He pointed to the one Hazel was holding against the glass. "No clouds. This is how your lungs will look after we make you well. Then you can go home."

Annie stared at the films as Caroline spoke. Lachlan's tutorial made the disease clouds on Annie's film seem obvious, but as she looked at them Hazel wondered if she'd be able to spot them on her own. She examined the old woman's face for slight shifts in expression, but Annie gave nothing away. She turned her head from the window and closed her eyes. She breathed deeply and seemed to have nodded off.

Lachlan waited and Hazel tried to catch his eye. How had he failed to reach her? A few tense minutes passed before Annie opened her eyes again. She slid one arm from under the covers and placed it, open-palmed, an inch above her chest. Her hand moved in a slow, clockwise circle. Her voice was steady and low. "*Silatsiaq?*"

There was a silent exchange between Lachlan and Caroline. Every molecule of the young woman's face seemed alive. "She ask, Clear sky?"

Lachlan pressed his lips together. He sighed and shook his head. "Not yet, Annie. Not yet. But after rest and medicine, your lungs will be clear. Silatsiaq."

LACHLAN STOOD IN THE CENTRE of the room, head bent over a small notebook he'd fished from his pocket. Of course he'd want to record the new Inuktitut word in his makeshift dictionary, though it seemed unlikely that he'd forget it. Hazel expected to hear it on the wards again, or read it in one of his papers. She made a few mental notes of her own. There were always calls for submissions from the field in *Canadian Nurse*. Lachlan checked his watch and started for the door, head down and still writing, and looked up just in time to avoid a collision.

"Morning, Doctor Wilcox." Charlie's trouser creases ran in unbroken lines to his shined shoes and his wooden posture suggested he'd been standing in the doorway for some time. The attitude in his stance was almost laughable. Lachlan closed the notebook and slipped it into his pocket. "What can I do for you?"

Charlie's smile was tight. "We should consult about the new patients, Doctor Davies." He emphasized Lachlan's title. "I've already seen to the children this morning. You're finished here?"

"Almost. One more room."

Charlie made a show of checking his watch. "Late start?"

Lachlan ignored the question. It was clear where this was going and plain that he'd been watching long enough to have marked the time Lachlan had spent showing the films to Annie. They had exchanged words on the subject before. This exercise was foolish and a waste of time, Charlie believed. Doctors spent years learning to read and interpret x-rays. How could patients, untrained and lacking a proper translation, possibly decipher ghosted marks on the film? The first time she'd heard him argue with Lachlan this way she'd held her breath, waiting for the verbal slap that would have come from any other staff chief she'd known. But Lachlan had only frowned, as if he'd been presented with a new and unexpected symptom, and let Charlie continue.

"You're giving them false hope," Charlie said now, with more force and less deference than seemed prudent. But Lachlan was unflagging, calm and resolute. Patients had a right to know what was going on inside their bodies. Even if they didn't fully understand what they were seeing, it was a way to make concrete what they were doing here. He was giving the most basic of explanations anyway, didn't Charlie agree?

"Don't you open the clinic right about now?"

"As a matter of fact, I do." There was no reproach in Lachlan's voice. The man was a paragon of control. "But if it's already nine I suppose they'll have to wait, and so will you. If you'll excuse me, I'll get on with it."

Charlie stepped backward stiffly and let Lachlan pass. He called to him once Lachlan was several paces down the hall. "We should meet today."

"Of course. I'm available to do that around noon."

The line of Charlie's jaw became hard, visible. "Fine. Cafeteria at noon."

"I'll be there as close to noon as I can, Doctor Wilcox. Get us a table, will you?"

Charlie didn't answer. Hazel watched him for a few minutes, but it couldn't be helped, certainly not by anything she could say or do. His hands clenched and unclenched at his sides, and he turned down the hall in the opposite direction with a clipped stride. She caught up with Lachlan, who was already entering the next room on the ward.

"Doctor Davies." Lachlan seemed almost surprised to see her standing here. "Why did you tell her the medicine will work?" The question seemed disingenuous even to her own ears, but that wasn't her intention. She was confused. She'd watched Lachlan use a range of means to achieve his purpose, but never an outright lie.

"Because it will." No hesitation.

"But you said we were flying blind."

"The streptomycin has been working miracles," he said, fiddling with the mask ties again and finally pulling it below his chin. "We can finally talk cure, Nurse MacPherson, after a long history with a disease that's been with us from the beginning. I assume you know that First Dynasty Egyptian mummies showed tubercular bone lesions. And now the end of it is within reach. We're the last generation of medics that will have to deal with it. The puzzle is in the dosing, but we'll do it. Look, Hazel." His use of her first name was rare. "Annie's stay here will be long. I need her to believe in what we're doing."

"So that she'll cooperate." The conclusion seemed obvious now, and also only the beginning of what she felt she needed to understand. It was not her habit to mollify patients with partial truths, and she'd never seen Lachlan make that decision, either.

"More than that." The uncharacteristic slow pace of his speech called her attention like the sounding of a bell. "The medicine can only do so much. If she can't see herself going home again, there's no chemical cure in the world that can help her. It's going to be hard for her here, much harder than it'll be for the younger ones. Her case isn't advanced but her body will be slower to heal, she won't learn the new language easily, if at all, and she'll have difficulty adapting to the rhythms of hospital life. If we're to cure her, we have to use any means possible to keep her spirits from flagging."

"Because the younger ones will be watching her."

"And that too." He smiled. "Exactly." The creases she'd noticed around his eyes a moment earlier were gone. He lifted one eyebrow. "Would you like to see something remarkable?" He leaned close enough that she could smell the coffee on his breath. "Won't take a minute." He didn't wait for a reply, just turned and walked out the door. She found herself following him down the corridor toward his office at the official start of her shift without once wondering who'd cover for her.

THE DOOR TO THE CLINIC waiting room, next to his office, was already open and she could hear voices, but Lachlan stopped at his office door and unlocked it. Every horizontal surface – his oak desk, the shortwave radio, the metal table in the centre of the room – was stacked with papers and books. The walls were bare except for the light box and a map of James Bay held there with several layers of tape. Lights blinked on the radio and she could hear static and tinny dispatches coming from the headphones.

"Come in, come in." He closed the door behind her. To her eyes, the office was a disaster, but he went directly to one of the stacks of paper on his desk and pulled out a manila x-ray envelope from the bottom of it, exactly the one he wanted. He clipped the film to the light box and flipped the switch.

The wing-like embrace of the ribs was distinct, but apart from that she wasn't sure what she was looking at. Were these normal or diseased lungs? Without a second film for comparison, she couldn't be sure. Even if using x-rays to diagnose the disease wasn't still so new, nurses weren't trained, or allowed, to read them. And yet he seemed to assume that she could follow. She wanted to.

"Six months on the plain streptomycin." She took this to mean that the x-ray was normal. "If we're vigilant, we can get it all. TB will be over, done, even up here among the natives, after all of these years." He folded his arms in front of his chest. "The next generation won't know its name. Can you imagine? Places like this will be empty!" He was almost giddy. She didn't know this side of him. "What will they do with the space?"

He turned his back to her and sifted through some papers on his desk. "Do you know how we used to control the disease? Have you read a history of treatment yet?" In spite of the extra reading she'd managed to squeeze into her schedule, she felt a sliver of panic at the ignorance her answer might reveal, but he flipped through a book he'd finally found on his desk. "By the time you started at Mountain we'd stopped doing collapse therapy, hadn't we? Here. This is it. Take a look. Bedrest was fine if you didn't have to work for a living. Scar tissue did the job nicely, held the growth of the tubercles in check. But if bedrest wasn't an option, if the lungs were in constant motion . . ." He turned the page and pointed to the photograph there, a woman naked from the waist up, her back to the camera, arms lifted over her head. Where her lower left ribs ought to have been, there was a hollow. "We had to make it rest. See, they moved four sternal ribs, front and back, to force the lung to collapse. I oversaw a few of these myself."

He paused. On the facing page was a front view of another woman. "Thank god we don't do that anymore. Seems barbaric now. See the way the skin sinks below her clavicle in this one? She's young in the photograph, but she's been marked by the disease. She'll carry it to her grave." He stifled a yawn. "We don't have to disfigure to cure anymore. See for yourself." He motioned toward the light box. "Some minor scarring in the lung tissue, that's it, and that's only because it had gone untreated for the better part of a year. Now he's back in his community." He leaned toward it, closer to her, searching for something. She became aware of the warmth of his body. "Incredible, isn't it? You know, you really ought to go out on the survey boat sometime, see a patient from start to finish with your own eyes."

She couldn't speak. To her enduring but unspoken frustration, she hadn't even been as far as James Bay. Women didn't go out in the survey boat. The bigger boats were gone for months, and even the smaller ones like the *Mercer* were usually away overnight. The men pitched tents, huddled around campfires, bathed in cold streams.

He was animated now. Instead of the loping awkwardness that usually characterized his gait, he was moving like a boxer, light and sure on his feet. This sudden shift, and the mention of the survey boat, propelled her to act.

"Could I see that again?" It wasn't the right question. "I mean, could I borrow it awhile?"

Lachlan wasn't an unhappy man, but it was rare to see the kind of unguarded smile he offered now. "Sure, of course. It's a good one, just came out last month. Keep it as long as you like."

"Thanks." Their hands brushed. The shift in their relationship that a loan suggested made her suddenly awkward. Fine, then, she'd make sure she was worthy of his attention. She'd study this and teach herself to read TB films. She did a few quick calculations. With a little discipline and slightly less sleep she'd be able to find at least two hours in each day. Most of the conversation in the nurses' residence bored her anyway. "I'll have it back by the end of the month."

"Fine, good. As I said, no hurry." His tone seemed cooler, almost dismissive now, as if it was of no consequence when or if she finished reading it. Well, then. She'd push herself to read and understand it, and she'd have it back when she said she would. He sat at his desk and began to leaf through pages of test results. This meant their conversation was over, she assumed.

"One more thing," he said. Her hand was already on the door. He tipped his head in the direction of the waiting room. "Sounds like a crowd in there. I'm going to get started. Finish rounds for me, will you? There's only that one room left on the women's ward."

On her own? Nurses didn't do rounds. Even if she'd come north for that possibility, the distance this strayed from nurse-doctor protocol was significant. Was this the beginning of a greater scope of responsibility? Where might it lead? It was impossible to imagine this kind of thing happening at Mountain, where most doctors were minor generals who jealously defended territory.

"Not much to do, really." He held out a stack of files. "Just make sure the new ones are comfortable. I'll check on them later."

"Of course," she said. This made more sense. "I'll see who's on for the strep shots."

"Fine." He stood and reached for the door that led from his office to the waiting room. A crowd of sounds invaded his office. "Come back as soon as you're finished, will you? I think I'm going to need some help in here."

Twenty minutes later, walking back toward the clinic, she went to check on Annie. The elder Inuit faced the window. Her diminished body made a slight ripple in the bedcovers. The window laid a lozenge of sunlight across her face, her arm and half the bed. Her eyes were open but staring. She was there in bed, in a hospital ward far from her home, and she was also somewhere else entirely.

THREE

FIVE HOURS PASSED GREENLY. GIDEON watched the rush of conifer out the window until the train's tottering, heavy-hipped sway lulled him to sleep. He woke with a jolt in Moosonee, end of the line, as far over the muskeg as rails would carry him. He tucked the photograph that had fallen from his hand inside the front cover of *Birds over America* and stowed the book in his pack. Then he followed the others from the train to the water's edge and climbed into a freight canoe to cross the water to the big island in the middle of the channel.

So this was Moose Factory. He laid his hands on the soil and closed his eyes. This stop was only temporary, but each decision must be deliberate. He'd been making plans for months.

He picked up an elbow of driftwood from the beach, sat at the base of a balsam poplar and reached into his wood box for the carving knife. Sheltered from the rain and snow for years, the words on the side of the box were still vibrant: *Pepper Sauce, Stickney and Poor*. It was filled with oily rags when he found it in a rail yard outbuilding before leaving St. Paul's, and, with an old leather belt screwed on as a shoulder strap, it was right for the journey he'd been about to take. His tools and books fit inside and he laid the umbrellas he'd found on the lid.

Stragglers made their way from the dock along the path into town and some paused to stare, but he was familiar with that sort of behaviour. He saw beauty that the common eye could not. The pepper sauce box, for instance, and his three-piece black suit and bowler hat, a lucky find at the Sally Ann. He was thinner now, so he'd cut a new notch in his belt. He'd given the rest of his belongings away. His life was simple.

Something near the dock caught his eye. Ankle deep in the dark water just offshore, a Cree man swung canvas bags from a rocking boat to his companion on the stony beach in an upward arc to where the gulls cried, circling in skirmishes a dozen strong. Gideon was caught up in their querulous motion when he saw it, higher still, almost lost to the altitude: a lone black mark in the sky, the telltale anchor-shaped silhouette above the gulls.

Gideon put the driftwood down. He slipped the knife into his pack and reached for his hat without breaking eye contact with the drama unfolding above him. The falcon was no longer idly pacing the sky, waiting for something to happen. She was climbing higher and there seemed a swift sureness to her trajectory. Gideon's body became taut, alert. He'd read about this but had never seen it: she was preparing to stoop. He watched her with singular focus, as if her entire attack could not be folded into the space of seconds but had a languid unfurling, a series of arrested movements that he could track and catalogue individually.

There had been months of doubt, maddening conspiracies between maps that guarded their secrets and eyes that were blind to
anything they might have revealed. But that was all behind him
now. Watching this, he was calm. The expression on his face was
open and untroubled. This sighting was confirmation of his decision and proof that his plans would reach fruition.

The falcon angled her wings to direct the wind, then pulled
them tight against her body. She revolved as if on an axis and
then hurled herself toward earth, wings held fast against her sides,
feathers quivering in the force of the air that rushed past her body.
The swirling mass of gulls, oblivious until the sudden violence
of her arrival, screamed and dispersed but the falcon's keen sight
tracked only one of them. She flung her body against the one she'd
chosen with the force of an iron ball shot from a cannon. The
dull crack carried across the water and the gull was claimed by the
rocks below. The falcon made an elegant midair turn, dipped toward the shore and seized the fallen bird. Then she carried it away,
a limp white cloth suspended from her claw.

GIDEON MOVED ALONG THE BEACH in the falcon's wake, outside
of thought. Clockwise once around the perimeter of the island,
and then counter-clockwise: it was important to have a body
memory of the island geography to choose the right spot. Now
he took fourteen paces to the water's edge, his compass held at his
hip, and looked down. The needle lay across the ornate script of
the capital *N*. North was where he was headed. It would bode well
for the success of the journey to orient his camp in that direction.
He shrugged the pack from his back and set the box down. How
his load had begun to weigh.

He lifted his face to the sun and closed his eyes. Midday. The
sand was warm and he eased the jacket from his shoulders and set

his hat beside him. Here were poplar leaves shifting in the wind, smooth stones, the slow eddy of the river and, in the distance, an expanse of water knotted to the horizon with a glittering, shifting carpet of light. Small islands led the way along the river toward the Northwest Passage like a repeating pattern.

This water came down from the high north deep into the belly of Canadian land. He'd been staring at the map on his bedroom wall one day when he'd noticed the peculiar way the land gathered itself into the shape of a hand. He'd traced its outline along the shores of Hudson Bay and James Bay, four fingers of water folded and the fifth pointing here, to Moose Factory. It was a message from the divine, telling him where to go. In the blue expanse of the Atlantic, he'd written a new name for himself: Gideon. It was majestic, a better fit for a man on a journey like this one. A new name for a new direction. Gideon would follow the water's lead north. He shed his birth name like an old skin and never called himself Daniel Pederson again.

He reached for his pack and untied the knot he'd made the day before in Timmins, unrolled the canvas and stood to shake out the tent. He was deliberate and unhurried. Everything weighed, even if this stop was only temporary. He'd read about the ancients, the way they oriented their temples so that the solstice light might penetrate to the centre and illuminate the drawings inside.

In the end it was not so much about protection or the way the light might strike the interior but the waking view: first impressions counted when the veil between dreaming and waking had so recently lifted. Here was a spot in the lee of a copse of trees. He knelt to sweep the ground of stones, branches and pine needles, then unrolled the tent so the door faced north and laid the compass on it. He shifted the canvas until the needle lined up with the *N* again. Then he searched for branches strong enough to serve as tent poles, humming as he whittled the offshoots from a good one, then another. He pitched the tent and stood back. The sun was setting on his first day in Moose Factory, but his camp wasn't ready yet.

He could dig in the dark, and he'd done it before, but to choose the spot required light. Gideon rested his palm at the base of one tree, shook his head and moved to the next, and the next, and the next. The light had begun to swirl around the drain of the day when he finally stopped at a white pine. He fitted his fingers into the sinews of the bark, laid his cheek against it and closed his eyes.

The trowel was in the side pocket of his pack. He'd dug this hole so often he didn't need to measure anymore. He traced an outline in the ground at the base of the pine, but then reached into his pack again for his knife. First things first: he could take the box into the tent for the night, but the marker could not wait. Before he slept, he needed to do this. He flipped the safety, felt the blade spring to life in his hand and sketched the first strokes of an arc that sheltered a sphere into the bark. By the time the moon rose, he'd carved the outline on the tree by feel.

FOUR

MY FINGERTIPS FIND A MONSTROUS and misshapen landscape where my face once was but you never seem shocked, Jude, not even when I feel it contort even more with the enormous effort of trying to speak. It's just one hopeless attempt after another. It seems that you are capable of holding secrets and tolerating uncertainties because here you are again. How many days have passed? There is no way to measure time in this hospital bed.

The day of the stroke I was already in the car and backing out of the garage when you arrived. I told you we were going to Martin's for chicks. The sweetish stink of the offal-saturated hunting bag I'd put in the trunk made you wince and roll the window down. The gamy smell of it no longer repelled me. You'll get used to it too. You've grown accustomed to things more objectionable than this in your life.

It was an established but unspoken agreement between us that every silence didn't need to be filled and so the lack of conversation during the drive to the Mennonite farm was neither uncomfortable nor unusual. The unsown winter fields beside the rural road undulated in a soothing way and you slept until the car jostled in the deep ruts that led to the Martin farm. Hens and roosters ran loose outside the barn and blue and white laundry on the line luffed in the breeze.

It was a Tuesday and even though your classes at the university were out for the summer it was unusual for me to break with the Sunday routine that had been in place for over a year. I didn't know why I'd called you that April day but I did. Ruth always said the body knows. I took the bag from the trunk and let you trail behind me like a lost duckling. The matriarch of the family sat on the porch in a rocking chair, peeling potatoes into a chipped enamel bowl in her lap and giving no sign that she'd noticed us. She didn't approve of falcon-keeping by an old woman who lived alone. This is my interpretation of her borderline hostility because she has never said as much but I've never known Mennonites to exhibit anything other than detached politeness. An unbroken spiral of red potato skin dropped into the bowl. "Amos is in the barn," she said. "About a dozen this time. That'll be five dollars."

I took the bill from the breast pocket of my plaid work shirt and held it out to her. She slipped it into her sleeve and turned back to her potatoes. We walked toward the barn. "She's not too friendly," you said. It made no difference to me. I wasn't there to make a friend. I just needed to feed the bird. The hunting season was closed and my freezer was full but I still had to exercise him.

Needles of light entered the barn through knotholes and splayed wallboards. Amos lumbered toward us in the gloom and his gloved hands were cupped in offering. He tipped them into my bag and the pile of slack yellow forms tumbled like so many rag dolls. Amos sexes the chicks soon after they're born. He keeps only a few of the males for breeding and drowns the rest. What he did with the tiny corpses before I came along as a ready market I have no idea but it was lucky for me or I couldn't have kept a falcon. In days gone by a falconer would have hunted for smaller birds to distract his falcon from what he'd caught. You'll have to take over now. You've been to Martin's. You know what to do.

We'd exercised the falcon together on only a handful of occasions before that day. Back at the lake I handed the hunting bag to you and we walked to the weathering shed behind the cottage. His restless gaze found me immediately and he began a steady pace to the end of his tether and back. I took what I needed from the storage compartment at the end of the shed and slipped the glove on my hand and the hood on his head without fuss. Each of us tolerated the other easily. Fifteen years will do that.

I unclipped the leather jess from the perch and offered my gloved hand. I didn't yet know what had begun and I braced my free hand against my knee so you wouldn't see how much pain I was in but I'm sure that you'd noticed that something had shifted by then. I'd never given you the bag to carry before and now I was handing you my spare glove. "Put it on," I said. "He's bound to notice that you're carrying the goods. If he flies toward you, just raise your arm and hold steady."

You followed me along the path that leads to the field. Out in the open all traces of snow and ice had disappeared but under the shelter of cedar and pine tenacious islands of ice clung to tree roots and cooled the air. The arm that carried the bird was tucked close to my body and he was tethered to my hand by the jess. Even if he knew I wouldn't fly him until we reached the open field the air around him vibrated with restlessness. His cloaked head was in perpetual motion as if he was trying to sense all that he couldn't see.

Did you notice the first falter in my stride? My free arm flung out and caught you on the chin. Your eyes betrayed nothing as you slipped your arm around me. You'd endured enough emotional pain in your young life to conceal a reaction without much effort. I'd seen that from you before. You'd make a good nurse. The bird struggled to keep his balance and managed to do so as I righted myself. I shook my head and shrugged off your protective embrace. "It's fine. Tree root."

It was a lie and we both knew it but you let me go. I thought if we were out in the open things would improve and ahead was the brightening that signalled the start of the farmer's back field. There was a hill on the left. It was a good place to launch him and I'd climbed it countless times over the years but I could barely catch my breath when we reached the top. The headache had intensified and I pressed three fingers to my forehead. You held your arm out. "No need," I said. "He'll be under his own power in a few minutes." I loosened his hood and lifted it off his head. He blinked and shook his feathers and stretched his wings.

"Steady now. Won't be long." My voice was calm for him but his gaze was still restless. Over the years I'd tried to imagine what he saw. What stood out from the bucolic snow-bleached landscape of long grass and trees and low hills? Did his restless eye seek perch or prey? Did his blood warm to the possibility of flight, a silver quickening as the wind lifted his feathers?

As soon as I released the jess he flew. At first I thought he'd gone straight up because I lost him but then I saw a slight but joyful agitation high in the pale sky. There was already a pattern to his flight. He moved in concentric circles that widened as he rowed the thin air. You saw it too.

"Will he –"

"Stoop? I think so." My own sensations receded for a moment as I reached into the pocket of my work jacket. "He shouldn't. That duck he has his eye on is out of season." The last words were mired and caramel-slow. The fuzzy lure I'd pulled from my pocket dangled from the ends of fingers that had suddenly become useless. But I found the strength for a half-hearted toss to distract him. The hunt he'd begun would have caused trouble if the ministry fellows were about but I didn't care. This wasn't something I could command.

This is what I wanted to say to you:

Every time he folds his wings against his body he feels death very near. It's there in the blood that calls him to his quarry. It's there in the hundreds of feet that separate him from earth and the wind that parts his feathers two hundred miles an hour sharp on his skin as he descends and the gravity that makes it so. He feels it to the hollows of his bones. Still he is unwavering. Still he climbs to the place where the air is thin and he has only one remaining purpose and no other choice. Watch, Jude. Just watch.

As if you could have done anything else. The falcon rowed the sky above us in a widening and inevitable circuit. I didn't have to say a word.

THE LIGHT WAS OCHRE WHEN we stepped from the bush. It had been a good hunt and I was pleased that you'd seen it. We found the falcon mantling over his kill in the field. I offered a chick with one hand and bagged the mallard with the other. When the bird finished his meal I offered my arm. He was hooded for the entire walk back but no longer restless. Like a horse in a stall he stood placidly on the hard leather of my glove, tranquilized by the spent adrenaline and the tang of blood. You carried the mallard in the soft leather sack I gave you as if you'd done it every day of your life.

We skirted the cottage on the north side. The day was glorious. When we reached the weathering shed I had to squat to set him down. I'd begun to feel dizzy by that point and the headache had grown steadily. But when the arm carrying the falcon lost all strength I knew. Too late. The falcon clawed at my glove and flapped his wings. He would have flown if not for the hood. You pushed your gloved hand under his belly and he clawed his way up your arm. My headache was blinding. Your free hand caught me under the arm as my knees buckled.

FIVE

HIS HEAD WAS HIDDEN BETWEEN two chairs, but it was clear to Hazel that the big Cree man stretched out on the waiting room floor was unconscious. He must have fallen or collapsed, and it wouldn't have been a first. The hospital had drunkenness to contend with from time to time, but more often patients presented themselves at the clinic only once they were gravely ill. In the past, she interpreted this eleventh-hour custom as distrust. Medical services from southern doctors were still a novelty in the community and used only as a last resort, but it occurred to her now that responding to illness or injury by going to the hospital might not yet be habit.

The boy at the man's side was the only other person in the waiting room and he had his back to her. He hadn't even lifted his head at the sound of her footsteps. She cleared her throat just in case. Nothing.

"What happened?"

Still nothing. She waited several minutes before saying it again. She stepped over the man's moccasins and crouched beside the boy. He raised his head, his expression neutral and unsurprised. Assuming that his deficit, whatever it was, hadn't affected his brain, he should have been expecting someone. These were clinic hours.

"How long has he been on the floor?"

The boy made a guttural sound, something strangled that fell between a grunt and a sigh. Ah. She sat on her heels. Knowing he was deaf didn't solve the immediate communication problem. Even if he could read lips, could he decode the shapes of English words? She touched his sleeve.

"Papa?"

The boy nodded and pointed to his own scalp, then toward his father's. She lifted a lock of hair from the man's face. The gash it hid was fresh and deep, and the trail of blood from it followed his hairline, ran past his ear and was already wicking into the collar of his flannel shirt. It had begun to clot but he needed stitches, no fewer than seven. His arm was dead weight when she lifted his wrist but his pulse was strong and he was breathing normally. She'd suture quickly and get him into a hospital bed.

She went to Lachlan's office, knocked and then tried the door. It was open. He must have been called away. His bag sat open on the exam table, but she paused before deciding that he'd want her to take care of this. She took a needle and black silk thread from his bag, gauze and alcohol from the cupboard, a clean sheet from the exam table drawer, and scrubbed her hands and arms. She'd sutured only a couple of times since nursing college but her dominant concern was not her own skill with a needle but the possibility that the man would regain consciousness before she finished. She knew nothing about him or how he came to have this injury; how would he react if he woke before she finished? She'd have to work quickly, just get it done.

"I'm going to move him away from the wall." She spoke slowly and mimed doing so. It felt idiotic to speak this way. She'd just mime what she wanted next time.

She lifted the chairs out of the way and tucked the sheet under the man's head. The boy understood her purpose and moved out of the way. She crouched over him, hands on his shoulders, and tried to push him away from the wall. He didn't move. He was heavier than he looked and at least a foot taller than she was, so she braced herself against the wall, tightened her grip and pushed hard. It was as though the laws of physics had changed: he moved away from the wall by at least a foot and she lost her balance. She caught herself just in time to avoid a position that might have hurt him and would have taken some explaining if anyone had walked into the room at that moment. She stood, smoothed her skirt and glanced at the man's feet, knowing too late that the boy was there. He sat on his heels, one hand on his father's leg.

Even this much commotion had not roused the man. She knelt beside him and brushed the hair back from his face. His lips were dry and cracked and there was sparse stubble on his chin. Near his left ear was a small scar that had faded to a scratch the length of a fingernail. His lack of consciousness masked his character: there was no jaunty curve of an eyebrow or deep furrow at the corners of his mouth to give him away. From the ruddy tint of his skin and the squint lines that ran from the outer corners of his eye to his hairline, she guessed that he'd recently come in from the trapline, part of one of the families in the tents on the shore just east of the hospital that were here for the summer to trade furs. She sponged the wound with gauze and alcohol. It was neither straight nor clean. A fish hook might do this, maybe a broken bottle.

Suturing from this angle was awkward, but the alternatives were no better. She drew the thread through the skin with careful, tight stitches so that the scar might eventually pass for a wrinkle. She'd soaked another gauze pad and was cleaning the dried blood from around the new stitches when he began to stir. He opened his eyes and tried to sit up, but she'd anticipated this and had her hands on his shoulders.

"Stay. You must be still."

He blinked and squinted against the light. "My boy."

"At your feet. He's been here all along."

The man closed his eyes and grimaced. He licked his lips and lifted a scarred and calloused hand to his forehead. He groaned softly when his fingers found the stitches. If she left to get an orderly and a gurney, he might try to stand and black out again.

"I'm going to check the back of your scalp." The ropes of his neck muscles went taut as she turned his head. "Try to relax." The sheet she'd put under his head was clean, no blood. This was good. But wounds could hide on a scalp with hair as thick and dark as his, the blood finally seeping through only hours later. She threaded her fingers through his hair, working upwards from the nape of his neck and along his scalp to the roots. The skin was unbroken but spongy near the crown.

"No cuts." She lowered his head to the floor. "But you've got a goose egg that needs ice and observation."

"Goosh egg?"

There was more emotion than logic in his response, and it was something his son didn't need to hear to interpret. Light as a spider, the boy moved to his father's side and crouched there, stroking his face, making small sounds at regular intervals. He might have been singing.

"Bump. From when you fell."

She'd been hearing a commotion at a distance for several minutes, and it was louder now. There was a crash and shouts in a mixture of languages. She looked out the door. Two orderlies and a nurse hurried along the corridor toward the men's ward across the hall. Joseph strode by, pushing a gurney, and then reappeared in the doorway.

"You need help, Nurse MacPherson?"

"Yes. Finally. Where is everyone?"

He steered the stretcher into the room ahead of him. "Emergency. Big fight in the men's ward."

That explained it. The Inuit and Cree patients in the men's ward had kept uneasy company since the hospital opened. There had been long discussions about the merits of having separate wards, particularly for the men. She stood and released her end of the gurney. They lowered it to the ground.

"My family is waiting." The big man lifted his head from the sheet, and Hazel caught him as he swooned.

"Not so fast." Lachlan stood in the open door to the clinic, his arms folded over his unbuttoned white coat. He stepped around them and squatted behind the man's head, motioned to Joseph and slipped his hands under the man's shoulders. "You hear that wet sound in your voice? That's the sound of two head injuries. One more and your hunting days are over."

IT WAS HARD TO DISMISS the idea of working on the survey boat, even if she'd never convinced herself that Lachlan's offhand mention of a trip on the *Mercer* was anything more than a careless remark, evidence only of his preoccupied state. But it had to be. He couldn't be serious. However different this place, certain rules still applied: she was neither a doctor nor a male orderly, and if she pressed the point, Lachlan would be forced to remind her of that. She might even lose ground in his estimation for raising it. He'd expect her to understand, implicitly, that it wasn't a real possibility. It was better, and safer, to avoid that conversation. She wouldn't mention it again.

The book she'd asked to borrow was something else. He'd loaned it without reservation but she'd detected a hint of surprise in his voice, as if he hadn't expected this from her. And why would he? None of the other nurses on the ward were doing extra study. Most had romance novels on their bedsides and movie magazines in the common room, if they read at all. She'd subscribed to and was intermittently receiving *Canadian Nurse*, but apart from a recent issue dedicated to tuberculosis nursing, the depth of discussion was limited.

This book was a text on the history and treatment of tuberculosis written for doctors, just out this year. She'd promised him that she'd have it back by the end of the month, but after the latest boatload of new patients she'd been working double shifts, able to dip into it only during her lunch break and for brief moments before sleep claimed her each night. It hadn't helped that two of the newest nurses had left to go home last week, finding the isolation of the place more than they could bear. Staying here required a constitution that half of the nurses sent from Ottawa found that they lacked within their first few months, so the hospital was constantly short-staffed.

Things had finally settled down. Today she'd managed to finish her work at the official end of her shift. When was the last time she'd done that? She pushed open the back door of the hospital and stepped outside. The air carried the mild green perfume of the river a couple of yards away. The first breath was a tonic, its organic sweetness a sharp counterpoint to the manufactured air inside the hospital. On the water ten feet away, ripples caught the sun. The watch pinned to her uniform read 6:05 p.m.

A single row of poplars marked the hospital's southeast perimeter, the remains of the dense forest that had been cleared when the hospital was built. She stepped between them and faced the water. If the island was small, the river was shimmering compensation: its restless movement was an unconditional offer of escape. On the opposite shore was Sawpit Island. Nurses, aides and orderlies used it during the summer for picnics and year-round for overnights in the cabins. It was a short paddle across, but she'd never done it.

Two hospital canoes rested on the shore. The river was calm and sunset was hours away. She could be across in minutes. She dragged the canoe toward the water and it occurred to her that she should tell someone where she was going. She didn't.

The canoe was made of birch bark and easily pulled to the water. She set the textbook and her notebook under the seat and launched the canoe without getting her feet wet. The rock and pitch of the river was a buoyancy she hadn't felt for months. Each stroke of the paddle seemed to connect with her gut and send her across the water, a bowstring drawn and released. She was almost disappointed to feel the scrape of Sawpit's shore on the hull.

Motion on the hospital dock caught her eye as she stepped out of the canoe and dragged it high on the beach. A figure waved, trying to get her attention. Probably Henry. It would be unlikely that he'd been sent out to find her, as he set foot inside the hospital only rarely; curiosity made more sense. He must have been near the dock when she paddled across. She started up the slope. Let him wonder.

One of the three cabins she'd heard about was directly up the slope ahead and half-hidden by the trees, a clapboard green-roofed structure. Judging by the blanket of pine needles against the door, it was not only empty now but had been for weeks. Even so, she stepped heavily up the steps to warn anyone inside before she pulled the screen door open. Whatever she might have seen through the front window was concealed by a red gingham curtain. She knocked and then turned the knob.

So this was it. She pushed the curtains aside and the single room filled with dappled light. To the left was a squat wood-burning stove, door open on a small pile of ash. A simple table and chairs were at the front window, a pale blue cloth laid across it. Under a window that opened on the thick poplar wood behind it was the double bed, stripped of linens but covered with a quilt. Hand built and sewn, all of it, by the first wave of staff at the hospital. Moose Factory was just over two miles long and less than a mile wide, and home to seven hundred Cree and one hundred hospital staff from the south. It wasn't solitude they wanted, it was privacy. She must have been the first person to arrive alone. She closed the curtains and stepped back outside, pulled the door shut behind her. Summer was so brief this far north. Mosquitoes be damned, she'd sit outside.

The top step was still warm from the sun. She laid Lachlan's book on her lap. Gold lettering spelled out *The Great White Plague: Tuberculosis in Canada* by W. H. Thomas. She set the spine on her knee and let the book fall open where it wanted to, a game she hadn't played in years. Only the cover fell aside, but the breeze lifted the first few pages and something handwritten on the title page caught her eye. In blue ink and a looping script almost as familiar as her own, there was an inscription: *LM Davies*. It was a surprise; he didn't seem the possessive type. That he might lend out a book and forget who he'd given it to seemed more likely.

She flipped to the centre of the book and stopped at a full-colour illustration, the human lung at high magnification. These drawings were the best she'd seen: on the left were the bronchioles, atria, ducts and alveolar sacs of a healthy lung. On the facing page, the same constellation of parts jostled for space with tubercles, the colonies of waxy beads that grew from the TB bacillus and shifted shape as they invaded lung space. She turned past the drawings she'd made in her own sketchbook of collapse therapy and sketched the smooth symmetry of the healthy lung, the branching trees of breath. "That's the nice thing about the body," Lachlan had told her once. "Everything comes in twos. We can compare." She'd always found the balance in the body's architecture soothing.

Her pencil lingered on the tubercles in the second sketch, adding shadow and dimension and fine detail with enough pressure to engrave the shapes on the paper. In the uneven, disordered beading of the disease, there was terrible beauty: it had created a compelling landscape of frenetic movement and sculptured chaos. It ravaged the calm uniformity of the lung. Her drawing of the diseased lung eclipsed the one she'd made of the healthy lung in every way.

She swatted at a mosquito on her calf and noticed that the sun had begun to set. She held her arm out, fingers stacked above the horizon. Another hour of light. She'd have to go soon. The next page showed a magnified cutaway drawing of one of the tubercles. The notation read, "liquefaction of caseous centre, advanced stage of the disease." She sketched its cavernous interior. How would these lesions look on a chest x-ray? Would they absorb or reflect light? Were these the nodes of darkness that told of advanced TB?

The facing plates on the next pages were x-rays of healthy and diseased lungs, but the notations were minimal and didn't connect them with the illustrations on the previous pages. Nor was it obvious what she should be seeing, even with a group of tiny white arrows that were meant to indicate the abnormality there. When Lachlan pointed to dark cavities in the lung, she'd always thought that the disease announced itself in unmistakable terms. Without his guidance, she was less certain. She tried again. On the left page were four x-rays of normal lungs. She stared at them, intending to memorize the features that signalled normalcy. On the right page was tuberculosis in order of its progress in the lungs, the final plate showing the most advanced case. Here normal, here diseased. She felt that she could discriminate between the absence of light that denoted a cavity in an advanced case, and a clear lung space. But in its milder forms the signature of the disease was far less legible, and she doubted that if tested she'd be able to distinguish a healthy lung from a diseased lung. Was that woolly tangle in the upper lobe a nest of tubercles that choked out the air, or a branch of bronchioles that carried it? Not even the trios of arrows helped. She drew hasty sketches in the failing light, trying to understand.

She knew that this exercise was for her own edification only. A scenario that demanded her interpretation of a lung x-ray was fanciful at best and a display of overreaching ambition at worst. And yet.

Lachlan had called her into his office that day and given her this book to read. She could help patients understand what they were looking at, even if only at a basic level. This might have been Lachlan's reason, and it fit his philosophy of rehabilitation. She wanted to be part of that. She wanted to help them understand that they would be well again one day. She wanted to give them hope for clear sky.

When she looked up from the page, the sun had already begun to intersect with the water. She stood almost involuntarily and the book slid from her lap, down the stairs. It would be foolish to be stuck here after sunset, no matter how brief the canoe journey back. The tides shifted without warning. She hurried down the stairs, picked up the textbook and her sketchbook and edged down the slope to the beach.

The canoe's stern bobbed in the river. Within the next half-hour, it would have been carried away by the rising tide. How careless. She might have been caught here overnight, and even if she could sleep in the cabin, they'd still expect her for her shift in the morning. She pushed the boat from shore and climbed in.

The current caught the canoe and carried it across the channel with little effort on her part, and as it approached the dock she noticed a figure slumped against a corner post. Henry, his cap pulled low over his eyes and his knees folded against his chest. He nodded to her as she reached for the dock. He didn't get up, even as she guided the canoe to the beach and dragged it high on shore.

"Everything okay, Nurse MacPherson?"

"Absolutely fine, Henry." She should have just walked away, but she didn't. "How long have you been here?"

"Since you went across."

"You can't have been sitting here the whole time."

He shrugged in his infuriating way, stretched his arms over his head and pushed himself to standing. "Strong tide tonight."

Dusk almost hid the cabin on Sawpit Island now, but he'd have been able to watch the river rise and lift the canoe from safety. "You did this on whose instructions?"

Henry's smile was crooked. "Mine. My idea."

"Yes. Well, I'm fine, as you can see. Thank you for your concern."

She walked up the dirt path between the maintenance buildings and the hospital, not sure whether she believed him and aware that she preferred not to. Ridiculous, of course. She'd chosen to inform no one that she was going nor did she desire to be watched over that way. In nursing stations along the coast of James Bay – Attawapiskat, Fort Albany, Povungnituk and communities smaller than these – she could be the sole medical resource for an entire community. In the previous six months, she'd frequently considered it, and Ruth talked about it too. As other nurses passed through the hospital on their way further north, they all did. You couldn't buy that kind of experience. If anything could draw out a passion for this work or kill it off for good, that would. Either way she'd find out what she needed to know. But with beds flowing out of the wards and into the hallways, and with nurses deserting for the resources and communities of southern sanatoriums, it was an idea that seemed almost self-indulgent. If she was going to make a move, she could wait until this epidemic was under control. Maybe by then she wouldn't want to.

She'd reached the corner of Centre and Thurston. Some of the lights in the residence had already been switched on. She heard voices through the kitchen window punctuated by shrieks of laughter. Ruth had to be involved, no question. Her skill as a mimic had earned her a hospital-wide reputation. She stepped into the main hall just as Hazel crossed the threshold.

"Oh! Hazel!" She wiped tears from her eyes. "There you are. Missed you at dinner." She noticed the textbook Hazel was carrying. "Working late?"

"You could say that." She'd tell Ruth about this, but later. It was enough that she'd remarked on it. The handful of nurses in the kitchen made their way to the door behind Ruth.

"Right." Ruth gave her a meaningful glance. Hazel willed the midwife to hold her tongue. "If only we were all as dedicated as you."

Hazel pulled the door closed behind her. The other nurses drifted back into the kitchen. "Did I miss anything? How's the chief?"

"Still coughing. Davies tried to get him into x-ray but he insists that it's just a flu and he's man enough to fight it."

Hazel shook her head. "I hope he's right."

SIX

A SOUND WOKE GIDEON FROM a deep sleep. He crawled to the
door and parted the canvas, first only an inch, then another and
then enough for his head and shoulders. He listened, barely breathing. It had seemed close, so close. His heart hammered. Were there
bears in these woods? He pulled his head back into the tent and
tied the door closed.

He sat up and listened, but heard nothing more. To calm himself he opened his box and set his books in a pile on the ground
beside him, one by one. *The Geographical Journal. Birds over America.
Edible Wild Plants. Roughing it in the Bush.* When he'd heard nothing more in a long time, he untied the flaps and crawled out. The
sky was pale rose. It was still very early. He glanced around his
camp and then turned back to the white pine.

Where was his knife? He was on his knees at the base of the tree now, scooping away handfuls of pine needles and earth from the tree roots. Nothing. He sat back on his heels. Last night he'd pitched the tent, started to dig, then etched the marker into the pine bark. He scanned the tree, roots to tip, and saw it standing handle-up in a branch. He shut his eyes and exhaled. His lips moved without sound and when he opened his eyes again, his breathing had calmed. He would not be so lax with his possessions again. He pulled the knife from the branch and finished carving the shape he'd outlined in the bark, chanting under his breath. The shape of the symbol was distinct now, the strokes of the arc smooth and sure, the sphere below it round and tangible. He stood back, crossed his arms and returned its fearless gaze.

He dug a hole at the base of the pine and lowered the box into it. A good fit. It would be safe there, but he needed it with him today. He pulled it out again and made a restless circuit of his camp, then picked up an umbrella and sat at the edge of the bluff. He'd found some on the way here, two for parts, two for mending. Together they would make a morning's work. He could take them into the settlement and sell them, buy some supplies.

The best one was first. It was locomotive black and the mercerized cotton still shone. The wood handle was only slightly scuffed, but two ribs had snapped. They were side by side and conveniently located near the twist in the wire. He found his smallest pliers, opened the wire loop at the base and slipped the ribs out of it. Then he found the matching join at the ring on the shank and performed the same operation. Now the broken ribs were free.

He reached for the umbrella he'd picked up for parts. A few good ribs remained. He loosened these in the same way, threaded them into the good umbrella and closed the wire loops. The open umbrella's canopy was smooth and ready for rain. Ten repairs in, he felt he'd finally earned the title he desired: Mushfaker. He liked the sound of it. He'd said it aloud a few times when he'd first read about Roving Bill's nomadic travels across the country, fixing clocks and umbrellas for his bread. It was an authentic way to live.

Gideon ran his fingers along the wood handle and found the places it might accept a new shape. It was a tempting thought and he picked up his carving knife and held it a few minutes, but put it down again. Not this one, not today. There was too much left to be done. He threaded a needle and replaced the three missing tips. The work he'd done on this umbrella was good. He smiled and reached for the second one.

BY THE TIME THE SUN laid down tracks across the fresh scar in the white pine, Gideon was gone. He'd slung the box over his shoulder, balanced the two working umbrellas on it and walked the path south toward the main settlement.

That was when he saw her, crossing the road in her medical whites with a determined stride. Hazel gathered her long hair and with deft fingers pinned it into a high knot as she walked. Gideon stepped into a copse of trees and tracked her progress toward the white building. His eye followed the milky curve of her neck, the sway of her hips, the mesmerizing turns of her ankles. Even after she'd passed through the doors and out of his sight he was still there, watching.

HE WOULD EAT TONIGHT. TODAY he'd found the trading post and sold an umbrella. His stomach rumbled as he took cans from his pack and piled them inside his tent. The beans didn't need heating but he wanted a fire. There was a good spot near the edge of the bluff. He hopped down to the beach in bare feet and lifted stones from the water to the lip of his camp. The last was much larger than the rest and he grunted as he hoisted it over his shoulder and rolled it inland.

A month into his journey, he was already practiced at making a tripod that wouldn't collapse into the firepit and take his meal with it. It was a lesson reinforced by hunger in his first few days on the road. He sat on the large rock with the longest, greenest branches he'd been able to find and laid lashing cord on the ground beside him. The downward strokes of the knife were quick and sure and he had two branches sharpened in minutes.

His hand was in motion with the third when a gull screamed, startlingly close and shrill. The knife missed the branch and took a clean bite from his exposed shin. It wasn't the first time he'd cut himself, but it was the deepest. He blinked in shock and gulped at the air, stared at the blood beading the surface of too-white flesh until he felt woozy. He shook his head. He let the knife fall to the ground and dropped his head between his knees. When a twig snapped nearby, he looked up. Henry stood at the edge of his camp.

"Hey," Gideon said, weakly.

SEVEN

HAZEL CHECKED HER WATCH TO be sure: eight-thirty. She was not late. And yet he'd started without her. Through the open door to the exam room she saw a young Inuit woman on the table against the wall, her shirt in a disordered heap beside her. This was odd. Things were different in the north but not so different; a nurse should be present for an exam of a female patient by a male doctor. It was standard procedure. Lachlan should know better. She caught his eye and raised her eyebrow. He shrugged and handed her the file.

The young mother had come in the night before on a small fishing boat, not on suspicion of TB but what Charlie's hastily scribbled note referred to as a breast abscess. Her baby was laid on the floor beside her, bundled in a long narrow ticknoggen with criss-crossed leather laces. That her left breast was an unusual size and didn't match her right couldn't be debated. But a breast abscess?

"This can't be right." Hazel handed the file back to Lachlan. The young woman's braided hair shone, her cheeks were plump, she was alert and smiling. "She looks too healthy."

"We're agreed, then." He tapped his pen on the table, scratched at the beginnings of a beard and leafed through scraps of paper on his desk. He swivelled the chair around and faced her.

"*Qanuippa?*"

The woman smiled again. "*Qanuinngittunga.*"

Lachlan frowned. "Needless to say, she feels fine. With an abscess that size, she wouldn't." He held a stethoscope to her chest. "Lungs are clear." He slipped the earpieces from his ears. "I wonder if it's her own baby. *Nutarait una?*"

The woman nodded. She motioned for him to come nearer, and then her gaze settled on Hazel, frank and inquiring. Hazel had a fleeting glimpse of her reflection in the shiny surface of the sterilizer and was suddenly aware of the pallor of her skin, the chemical whiteness of her uniform, the starched folds of her cap and the unnatural orderliness of her hair. If not for the pressed and spotless lab coat provided for him every morning, Lachlan looked as though he'd just rolled out of bed. He'd certainly been awake for hours and he was smiling now. A puzzle like this was a satisfying way to start the day.

The woman motioned again for Lachlan to come closer. He leaned toward her, his face now no more than six inches from her left breast. Any sense of decorum he might have possessed was gone. He'd given over to his greater desire for an answer. The woman's neck and shoulders were free from visible tension and there was a glint of mischief in her dark eyes. She was in no hurry. In fact, there was a languid quality to the way she raised her hand to the larger breast and massaged it.

Lachlan sputtered and slid his glasses away from his face. He held them at arm's length from his body between finger and thumb, allowing the spray of breast milk that had caught him full on the face to drip to the floor while he reached to the shelf above his desk for a tissue. He blinked and wiped the milk from his face, reached for his chair and lowered himself into it. As he wiped his glasses, he straightened his back and closed his eyes a moment. Then he put the glasses back on and turned toward the desk and wrote. His restraint was admirable. Almost inhuman. Hazel bit her lip, in imminent danger of losing her composure.

After what seemed an eternity, Lachlan turned to face the Inuit woman. "That's one leaky abscess." The angle of his eyebrows was stern, but the corner of his mouth was beginning to twitch. "One of a kind, I'd say."

The end of the sentence hadn't made it out of his mouth before Hazel surrendered to a most unprofessional burst of laughter. His comment had been in English and clearly for her benefit, but the woman needed no translation. She gestured toward her sleeping baby and chuckled softly. Lachlan pointed to her smaller breast and mimed a squeeze of his own. She shook her head, serious now, and spoke a few words.

"Well, Nurse MacPherson, that's as far as we get without a translator." He leaned back in his chair. "She seems in no immediate danger, as you have seen, and her sense of humour is intact. But the size difference between the breasts is remarkable. I see why Doctor Wilcox sent her." He stroked his chin. "See if you can find Joseph."

"On my way."

She thought she'd heard his voice in the hall a few minutes earlier and she was right: there he was, crossing the hall in the men's ward. By the time they were back in the clinic the baby was awake and moving his head side to side, beginning to root for a feeding. Joseph nodded once to the woman. "Aye."

The woman nodded and smiled. Lachlan shifted in his chair. "Ask her if she knows why her left breast is so much larger than the right."

The two exchanged words, the woman gesturing toward her baby and then to herself. Joseph faced Lachlan. "She says her first baby died while feeding." His tone was characteristically flat. "She fell asleep and the baby couldn't get air."

Lachlan frowned. "Fine, but that shouldn't affect her production of milk for this baby."

Joseph paused. "The right side is unlucky now. She will not feed the baby on that side."

"Ah." Lachlan stroked his chin again. "She does realize . . ." Joseph's slow blink was a direct challenge and Lachlan's voice trailed off. This was something Hazel hadn't seen before. "Never mind. Please tell her that unless she has any other health concerns, we will arrange for her return to her community as soon as possible."

HAZEL'S FIRST GLIMPSE OF THE hospital was from the compact window of a Cessna. Dead of winter, six months earlier, she'd stepped off the train from Toronto to Cochrane and found Lachlan waiting for her on the platform. She had a ticket for the five-hour train trip to Moosonee, and from there a Bombardier would have carried her across the frozen river to Moose Factory, but Lachlan had arranged to be on a supply plane to Cochrane that day. They sat among the cargo and were circling Moose Factory an hour later. The 163-bed infirmary had been impossible to miss, dwarfing every other permanent structure on the island.

"Notice the shape of it?" He sketched it on the back of his file folder, a centre staff with a set of parallel arms. He hadn't waited for her answer. "Cross of Lorraine. Like Joan of Arc wore." He'd smiled when she said, "A different kind of crusade."

In the six months since her arrival she'd spent more time in this place than anywhere else on the island, but she was still waiting to feel devoted to the cause. She picked up the envelope Lachlan asked for and started back down the hallway.

The door to his office was open when she came to it, but he didn't notice her, not even when she stepped inside and stood there a few minutes, waiting. This was nothing new, but that day she wished she could be spared the indignity of having to draw attention to herself. She'd encountered the depth and quality of his concentration repeatedly in the years she'd known him, but once in a while came this shift in expectation, this need to be more visible to him than anyone else was. It didn't help that in this habit he was utterly democratic; if he'd descended to the bottom of his well of study, the world and everyone in it disappeared, no exceptions. The fact that she fell into that undistinguished population was no consolation. She took a step closer and cleared her throat.

"Nurse MacPherson. Oh. Yes. Thank you." He was startled. There was that, at least. He took the envelope, but she didn't turn to go. His eyebrows lifted.

"The waiting room is clear. It's five."

He pushed his chair out from his desk, in line with the door to the waiting room. "So it is. We're done for the day, then. Please lock up."

"You don't need anything else?"

"Not a thing. See you tomorrow."

"Sure." She pulled his door closed behind her. The waiting room was quiet now but showed signs of the day it had been, the chairs in disarray, one of the TB prevention posters hanging by a single pin, the old magazines sent by the volunteers in Hamilton in a heap under the chairs. She picked them up and lined the chairs against the wall.

There was a knock at the hollow metal door that led outside, two sharp raps. She noticed the shape of him first, a reedy upward spill that flowed almost to the top of the door frame. The man standing there pushed his shoulders back and settled his black bowler hat on the nest of his dark blond hair. Even through the reinforced glass she could make out the blue burn of his eyes. His three-quarter length coat was black with wide lapels and outdated by a decade or more, and he wore it over a black vest, dirty white shirt and black trousers. He carried a wooden box by a leather strap over his shoulder with an umbrella laid on the lid.

"Hey, nurse." He pushed the door open. "I'm the mushfaker. I've come about the umbrellas."

For a few hallucinogenic moments, she could think of nothing to say. Her mind chased the details of the end-of-day events, as if tracing that trajectory could answer to this aberration. She'd set out patient history sheets for the next day's appointments and made a list of supplies the clinic had run short of so she could pick them up from the dispensary before her shift started. She had fetched the x-rays and delivered them to Lachlan. She'd tidied the waiting room. All unremarkable. All routine, all done in the usual way.

And yet, there he stood as if he belonged. Disconnected pieces of language floated unhelpfully around her mind. She shook her head. "I don't..."

"That's why I've come." He winked. "May I?"

He was already stepping across the threshold. She became aware of a thudding in her chest and tried to talk herself out of it. Lachlan was just in the next room. Could any of this commotion penetrate his deep focus? Never mind. She should be able to take care of herself. She reached for her purse.

"We're just closing up for the day." The voice belonged to a no-nonsense nurse, and it was a relief to recognize it as her own. "Is there something you need?"

The man's smile was dazzling, assured. "No, like I said, I'm here to help you. I can fix all of your umbrellas. It's much cheaper than buying new ones from the store up the road. Look at this one. Good as new, now I've mended it, but can you believe I found it in the trash by the road on my way up here? See the workmanship on the handle? And the cloth, mercerized cotton, heavy duty and smooth as silk. Don't make 'em like this anymore." He pushed the lever to open it.

"Not inside, please. It's bad luck." Why on earth had she said that? She tried to laugh, but the tightness in her throat made it come out like something between a cough and a sigh. With him in it, the room had become small.

"Ah, a superstitious one." He rubbed his hands together and flashed a brilliant smile. She noticed the sheen of worn fabric on his lapels and shoulders, the fraying at his cuffs and his clean-shaven jaw. "My favourite kind."

His face was a lantern now, and the blood in her cheeks mimicked it. Her heart was beating too fast. Who did he think he was, assuming such familiarity and staring at her so frankly? She folded her arms across her chest. Surely Lachlan could hear what was going on. Surely the sound of a foreign male voice would rouse him.

"Is there something I can help you with?"

Lachlan's door opened. Finally. "Another patient, Nurse MacPherson?" His appraisal of the man was clinical and frank. "Do you need a doctor?"

"No, sir, I do not, though I appreciate the offer. I'm here to fix your umbrellas. Gideon Judge." He said his name as if it should explain everything and extended his hand. "Mushfaker."

Hazel thought she'd known Lachlan long enough to decipher his expressions, but this one was new and unreadable. He raised his eyebrows and ignored Gideon's extended hand.

"Mushfaker."

Gideon grinned. "Umbrella mender. All-round fix-it man. At your service."

"Very well. Doctor Lachlan Davies. Nice to meet you." He waved away the umbrella that Gideon was holding out for him. "We've no work for a mushfaker at the moment. To my knowledge, all of our umbrellas are in good working order, but we'll keep you in mind should any such emergencies arise. Nurse MacPherson will show you out. Good day." He caught her eye, nodded once and closed the door behind him.

"Well, then, sir." She reached for her coat. Lachlan's presence had helped her right herself. She walked toward the outer door and opened it. "We do appreciate your visit. Perhaps you'd like to leave a card?"

Gideon cocked his head to one side and smiled. "Doesn't work that way. I'm here while I'm here. A place can't hold me long." Later, when he'd gone, Hazel would consider what she'd say to Ruth. News of this visitor would reach her by the end of the day in a community this size. There was no way Hazel could give over the totality of the man in words alone. Neither would a photograph have done justice. She could describe his manner of dress, the way he held his body, the odd assortment of goods he carried with him, the various inconsistencies among these. But none of it would add up to the unsettling sum of his presence.

He studied her face as if to memorize it, then pushed his hands into his pockets and turned to walk out. She had her hand on the door to close it when he stopped on the threshold.

"Well." His face was tilted toward the sky. "Would you look at that."

She released the doorknob. "Look at him, wheeling around, the way he paces. Come on out here, you'll get a better view." He spoke as if sharing a confidence and stepped out to the hospital lawn without breaking eye contact with whatever he saw. She glanced over her shoulder. Lachlan's door was still closed. Could he be listening? She hesitated a moment and then stepped outside. A few gulls, a duck, a couple of clouds.

"No, nurse. Higher. Way up." He nudged her and pointed. "There."

She saw the bird then, a solitary presence far above the others. It rode the wind for only brief moments and then began pulling itself across the sky again, making tight turns.

"I read that falcons were plenty up this way, but to see one again so soon . . ." He hooked his thumb into his shoulder strap. "And he's hunting, see? Lots to choose from up here, but I guess he's after those ducks just now. What else do you see around here? Geese? Snow buntings? Gulls? Starlings? Maybe some grouse?" She couldn't see his face but there was a smile in his voice. "Ah, what a beauty. The way he flies! No hesitation. He owns the sky, and even if the wind offers it he won't rest until he's got what he wants." He reached into his breast pocket and pulled out a small pair of brass binoculars. "Oh! He's a she. Here. Take a look."

It was a simple thing, and taking them from him would have been a natural response, but she resisted it. He was already too familiar with her and they'd only just met. He lifted his extended arm again.

"Go on. It won't hurt you to look."

She shook her head. The refusal felt a little ridiculous but doing what he asked would only encourage him. He waited a few more moments and his hand dropped. He shrugged and raised the binoculars to his face again. "Suit yourself."

She turned back toward the clinic door and set one foot on the step. She was probably overreacting. What was the harm? Lachlan was within hearing range. In a few minutes this man would be gone and she'd be making the short walk to the nurses' residence. It was a good day for a walk before dinner. Nothing had changed.

Children played in the yards of the staff houses behind the hospital and their shrieks filled the early summer air. The sun was hours from setting. She'd never seen a falcon.

"Maybe for a minute. Then I have to get back."

"Sure, sure, of course." He handed the binoculars to her. The metal was still warm. "Just watch how she circles. See that? She's hunting. Something for the little ones."

"How do you know it's female?" Even with the binoculars, she could only pick out colour and shape. The bird moved so fast that she lost it from view, twice.

"Look how big she is. A male couldn't be. Girls are always bigger ..." He turned to her. "In birds of prey." Heat rose from her collar like a flow of lava, and she knew her skin would be as red. She turned away and tried to spot the bird again. He stood behind her, close enough that she could feel his breath on her neck. Her shoulders locked and the muscles around her spine clamped down defensively. She willed herself to relax. There was nothing to fear here. They were standing in the open where anyone could see them.

His voice dropped to a whisper. "You're four, five hundred feet off the ground, Nurse MacPherson." She shivered at the sound of her name on his tongue. "You're one with the air to the hollows of your bones. The wind buffets you, but only if you feel like playing; your wings are strong, all sinew and muscle. A single flap lifts you out of danger. You pull your feathers in sleek against you. You're gliding, wheeling. You can see forever! You're in the mood to hunt, you always are, and then there's a starling just below you, and you want it for your little ones. They're crying in the nest and you can feel it in your gut. You wheel around and turn tight. Then there it is: the starling snaps onto your grid and you lock on him like a missile, and you know that when you pull your wings in against your body and drop like a stone down, down out of the sky, he'll be exactly where you expect him to be. You're falling, falling, the wind licks the tears right out of your eyes and parts the feathers on your chest, two hundred miles an hour sharp against your bare skin. And at the last possible moment, just as the ground is rushing up to claim you, there he is, a breath away. You could knock him right out of the air but you don't, you kick out your leg instead, your four toes snap wide and with a single slash you've laid his head wide open. In the next second you feel the nerves electric along your wings as they unfurl, whomp, and you open your beak and snap it shut on his neck. The down feathers are soft and warm on your tongue. Starling blood trickles down your gullet and it tastes . . ." He brought his mouth close to her ear and lowered his voice. "It tastes like lightning."

There was a sharp intake of breath that she almost didn't recognize as her own. She swallowed, the metallic tang of her own blood in it. At some point she'd closed her eyes; when she opened them, he was standing right there, nodding.

She felt thrown clear of her skin. Her top lip slid over bottom and found the break in the skin, a ridge of cells rising. "I . . . I have to go now." She shoved the binoculars at him and pushed open the door to the clinic.

EVEN FROM A DISTANCE, THE umbrella mender was unmistakable. Of course he was. She rounded the bend past the church and spotted him on the slope at the far side of the main docks. No one on the island bore the slightest resemblance to him, but it was too easy to reduce his singularity to an eccentric suit.

Now his head was bent over his work and something in his hand caught the sun. He was a magpie huddled over his treasure, so intent on his work that she doubted he'd notice her, and she preferred to keep it that way. Once today had been plenty. She was just out for a walk, as usual. This is what she told herself.

A cloud of biting insects hovered in the air around her head and she waved them off. The man in the freight canoe just off-shore raised his hand in response. She squinted and waved again. Had she treated him in the hospital? Maybe, but not necessarily. The people on the island were friendly and quick with a joke, not the reticent population she'd expected when she'd decided to come to Moose Factory. Even the landscape was more lush and familiar than she'd pictured. The place had required less adjustment than she'd imagined, and she'd felt oddly disappointed about that. It wasn't that she'd hoped for hardship, precisely, and there was the isolation of the place to contend with, but this wasn't the exotic frozen tundra she'd imagined, either. She'd have to go further north for that, and she intended to.

Ordinarily she'd have continued past the main dock, but today she edged down the hill toward the water on the near side of the dock. Her shoes slid in the soft earth. She told herself that it had been too long since she'd sat at a water's edge. She took her shoes off and burrowed her toes into sand still warm from the sun. It was impossible to ignore the fact that the umbrella mender was a few hundred feet upstream. When he lifted his head in her direction, she froze. She closed her eyes and wished herself invisible, or at least unrecognizable out of uniform. And she was, it seemed. When she opened them again he'd turned back to his work with no sign that he'd seen her.

She exhaled and became aware that she'd been holding her breath. This was ridiculous and unlike her. She untied the scarf around her neck and covered her hair with it, and lay back on the sand. The day had been long, that must be it, beginning with the curious breast abscess. Mother and baby were settled in an empty triage room for the night and scheduled for transport back to their community in the morning. Annie was doing well enough, too, Lachlan said, though when she'd asked Sally about the elder

Inuit's appetite, the nurse's aide shook her head. That was normal as they settled in and learned a different diet, but she'd mention it to Lachlan.

The slow sail of the clouds was mesmerizing and she was tired. Her eyelids were heavy when a child shrieked at close range. She sat up too fast.

"Did we wake you, Nurse MacPherson?" It was an accusation, not an apology. There was always something hostile in Nell Moore's tone. It was no secret that the factor's wife had been petitioning her husband for a transfer to another Hudson's Bay post almost since they'd arrived a few months earlier. Since she'd volunteered to help Nell with the children on Sundays at St. Thomas's, Hazel had noticed a slight thaw in her attitude.

"Oh, no, of course not, Mrs. Moore." Hazel stifled a yawn. "I just came to sit a minute and ..."

"That's far enough, Reginald James. It's not nearly warm enough to swim yet." The woman's voice grated. Her blond preschooler had run to the water's edge, kicked off his shoes and splashed into the water. "Such a little daredevil. Just like his father." She pulled the brim of her straw hat lower on her forehead and scanned the shore.

"Still there, is he? Thought he'd gone back by now." She tipped her head in Gideon's direction. "That fellow over there, dressed like an undertaker. Did you see him today? He came to our door offering to fix umbrellas, or sell them. I don't really know what he wanted. Gave himself a funny-sounding name, something foreign."

"Mushfaker?" Once she'd said it, the word seemed a confession, and Hazel wished she hadn't.

Nell raised her eyebrows. "That's it. I suppose he came by the clinic, too?"

"Less than an hour ago, just as we were locking up. He walked right in."

Nell shook her head. "Oh no, my dear. You shouldn't have let him. Next thing you know you'll have a clinic full of them, cracking body lice with their fingernails and begging for bread." She shuddered. "His kind, you never know."

"I didn't. Let him in, I mean. He just walked in."

"Well, a young woman like yourself ought to be more careful when you're on your own." This was maddening. She was no more than two years older than Hazel.

"The hospital is a public space, as you know." Hazel's need to continue to argue this point was vexing, but she couldn't stop herself. "And Doctor Davies was just in the next room."

"I suppose he would have protected you then, wouldn't he." Of all possible responses, this one cut the deepest, but she'd walked right into it. She was not like Nell, not remotely. She could take up a post further north if she wanted. Alone. She depended on no one. "We'd better go, Reggie-dear. Your father will be wanting his dinner soon." She shot Hazel a tight smile and reached for the boy's hand.

Hazel watched them climb the slope, then stood and brushed the sand from her trousers. She no longer felt drowsy, and even when she finally climbed into bed, the questions rode long into the night. She closed her eyes and saw the falcon circling, felt Gideon's breath on the back of her neck, and when she finally dropped into sleep he was there, too. She twitched awake and picked up her wristwatch. Five a.m., a single hour since she'd finally fallen asleep. She ran her top lip over bottom. The split had healed to a swollen bead. She probed it with her tongue and vowed that he'd never cost her another night.

EIGHT

IN WINTER, THE SAWTOOTH EVERGREEN horizon behind the hospital had to be taken on faith until nearly nine in the morning, but this was late June. At six-thirty, only the shadow side of the hospital lawn wore a patchwork quilt of light reflected from the windows. Even if she hadn't slept properly, it felt good to be here this early. It always did. The cushion of time before her shift officially began made all things seem possible.

Today she wasn't alone. She'd come down from her room and found Ruth on her way to the hospital. "Come watch this with me." Ruth held up the package she was carrying. "We'll take some eggs up there with us."

Hazel pulled open the door to the flagpole entrance and nodded to the commissionaire. The smell of coffee in the front hall was an undertow. "I assume we're going to the auditorium?"

Ruth nodded. Her hair was wet and pulled back from her face, tidy as long as the weight of water held it. "But we'll have to check with the aides. They have early morning demos up there sometimes." She handed the package to Hazel. "Queue it up, will you? Try the supply cabinet at the far end if the projector isn't already set up. I'll go for breakfast."

"And coffee."

"Duly noted, Captain." Ruth gave her a mock salute. They'd been out canoeing on the Moose River a few months earlier and Hazel had steered them in the wrong direction. It was a title she'd earned, Ruth said dryly. "Coming right up."

Hazel opened the door to the stairs. The stairwell was an oppressive chimney of heat; the combination of fire doors and stairwell radiators that seemed to be on whatever the season ensured that it always was. She took the stairs by twos.

"Whoa, Nurse MacPherson. Where's the fire?" Lachlan noticed the envelope in her hand. "Oh, yes, good. Watch it together. Fine idea."

Ruth described the film as an educational short, and until it arrived from Mountain yesterday they'd had nothing like it in half a year. Lachlan insisted that it suit the northern audiences, most of whom still spoke only scant English, and asked her to screen it first.

"It's no run-of-the-mill health ed. picture, did Ruth tell you? The director has a reputation. I think they might get something out of it."

She slid the grey metal case from the envelope. *Goodbye, Mr. Germ.* For children, surely, but Lachlan would be counting on the simple language to make it suitable for patients new to English. It could work. Even if they could understand little of the dialogue, the Inuit and Cree patients were keen on the moving pictures they showed on a sheet strung across one of the lesser-used hallways on Saturdays; since Lachlan had hit upon the idea there had been a consistently robust turnout. Even the most despondent patients found their way into chairs.

"Saturday afternoon at the movies, Doctor Davies?"

"Exactly what I had in mind. What else have we got?"

"We still have *Key Largo* and *Treasure of the Sierra Madre*."

"Last week was *Casablanca*, correct?"

"A regular Bogart festival."

Lachlan smiled and reached for the honey-coloured wood handrail. The builders had used the poplar trees growing where the hospital now stood, and it was the one nod to their northern location in the hospital's otherwise stark and pragmatic interior. The rest of the building was standard government issue, low-ceilinged and white-walled like a battleship.

"Let me know what you think. Maybe we could show it to the children, too."

She nodded and climbed the final flight to the third floor. Only nurse's aides lived here now. That it was a riot of domesticity was always a bit of a shock after the quiet order of the wards. Today clusters of young women in housecoats and curlers dodged an orderly steering a floor buffer in the hallway, trading gossip and stockings as they moved between showers and breakfast.

Hazel had never known sleep inside the hospital walls. The day she arrived in Moose Factory, a room had been ready for her at the new RN residence on Thurston. Her room was a monk's cell, large enough for a single bed, a chair, a narrow closet and a metal dresser, but for the privilege of living apart, for the small interval of space and time at the end of each day, she was grateful.

She heard Sally's voice in the kitchen and stopped in the doorway. The Cree nurse's aide frowned in concentration as she pinned up her dark hair, holding hairpins in her mouth while carrying on a conversation with an older woman that Hazel recognized from the island community. She must have just started working at the hospital.

"Anybody need the auditorium in the next half-hour?"

Sally patted her hair. "Oh-uh-yeah. We do. We were just going over there. Saturday morning is poker, eh, Mary?" She winked at the other aide and they giggled. "Only joking, Nurse MacPherson. It's all yours."

Another peal of laughter followed her along the hallway. She ducked into the corridor that led to the auditorium. She was not in the mood. Her head felt brittle from the lack of sleep and she needed caffeine. It was a chemical dependency that she resented, but she was on the wrong side of a ten-hour shift for this level of lethargy. There was work to be done and few hands to do it. The survey boat was going out for a couple of days; the pace would only increase while it was gone. The fact that the umbrella mender had cost her a night's sleep was an irritation. She was no flighty girl. How could she have let herself be taken in?

The doors to the auditorium were closed but unlocked, and when her eyes adjusted to the half-light she saw that a screen was already set up. She went to the bank of windows and faced the channel, thinking some fresh air would do her good, and noticed Henry at the dock readying the *Mercer* for the trip, lifting and swinging packages of supplies on board with practiced ease. She pushed a window open, undid the latch to the door of the flat roof and stepped outside.

The sun slipped over the horizon and lit the channel behind the hospital, picking its brilliant way across the goosebumped surface of the water. She saw Henry lift his head in response. She turned to face it, toward the shore that until a few weeks earlier was a wild heath that overlooked the bend in the river. Cree women moved between cookfire and tipi, tending pots and babies. She was still getting used to the city of tents, there for the summer trading season, that had appeared almost overnight and crouched along the water's edge. Curls of smoke lifted above them and caught in the pine branches. Gulls cried and circled overhead. She followed their flight path until she faced the dock again. There was variation in their calls, a constant and looping relay that was a conversation she could almost understand. How had she never noticed it before?

"Thought you were desperate for coffee."

"I am," she said, with reflexive sharpness. She hadn't heard Ruth come out.

"What's happening?"

Charlie had joined Henry on the dock, hands on hips as he supervised the boat's preparation. Since the river opened up, he was spending more time on the survey boat than in the hospital. "Nothing special. The *Mercer* goes out again today."

Ruth tipped her head toward the door. "Well, then? The eggs are lukewarm and it's six-forty-five. I have to be on the floor in fifteen minutes, which happens to be the exact length of this movie. Shall we?" She turned and began walking back, not waiting for Hazel's response. A few stray gulls circled the dock.

Ruth had left the lights off and was sitting cross-legged in the front row, breakfast plate balanced on her lap. She motioned toward a plate beside the projector. "They've run through all of the bacon already. Turn the projector on, will you? I've set it all up."

Hazel's hand shook as she flipped the switch. She'd been awake for hours but hadn't eaten. She picked up her plate and sat beside Ruth. After the first forkful it hadn't seemed possible to swallow fast enough, and in minutes she'd devoured the breakfast and washed it down with coffee that was as hot and strong as she'd hoped it would be. Another cup and she'd be back in fighting shape, ready for anything the shift might throw at her.

Ruth shook her head. Her own plate was still half full. "Did you taste that at all, Captain?"

Hazel shrugged. "I was hungry."

"Well no wonder." The opening credits scrolled up the screen. "What with the schedule at the clinic yesterday."

This was new. If Ruth had seen her with the umbrella mender, it was unlike her to play games like this. Hazel focused on the screen. Cartoon children gathered around a cartoon father, poring over the science book he held in his lap and talking about bacteria. Though this was an angle she hadn't seen before, she expected it to end predictably, as these things generally did. But the narrative took a radical turn when the father wondered aloud about inventing a special radio that could hear what the germs were saying. The family gathered around a microscope in their home laboratory and listened to a molecule of mycobacterium tuberculosis introduce himself and tell his story. It was unconventional and silly, but it worked. She pulled her notebook from her pocket and sketched the cartoon molecule.

Ruth's fork clattered to her empty plate. "The clinic must have been overflowing if you needed to examine patients out of doors."

So there it was. On closer examination, she wasn't sure why she'd kept him to herself. On the face of it, there was nothing to tell. An unusual man had appeared in the clinic, offered to fix umbrellas and then told her about a bird. But if that was all, why hadn't she slept?

She looked away from the screen and into Ruth's unflinching gaze. "Didn't have a chance to mention it yet." She tried to sound nonchalant. It was a stretch. "Nothing to tell, really. He was a bit of an odd duck, a sort of travelling salesman, so he said." She turned back to the screen. It was enough that he'd cost her the night's sleep. She had work to do. The movie was outlandish but engaging. These things were necessary and rarely interesting, but this director had made an effort. Mr. Germ was conducting a tour of the body now, indicating his path in. "This isn't half bad, you know. The animation is quirky but not dependent on dialogue. He seems to have considered the language issues."

"And you have no recollection of what he was selling."

Ruth and Hazel had known each other for only six months, but Hazel never had to wonder what was on Ruth's mind. Yes, her answers were evasive and Ruth wasn't fooled. Yes, she was protecting the episode for reasons that were still unavailable to her. She shrugged. "He was selling umbrellas, some old ones he'd fixed. As he was leaving he saw a falcon and wanted me to see it too. He was quite insistent on that point. That's why we were outside."

"And so you did?"

"The clinic was empty and it was the end of the day. And you already know the answer to that question." She didn't owe Ruth an explanation. "So? Can we move on?"

"So nothing." Ruth set her plate on the table, and the downturn in her voice doused the anger Hazel felt flaring. The man was an interesting diversion in an isolated place that Ruth was obviously sorry to have missed, and Hazel was holding out. "Yes, the animation is clever and the language is simple. We can show this to our patients and they will probably understand it." She paused. "Did you buy one, then?"

Hazel realized that she couldn't remember whether he'd picked up his case before going out the door. Her lasting image of his departure had been the way he'd swung his arm as he'd walked away. He must have taken his case with him. If it was still at the clinic, surely Lachlan would have noticed and said something this morning. Unless he hadn't been there yet. She wanted to go check.

"I didn't need one. Or have one that needed fixing."·

Ruth snorted. "For a woman of fairly good brain, Hazel, sometimes you are daft. *I didn't need one.*" She mimicked Hazel's inflection and tone with alarming skill. "Even if they were ordinary umbrellas, and I'd wager they weren't, you ought to have bought one." Ruth's assessment was so accurate it was uncanny. Either she'd seen them from a window or someone had described it to her. At that moment Hazel found she didn't care which it was. She had nothing to hide.

"As you say. Old-fashioned mercerized cotton, if you want his description. Anything else?"

"No. Not unless there's anything you want to tell me." Ruth waited a couple of minutes and then went on. "From where I was standing, he was darling – that sweet crazy suit and hat he was wearing." The end of the film slid through the machine and ticked around the back reel. She stood and turned it off. "What d'you reckon?"

Heat rose from Hazel's collar to her hairline and she was grateful the room was dim. She shrugged. "If you like that sort of thing." To her own ears, she'd managed an offhand tone. "I had the impression he'd been sleeping rough."

"I meant about the movie." Ruth fit the reel into its metal case and sat down beside Hazel. Her eyes narrowed. "What happened to your lip?"

"Nothing. I bit it." She reached for the lid and closed the film case. "I think it's fine for children and adults. You?"

"Agreed." Ruth stood to face her.

"Good. I'll let Davies know." She made her way to the door. "I didn't invite him in, you know."

"Of course you didn't." Hazel heard her stacking the plates. "Did you get a good look at the bird, at least?"

"Yes." Every impulse told her that the conversation should end there, but she couldn't stop herself. "Ever see a falcon?"

"Sure. Back in Australia." There was a smile in her voice now. "My baby brother lived for hawks, was forever at the skies with his binoculars." She paused. "Shall we show this after rest period, with the Saturday afternoon movie?"

"Sure. I'll start setting up about quarter to two. Coming?"

"All else being equal, Captain. It's a full moon and we're expecting a few babies around here."

Watching plumes of soapstone dust rise from the seated figures of six Inuit men in the craft room, Hazel felt a rare and fierce swell of pride. Two years earlier, these men would have been listless and confined to beds, now and for an endless procession of months, even years. But here they were on the main floor of the hospital, not only up from their beds but well enough to squat on the bare linoleum floor, a lump of soapstone in one hand and a file in the other, for a couple of hours a day. Lachlan's enthusiasm was justified. The new drugs were working, and quickly: some of the men in this room had arrived only a month earlier. Sonorous bursts of Inuktitut traded throughout the room, and though she caught only a word here or there, it was clear that wit was the currency. Gains were measured in laughter from the others, and on this count the man near the left wall, his hands gloved in white stone dust, was ahead.

Suujuq. The one who'd arrived wearing a ptarmigan coat and snow goggles. She remembered his fury and glanced at his hand. There it was, the scar standing out against the powdered whiteness of his skin. She'd made sure that he was accepting food by the third day, but for the first couple of weeks after his arrival, his dark, serious eyes were unreflecting as river stones and the slack attitude of his body in the hospital bed had put him on the suicide watch list. She'd resolved to find a way to draw him out, but they were over capacity and had been since he'd arrived, the

163-bed hospital hovering in the low 200s, beds packed into the wards, in the hallways and sunrooms, and outside on balconies in fine weather. But his presence in the craft room was evidence that Lachlan had managed to keep the man in his sights: this room, once a linen closet, had enough room for six men at a time, and only just. The competition among the patients for this privilege, for the chance to relieve their boredom, was fierce. Doctors decided who was well enough to be here.

Intent now on the figure emerging from the stone, Suujuq was changed utterly. The harsh angles of his high cheekbones had softened and his hands brushed the dust from the sculpture in sure strokes. Hazel made out the soft peak of a parka hood and a raised arm. He blew dust from the figure, turned it over and over in his hands, and held it at eye level. She'd long been cured of the impulse to offer prognosis, and she wouldn't have said it aloud, but she made a mental note to find out where his coat had been stored and keep tabs on it. He'd need it again.

The door swung open and Joseph staggered in with a new load of soapstone. She'd watched him carry shipments of the raw material into the room by hand since they began arriving in the hospital a month earlier; his energy seemed to well up after the late-night blitz to empty two linen closets so they could be used for craft-making, one for the men and one for the women. Ruth said he did the work of three men that night, long after he'd finished a twelve-hour shift, carrying out stack after stack of sheets and flannel nightgowns, and lifting shelves from brackets to clear the rooms for carving and needlework. She was going to comment on the weight of the load when she noticed the focus of all six men shift in response to his footsteps. Each man nodded gravely in turn and then resumed his work. Joseph lowered the cloth bag of stone to the table and returned the nod. She opened the door and slipped from the room.

The door to the women's craft room was slightly open. Hazel heard the murmur of female voices and Caroline's high, clear laugh. Since the cloth and thread had arrived she sewed most days, here in the craft room or in her bed during rest time. Once a week, the hospital held an auction of the parkas, mittens and sculptures that patients had made; the intake nurse kept the accounts, subtracting the cost of the materials from the sale price. Patients earned what remained. Caroline's handiwork was always in demand, and she saved her earnings in a small purse she'd sewn for this purpose. She told Hazel that she planned to buy a new dress from the Eaton's catalogue for her mother once she was well and could go home.

Hazel pushed the door open. Caroline was working a design into white wool cloth for a pair of mittens. A team of dogs sprinted across the back of the left hand and she was putting the finishing touches on the driver and his sled on the right. She looked at Hazel and smiled shyly. "I like to sew."

"I've noticed." Hazel picked up a mitten Caroline had already finished and slipped her hand into it. Lined with soft white fur, probably rabbit, this would withstand anything that the winter wind could bring. "You have talent with a needle. Did your mother teach you?"

Caroline nodded. "Before I came here, I make clothes for my whole family."

The other women in the room had stopped talking when Hazel walked in and were bent over their work now, sewing in silence. Three worked on parkas, another on a blanket and one on a piece of tender birch bark that she'd folded and was biting at intervals. This was a new craft room activity, introduced to the Inuit women by a Cree nurse's aide. The woman unfolded it and held it to the room's only window. Light came through the impressions her teeth had made. She was already accomplished at this art; her designs were complex and sold out at the weekly market. Last week she'd made frogs on lily pads, one for each of the four quadrants on the sheet of bark.

The level of happy industry was as high here as in the sculpting room next door, and compared to the Inuit patients she'd treated in Hamilton, the difference in morale was marked. She laid the mitten back on Caroline's lap and stood.

"I'll look for these at the market. I could use a pair." Caroline smiled again and turned back to her work. Hazel stepped into the hall. The women's chatter resumed almost immediately. Joseph stepped into the hall carrying the empty cloth bag.

"Going back for another load?"

"No more today. Tomorrow more will come."

"That must be a relief. It looks heavy."

"No." His voice was louder than usual. "I could carry three times as much."

"Of course." She searched for a fitting response. "They need you."

"They are my brothers."

Hazel nodded but couldn't look him in the eye. He turned and started down the hall. It had been a conceit to think that because she'd lost an aunt to the disease she could understand how he felt. She knew it even then.

EVEN IF HIS LOPING STRIDE had not given him away, Lachlan would have been easy to spot by his necktie alone. His lab coat was unbuttoned and the orange and brown flowers on his tie were distinct at twenty paces. Where did he find these things?

"Nurse MacPherson." He lifted his hand.

She glanced at her watch and realized that she'd been due in the women's ward ten minutes earlier. "Apologies, Doctor Davies. I stopped by the craft room for a few minutes and lost track of time. Just wanted to see how they were making out."

Before she'd even finished her sentence, his usual preoccupation dispersed like loose mercury. "The calibre of the sculpture coming out of that room has been a pleasant surprise, hasn't it?" There was no trace of self-congratulation in his tone, though he was owed; the craft room had been another of his inspirations. She'd seen this happen with a few other ideas of his, like the curling rink he'd arranged to be built in an unused maintenance shed for staff use during the long dark of winter. Lachlan could have been described as neither self-effacing nor selfless but once an idea had been living outside his imagination for a period of time, he treated it as common property. If he was generous with his thoughts and impressions it was only to advocate for ideas as entities apart from himself. "If they can't hunt again, the men will have something else to turn to."

On the matter of the craft room, she could recite Lachlan's thesis on rehabilitation and retraining for TB patients chapter and verse. She'd heard it from his own mouth when he'd first established the program and read it in an article he'd published recently, but she didn't mind the repetition. To be in the same orbit with a doctor with ideas like this was the reason she'd come to Moose Factory.

"You should see the piece Suujuq is working on. It's a hunter." She lifted her arm to mime the pose she'd watched him creating in stone. "His sculpting skills are sophisticated."

"Yes, but did you look at the man? He's putting on weight, his cheeks have good colour and his eyes sparkle. Drugs alone can't do that much, no matter how good they are." Lachlan was genuinely animated by this. Would anyone ever say the same about her? She wanted to feel that kind of passion for her work. The longer she stayed here, working with Lachlan, the more likely that seemed.

"He was changed so much I almost didn't recognize him." She pictured him as he'd been the day after his arrival, subdued but still defiant. "Remember the noise he made that first night?"

Lachlan frowned, seeming to rifle through the stores of his memory until he found the episode he wanted. He couldn't have forgotten such a violent outburst already, but it wasn't a stretch that he might consider the matter superfluous now that the man was recovering. Apart from the scratch on his hand, it hadn't affected Suujuq medically.

"Yes, yes, right. He was a handful that first night, wasn't he? He has a child on another ward, I believe."

"A wife." They'd reached the stairs to the second floor. Charlie Wilcox's narrow face appeared behind the glass. He glanced at her and then at Lachlan, pulled the door open and stood stiffly, holding it for them. The grim turn of his mouth was not uncommon for him, but the resignation in it caught Hazel's attention. "He's been at her side every day since he's been allowed out of his room. The aides tell me that it's all quite touching, but they have to enforce the visitation rules almost every day."

"We have to expect some resistance." Charlie called his name and Lachlan stopped. "Yes, Doctor Wilcox?"

"Could I have a word?"

"Of course. I'll meet you in the women's ward, Nurse MacPherson."

"Actually, I'm going that way too." Charlie released the door. "I came down to look for you."

"Well, you found me," Lachlan said. "What can I do for you?"

"I need a consult." Charlie followed Lachlan up the stairs. He held the door at the second floor landing and motioned for Hazel to go through. "That new batch of x-rays you asked me to review. We should talk about one of them."

"Fine. I'll be there as soon as I finish in the women's ward. Say twenty minutes? Of course you're welcome to come with us for rounds."

Charlie blinked and shook his head. "Twenty minutes is fine. Meet me in my office." He glanced at Hazel and started down the hall.

Lachlan began to walk in the other direction. There was no indication that he'd noted the other doctor's displeasure. "Some of these people have never before known doctors, let alone had to abide by the wishes of a hospital full of them. Something of a shock to the system, I imagine. But they all adapt." He said it with such certainty that it felt true to Hazel. "They must, if they want to do well. In return, we must do everything in our power to make sure they do."

"Even if it means imposing unpopular rules?"

"Even then." Lachlan led the way toward the women's ward at the end of the hall and stopped at the nurses' station. "You know, I was thinking that I'd do the exam and leave the rest to you, but maybe I shouldn't go in there at all." He threaded one arm into a ward gown and then turned to her. "Let's try something different this time, shall we? I can't be sure that Annie will respond better to a woman, but it's worth a try. Could you handle an exam on your own?"

She imagined Charlie's response to learning that Lachlan had sent a nurse to do an exam. "Sure. Should I be looking for anything in particular?"

He raised his eyebrows and sighed. "With this one it's a matter of morale, as you know. She hasn't been eating well. Her face seems thinner but she tucks her covers tight under her chin when I enter the room. It's hard to tell how much weight she's lost without taking a hard line with her, which I know will be counterproductive. Sometimes she won't even make eye contact."

Hazel wrapped the gown ties around her waist and tied a knot at her left hip. "Can't we check her entry weight?"

"Of course. But it's not really about a number. A number won't tell me why she refuses food so often. They tell me she's living on coffee and bread. She's stubborn and I'm sure she's weak. You must have noticed that yesterday when you took her to x-ray. See if you can get a sense of this. Maybe I'm missing something."

"Is the treatment working?"

"Minor improvement, but it's an improvement. Here." He took an x-ray envelope from her file and flipped the light box switch on the wall beside them. "See that pocket right there? That was a month ago, when she was first admitted." He clipped a second film beside the first. "It's still there, but diminished. See?"

Hazel nodded. She was fairly certain that she saw what he wanted her to see. She picked up a face mask and held it in one palm, then lined it with a double thickness of gauze. Cloth face masks were better nets than shields, according to the latest journal reports, and fewer than half of the nurses wore them now. The disposable masks had been ordered but had failed to appear in the last three shipments. "Do you want me to show these films to her?"

"Seemed to help last time." He hung his gown on the peg below his name card. "I'll be down the hall with Doctor Wilcox."

ANNIE'S ROOM AT THE END of the hall was built as a sunroom, meant for daytime use by all patients, but it had only briefly served that purpose. As survey boats returned with load after load of coughing patients, orderlies replaced couches with beds in the sunrooms on every ward. When Hazel walked into the room, the elderly woman appeared to be sleeping, but she was still the obvious locus of power whether awake or asleep. As the younger women returned to the room for lunch, they deferred to her with nods or furtive glances in her direction.

Hazel crossed the room and stood beside Annie's bed. The old woman's eyelids snapped open and she appraised Hazel with a cold, fleeting glance before she turned to face the window. Her lips were moving in silent prayer or indictment, Hazel couldn't be sure. When she laid two fingers on Annie's frail wrist, the old woman flinched. The procedure could be nothing new. Temperature and pulse were recorded morning and evening without fail. Hazel moved to the other side of the bed and blocked the window. Annie didn't turn away, but she wouldn't look at Hazel, not even when she laid a hand on her shoulder.

That she could feel the hard angles of the woman's bones through the thick cotton flannel was no surprise. Annie hadn't been a substantial woman when she'd arrived last month. And now she seemed more spirit than corporeal, her thinning black hair lank on the pillow, her face gaunt and quilted with long sorrows and deep joys. But when she lifted her chin, proud and undiminished, Hazel felt a surge of hope: she had not acquiesced to the disease. Yet she refused meals on a regular basis. How to reconcile these opposing facts?

"I have something to show you." She held the new film to the window. A translation seemed unnecessary. Annie had understood what they were doing last time intuitively. "You're making progress."

A flicker of recognition was the most Hazel had hoped for. But Annie's voice was clear and strong. "Silatsiaq?"

It was inconceivable that she had read and assimilated the changes in this new x-ray already, and Hazel was stunned. She hadn't even shown the earlier one for comparison yet. A second voice filled the silence. "She ask, Clear sky?" Having only just climbed back into bed for lunch, Caroline pushed her covers back and swung her legs over the side of the bed.

"Yes, Caroline, thank you. I did remember." Someone had braided the younger woman's hair and tied it with red ribbons. "No, no. You stay in bed now. Lunch is on its way." Annie seemed to understand much without Caroline's translation, and Hazel sensed that the intimacy of this exchange was making it work. The young woman slumped back down in her bed.

Hazel turned back to Annie. "Not yet." She reached for but

couldn't recall the Inuktitut words for fog, clouds, or heavy sky, not a single descriptor of changeable weather. It was like working with one hand tied behind her back. "Some clouds still." She held her thumb and forefinger an inch apart, and then remembered. "*Tatsiq*. A little fog." One of the nurse's aides pushed the lunch cart into the room. Even through the triple thickness of her mask, Hazel's mouth watered. The rich aroma of roast beef was comforting, evocative of Sunday dinners at home. She was famished and could have cleaned the plate herself. She motioned for Mary to bring a plate to Annie. "But you must eat to stay strong." She took the plate from the aide and lifted a fork to the old woman's mouth. Annie closed her eyes and turned her head away. How was she going to reach this woman? "Come on, Annie. Eat. You have to eat."

A voice from across the room was timid but insistent. Caroline's head was bowed and she wouldn't look at Hazel. "She does not want that food. For her it is not good food." She paused. "And her name is not Annie."

Hazel blinked. She picked up the old woman's chart. She'd been known as Annie since she arrived, but whether that name was given by someone here at the hospital or in her community at some point, Hazel had no idea. "What's her name?"

"Ulluriaq."

There was silence in the room. The rest of the women turned toward Caroline. Hazel glanced at Mary.

"Okay. Thank you. Has no one offered fish to Ulluriaq?"

Mary nodded, her eyes wide. "We have, Nurse MacPherson. Several times."

"Try again." She covered the old woman's veined hand with her own. "If you have trouble getting it, come talk to me."

"And my name is not Caroline." The young woman met Hazel's surprised glance. Her cheeks reddened and she was not smiling. "I am Pitsiaq."

NINE

I CAN SEE HIM STANDING on the other side of the clinic door and tapping out a strange melody. Gideon had taken to showing up at the end of the day to ask for something small. A strand of suture thread or a ball of cotton or salt or two buttons. One time I'd already gone for the day and when Lachlan answered the door Gideon asked for violin resin. I laughed when I imagined Lachlan's expression. Can you believe it? Violin resin. I can't say what he meant to do with it but logic never seemed to have any hold on him. He seemed to actively move away from anything resembling what I understood to be sense. I never saw him with an instrument of any kind but he spoke and I heard music.

He wanted a nickel. Picture him if you can, Jude: black bowler hat on a nest of unruly dark blond hair. Shabby three-quarter-length black jacket with outlandish lapels and matching vest and trousers whatever the weather. It was 1951 but he might have walked out of a photograph taken twenty years earlier. As far as I know these were the only articles of clothing he owned.

I decided to hazard a question about his getup once and his reply disarmed me completely. He said hobos were kin. They had a moral compass that protected them from the evils and failings of modern society. He said it just like that and he might have even used those words. I knew he meant it. Everything about him said so. The blue of his eyes seemed incandescent through the mesh in the glass. His gaze penetrated like x-ray through skin or sun through a magnifying glass. It left nowhere to hide. He saw me.

I started to dream. Oh the dreams! I felt more alive in the hours between midnight and six than during the day. I saw the endless curtain of the northern sky. I felt his breath on my neck. I heard his voice calling my name. Once I turned to face him and his mouth opened wide and the head of a raven emerged like it was being born from deep inside him. The bird lifted its shoulders up and out of Gideon's mouth and sloughed off his clothes and skin. A wrinkled pile of what was left of Gideon formed around the bird's yellow feet. It lifted one wing and then the other and held them out as if to dry them. It said something I couldn't hear before it lifted its wings and disappeared into the sky over the Moose River. Gone! It was gone and he was gone. And then I was rowing the air beside the bird. All the world was laid out in exquisite detail far below, but I was free and I could see forever.

FOCUS IS AN ELUSIVE THING now. It hides behind the first line of trees with a fox's wily stealth. It's no longer my familiar. If I am ever to give this over to you I must court it with stillness and patience and coax it to come nearer.

The northwest side of the island was unpopulated owing to the winds and tides and dense forest until Gideon arrived so it was easy for him to claim. If you went to Moose Factory and took the Bay Road to the west shore and then walked north along the beach some distance you might still see an exposed ledge of shoreline that stands ten or twelve feet above the sand. This would be at low tide. I suppose it was for high tide that he'd chosen that place to pitch his tent. The water would have lapped against the exposed earth a few feet below his door.

Over the years I've replayed the chain of decisions that led me to his camp and tried to understand what illogical impulse guided me to stay. That first time, a broth bubbled and clothes dried and a shaving mirror perched: I suppose the sum of these domestic familiars and the surprise of finding him prone to such habits was calming. In his own peculiar way he kept house.

With that outlandish getup he wore it's clear to me now that concealing himself was a low priority but neither did he seek the company of anyone else in the community. Once he'd made the rounds a few times offering to fix umbrellas he mostly kept to himself. It was easy enough for the island residents to avoid him or forget him altogether.

But not for me. Like a bell on a distant buoy his presence was impossible to ignore. I had just turned twenty-one. Your age. I listened to his talk about falcons and symbols and backward economics until the lights of the hospital and all that I'd worked for began to recede. I could feel it all slipping away but I wasn't alarmed. On the contrary.

A nickel, he said. If he had asked for gauze or medical tape or iodine or even antibiotics I'd have given him what he wanted but money was something else. I had only a small salary. With a nickel I could buy a loaf of bread or a bar of chocolate. He'd upped the ante and we both knew it. I hesitated a moment and noticed a stack of firewood that needed splitting. At the suggestion of labour one side of his mouth lifted. He would not chop wood but he did promise to repay the nickel with a nickel. This I hadn't anticipated and the words were out of my mouth before I could call them back: "Why bother?" Even now my lack of imagination humbles me. He smiled and said, "Trust me."

TEN

IT WAS A CURIOUS THING to find her outside, uniformed and idle, in the middle of the day. Gideon plucked another strand of usnea from the skeletal remains of a tree and glanced toward the dock where she sat, unaware of his presence, leaning against a corner post. He lifted another clump of the pale lichen from a higher branch. It was so like balls of tangled hair that he'd imagined a bizarre native ritual the first time he saw it draped on the branches, but now he carried a store of it with him at all times.

The weight of the lichen in his pack was inconsequential. He marked the quality of the plant in his mental notebook on the subject, scarcely believing he'd found an organism that embodied perfection this way, this heady marriage of insubstantiality and potency. He glanced at her again. There she was on the dock all alone, warming her bare legs in the sun. Until now, he'd shared this with no one. Would she understand this kind of magic?

He had become adept at roaming the forest on silent feet and edged closer to the dock along the path that hugged the shore without attracting her attention. He was like the thing he carried. He was untethered, weightless. The thought gave him courage and he inched closer still.

The low drone of a small motor caught his attention. A freight canoe emerged from the channel between the two smaller islands across from Moose Factory and rounded the bend toward the hospital dock. Her head lifted and she stood. He was awash in regret, sick with it. If only he hadn't hesitated. Even at a full sprint he wouldn't reach her before the boat did.

He swung his pack forward like a shield and wrapped his arms around it. This was a gift in disguise! She hadn't been part of his original plan and this minor disappointment was a reminder. His discoveries had to be his alone. The clock ticking in the distant reaches of his mind was audible again: well before the season's end he needed to be gone from this place. He stepped into the shadow of a poplar and sat to watch.

The meeting hadn't been pre-arranged. She raised her arm and the old man at the motor adjusted his speed and changed course. The constant hum of the engine stopped abruptly and Gideon watched the boat's wake nudge it toward the dock. She braced herself against the railing as the dock rose and tipped beneath her. Gideon's lips began to move in cautionary phrases, *be careful, steady now*, and when the boat's wake rocked the dock, his arms shot out as if to brace her.

It had never been a skill he'd perfected but Gideon gave his entire focus to the task of decoding the brief exchange between them, watching the shapes their lips made. A few words offered themselves to him, *fish* and *yes* and *you*, the last of which resembled a kiss. He blinked and studied the attitude of her body. No, she couldn't mean to kiss him, that much was plain. The old man nodded, pushed the boat from the dock and restarted his small engine. Gideon watched her watch the boat until it disappeared around the bend, and then he followed the path toward the dock.

Her face came into focus now as though a mist had cleared. The distance between them was finally closed. She tipped her head to the left and cleared her throat.

"Hello." Her voice was tremulous, shivery. "Lovely day."

He laughed. Her optimism cheered him. She was an eyas, that's what she was. A nestling. She was yet in the act of becoming. "The loveliest. Yes, it is. This is the loveliest now that ever was."

She shifted her weight from one foot to the other and cleared her throat. He was blocking her path. "The fish are biting," she said.

"Your Indian said so."

She blushed and glanced toward the hospital. He'd just confessed to having watched her. "Oh. Yes. I came out to get fresh fish from one of the returning boats for some patients. Well, one in particular." She was stumbling over her words. "Cook sent me out here. He said I only had to wait a short while and a fisherman would be along. He said the river would be thick as porridge with fishing boats at this hour. He may have exaggerated, I guess."

"Afraid I can't help you there, nurse. Not a fisher, myself. Not for fish." He smiled at her and made a decision. He wanted to show her. "But I've got something else." He reached for his pack.

"No, no." She held up her hand and shook her head. "No need. He'll be back in a little while with whitefish. He said he'd bring it to the hospital kitchen." She gazed in the direction of the boat now gone. Her words strung out in clean, official lines. "And I should be getting back. Lots to do." She began to walk toward the hospital. She was halfway up the slope behind him when he called out.

"Ah, but you haven't seen this, have you?" She stopped. The pack slid easily from his shoulders and he thrilled, again, to its weightlessness. He swung around to face her and worked the buckle without breaking eye contact. The leather pack had belonged to him since he was a child. He could do this with his eyes shut.

The dry, spongy sensation of the lichen was a familiar pleasure and he studied her reaction as he gathered a small clump into his palm and held it out to her. Whatever bemusement she experienced passed like an electrical discharge in an otherwise clear sky. She took it from his hand.

"It's lichen, isn't it? Grows around here, on the trees?"

"In the woods just behind us, Eyas." The name slipped and there was a new crease in her brow. "Just there. And there. And there!" He made a grand gesture with his arm to distract her. "And all over this charmed island."

"I've seen it. You have a whole bag full?"

"Of course. It's useful to me. Look here." He lifted his pant leg carefully and unwrapped the strip of cloth that held the plant against his calf. The clump of lichen dropped to the ground. A trace of pink remained but the open wound was docile now, not the furious blood riot it had been at first. Gravel crunched under her feet. She was nearer now. He could touch her bare arm.

"That's quite a wound. How did it happen?"

"Knife slipped. I was careless. But see? Only three days ago."

"Three days? We might have stitched a cut that long if you'd come into the hospital."

"Yes, indeed," he said, as though a hospital visit had occurred to him. It hadn't. "She's a powerful plant, usnea. Old man's beard, if you like. That's what the Indians call her." The nurse was probing the skin near the wound now, the tips of her fingers at the edge of it. The sensation perched tantalizingly close to the axis of pleasure and pain.

"The healing that has taken place ..." Her brow was creased again, but there was awe, not consternation, in it. "Three days? Are you certain?"

"The measure of time is less important to me than to you, perhaps." He could concede that much. The length of a day was pliable and so was an hour, if the situation demanded it. Time itself was an artificial construct. This truth proved itself steadfast since he'd first observed it at a concert years ago. Gideon had waited hours at the back door for the musician with the flying fingers, every molecule of his skin alive with one question. The man's answer: *You just open up the minutes, cat. That's how.*

"You've studied the medicinal properties of this plant?"

The question jarred and he frowned. "You might say so," he said, playing the words out as yarn from a skein. It was true: there had been a period of intense study in the minutes following the slip of the knife. He'd observed the steady flow of blood from a clean tear in the shin as he'd waited for it to clot. He'd begun to notice a subtle change in colour – scarlet going to brick, perhaps – when Henry had happened along and showed him what the lichen could do, forcing a premature end to his experiment. But the introduction to usnea was worth the loss. Each day since, after he'd lifted strand after strand of blood-saturated lichen from it, he'd repacked a cleaner, calmer wound that was less prone to the ticklish sting of foreign objects on raw flesh. Yes, he'd studied the medicinal properties of the plant. "But you don't have to take my word for it, do you? It's all right here, flesh and blood."

"Please don't." She was refusing again, but the concern in her voice seemed genuine. "You mustn't disturb it so often or it won't heal."

"Now, now." He could be patient. "How will you understand this plant, how will you accept the intelligence it offers the universe, without a little disturbance now and again?"

She stood. "Let me get some sterile water to clean it," she said, almost to herself, as she climbed the slope toward the hospital. "There's some in the clinic."

"Unnecessary." He found the word in time and sent it like an arrow. She turned. "Not a drop of water since the skin was opened, and you've seen the progress. Ask yourself, nurse. Does this injury need the hospital's water?"

She bit her lip and her free hand fluttered at her side. She didn't answer.

"Take it to them. I don't need their water, but you can give them the lichen." He reached into the sack for a piece of fresh usnea and laid it into the wound, unwilling to watch her go.

ELEVEN

EXPOSURE TO THE WHITE NOON light was a handicap once she'd passed through the doors of the hospital. Sun-blind, she stood at one side of the stairs and waited for her pupils to readjust. In the palm of her hand, the lichen was a ticklish combination of presence and absence. If she dropped it, it wouldn't make a sound. She lifted it closer to her face. She'd noticed the shaggy growth on the trees during her walks and had always told herself that she'd ask about it, but never had. The hair-like tendrils of the pale green plant were malleable yet held their shape and cushioned without pressure, but none of this explained how it had done what Gideon claimed. *How will you accept the intelligence it offers the universe?* She took the stairs to the main floor toward the kitchen. How indeed?

"Nurse MacPherson." She braced herself for the reprimand or complaint that usually followed, but Charlie was less guarded than usual. His tone was almost jaunty and he was wearing scrubs. If there was ever a time to find Charlie Wilcox in a good mood, it was after a successful surgery. "You'd be wise to watch where you're going. Some of the orderlies go at a pretty good clip around here."

Hazel became aware of the lichen in her hand. She closed her fingers around it and slipped it into her pocket. "You're absolutely right, Doctor Wilcox. I'll be more careful. My apologies."

"No, no, not to worry." His gaze settled on her pocket. "What have you got there?"

The question was a surprise, and not because he'd noticed her attempt to hide the lichen. Even as she slipped it into her pocket, she'd assumed he would. Charlie was nothing if not a keen observer; his sharp eye made him a good surgeon. But this was something else. His tone wasn't accusatory and he seemed genuinely curious. Was he making conversation? "Just a plant from the woods. I went outside to eat my sandwich."

"Old man's beard. Correct?" He was almost friendly. Now she was certain he'd just come from surgery.

"You've heard of it?"

He smiled. It was such a rare expression that his face became unfamiliar. She wondered if they'd all misunderstood him. "Can't work in an emergency room in these parts without coming across it ground up and stuffed into cuts. The Indians like it. It's one of their home remedies."

"Does it work?"

"Well, Nurse MacPherson." Now she heard the disdain she'd been expecting. "If it did, would they end up here?"

"But I've just . . ." She stopped herself. However friendly this exchange, relaying the story Gideon had just told was risky. She caught herself and cleared her throat. "Some of the aides have mentioned it. Their mothers and grandmothers use it as an anti-septic, I think."

"Yes, as I said. They'll want you to believe that you should take a preparation of it orally, too, to cure TB." He smirked. She had a sudden image of him as a taunting older brother. "A few months ago a local man brought some in, dried and pounded into a pow-der, for an ailing wife. Expected us to make a tea of it." He snorted and shook his head. "Can you beat that?"

She sensed that pursuing this line of conversation would be unwise, but she couldn't let it go. Later, examining her behaviour, she knew that his earlier, unexpected affability had played a role. "But...when you examine a wound that they've packed with this, have you found no difference at all? It isn't cleaner and beginning to heal?" She stopped herself. "I mean, that's what I've heard."

"Whether it works or not, we have no scientific evidence to support its use." His breath smelled of peppermints and his curly hair was tidy and recently barbered. "It is untested and unstudied. These people are free to use it as they wish outside our doors, but here we are obliged to use what we have studied and know to be safest and most expedient. *Primum non nocere.* First, do no harm." He stopped and cleared his throat, pulling himself back from the edge of a passion she'd never seen before. "We have good antibiotic creams now, properly tested and vetted. We have streptomycin to arrest the growth of tubercles. As you're well aware, we're curing people with these drugs." He patted her hand. The gesture was so foreign that she pulled back reflexively.

Charlie flinched and straightened his shoulders. "Curing, Nurse MacPherson. What we're here to do. These things work. This plant, I really couldn't say."

His tone was gentle and free of mockery, and his response kinder and more patient than she'd ever known him to give. Yet his answer abraded. She was no child. Of course they must use what they knew to be safe. Not for the briefest of moments had she considered presenting the plant for use in the hospital, today or anytime in the near future. But his easy dismissal of it was vexing. Couldn't he even entertain the possibility that there were different answers to the questions they were asking?

She pulled back from the edge of her own zeal. He was pushing her to defend something she herself wasn't convinced of. She reminded herself that he would not have been her first choice for a discussion of this nature. She hadn't sought him out. She gave him a tight smile, wished him a good day and took the stairs to the second floor.

There were facts to be aligned, expectations to be adjusted. The sky was searing blue, no clouds, midday: she was rarely outside at that hour, but she'd been up half the night assisting Lachlan at autopsy and he'd sent her home to get some rest. She lay half-clothed on her bed awhile, knowing sleep wouldn't come, and dressed for a walk instead.

It hadn't rained in weeks and the dirt road felt like stone underfoot. The flag at the police headquarters, hung at half-mast, lolled in the breeze. The police chief's death shocked them all, and not because it had been sudden. He'd come back from an extended trip north two months earlier coughing and fevered, and though Lachlan tried to convince him to be x-rayed, Chief McLean had refused. He would have been a difficult patient on the ward even if he had agreed to be there. Hazel knew the type. Lying in bed all day was the purest form of torture.

The cough didn't clear and his weight began to drop. His cheeks had the telltale rosy glow and his eyes were glassy. Still Lachlan couldn't force treatment. McLean maintained that he was fine and the hospital community's acceptance of his assertion was driven by self-interested denial: if he was invulnerable, so were they. The new treatments had slowed the death rate to the point that they had begun to feel superior to the disease, as though the mere presence of effective drugs somehow sapped it of its virulence. Regular tuberculin testing among staff fed this conviction, yielding occasional positive results but most often an asymptomatic disease. Everyone carried on as usual. Even when no one had seen him in two days and Lachlan sent Henry to check the chief's small room behind the police headquarters, no one expected he'd find a dead man.

It had to be the miliary strain to take him that fast – bloodborne, millet-sized, easily deposited anywhere in the body – but Lachlan autopsied to be sure. The unspoken wish that he'd find something else was palpable in the conversations that moved like fire through the wards once Henry returned with a request for another orderly and a stretcher. Even during her early days of tuberculosis nursing, Hazel had never felt particularly vulnerable to the disease, and she still didn't, but the chief's death marked a shift in her respect for it. There would be no cavalier disregard of the established hygiene rules. She did not intend to die here.

A week had passed since she'd last seen Gideon. She couldn't be sure that he was still on the island, but he wouldn't have made his home near the main settlement. She turned the corner at the stand of trees opposite the graveyard and her feet propelled her across the Bay Road. The lack of sleep and the death of a strong Mountie had peeled off the veneer of sensibility that ordered her days and held her impulses in check. Anyone who'd seen her walking away from the main settlement alone might have remarked on it, but she didn't care.

The Bay Road led to a short, muddy boat launch. Two canoes were pulled up on the bank in deference to high tide, which had swallowed the beach and the slope to the woods and then started to recede, leaving a strip of waterlogged clay in its wake. She tested the ground, thinking she'd follow the shore as far as she could. A few steps along she sunk into clay to her ankles. She reached for an overhanging branch, hauled herself up the slope and followed a footpath inland.

Broken twigs and bent grass led through the trees, close enough to shore that she could hear the river. Spent bushes of wild rose, their petals curled and dry, scratched her bare legs. Biting flies swarmed. Twice she began to retrace her steps, and twice she turned back around.

The path cut closer to the shoreline, then turned back inland and opened on a natural clearing in the woods. Milky columns of slanting afternoon sun found a grove of poplars, cedar saplings, black spruce, hoary lichen and poison ivy; soft moss carpeted fallen trees, their trunks greenly decomposing. Old man's beard hung cobwebbed and draping from the dry branches of dead poplars. Exposed roots arched their backs across the path.

The impatient squawk of a crow at close range broke the silence. Perched on the highest branch of a tall poplar that brooded over the water, the huge black bird fixed a glittering eye on her. Hazel's heart beat an insistent tattoo, and she felt foolish: all of this for a common crow, which by then had lost interest and hopped away. Her reaction was a clear enough signal of how edgy this walk was making her feel. She had to shake this off. She glanced over her shoulder before continuing. Nothing. She was alone.

Around the next bend, the path opened on another clearing that perched on a low bluff. The water glinted just beyond it. She saw the tent first, a canvas one-man that was pitched as close to the edge of the bluff as could be practical. The door wasn't visible from where she stood. Steam rose from a blackened pot over a firepit ringed with beach stones. Articles of black clothing, splayed on the lower branches of a tamarack like lifeless crows, dried in the sun. A white shirt fluttered from a branch.

She stepped closer and there was a pop of white light. She tried to find it again but there was only the measured glow of filtered sky and the shimmer of the sun on the water. Something occurred to her and she shifted her weight from back leg to front and back again. There it was, over and over, a brilliant flash low in the tamarack: a shard of mirror.

Her defenses stood down. It was for shaving, she presumed. She moved further into the camp and saw something carved into the bark below the mirror. She traced the shape with her finger.

"It's a marker."

For the second time that morning, her chest didn't want to contain her heart. Yet, she'd expected him. Even the most cursory probe of her conscience would expose that truth. But how had he managed to move with such stealth? And how had she left herself so vulnerable, again?

Wearing only trousers, Gideon seemed very young. The hair on his chest was soft and fine and his nipples were tender pink. His skin sank around his ribs. She had the sudden impulse to feed him a hot meal and tuck him into bed. His smile was lopsided.

"You are one gone chick."

A moment passed before she found her voice. "Pardon me?"

"It's a compliment." His face was open, untroubled. "Came all the way out here to find me?"

She hesitated. "Not exactly."

He shrugged. "It's a good place. I don't have to share it with anybody."

"I suppose not. Don't you find the wind a little much?"

He cocked his head to one side. "Anything's bearable, honey, if you want something else badly enough."

She turned away. His intimate way made her want to run

toward and away from him at the same time. "Hazel. Please call me Hazel." She needed to shift the conversation to more rational ground. "That carving. Did you make it?"

"Sure."

He was going to make her work for a better answer. "Well, what does it mean?"

"It's a marker, like I said." He was patient, as if explaining to a child. "In the language of a sophisticated brotherhood, it signifies. Few know it. I didn't expect that you would." He reached for his shirt. "I thought it was too late." He seemed to be speaking to himself as he dressed. "But it wasn't."

"Too late?" She felt a little faint. Was that a vague threat?

"To be part of it. That kind of purity, that unfetteredness." He sighed. He seemed tired of the explanation now. "I was too young, understand? I was only a small child in my father's house of excess and they were inches above the rails, oily dust blowing into their eyes, certain death a breath away . . ." He gazed at the water. The tension that had been building in his body found expression in his arms. He held them open to the sky. "They were riding for their lives, cutting their own swath of truth from one side of the continent to the other! They were shooting stars, brilliant ephemeral light." He faced the water, and his shoulders rose and fell. "I couldn't have known. I accept that now. I was formed in a den of capitalism." He spat on the ground. "But I'm starting it anew, Eyas. They wanted too much from me. They tried to take it all. It couldn't be allowed."

Her head swam. Who was riding for their lives? What shooting stars? And that name he'd called her that day on the dock, spoken like a shared confidence. Could she have missed something he said? She felt she'd fallen down a rabbit hole. She tried to shake it off. Lost sleep might affect her this way, distort things. She'd been up all night and she needed to remember that. He walked toward the fire, murmuring to himself, and she followed. Inside the pot, greens bubbled in a grey broth.

She thought how easily she could bring him a few tinned goods. He'd probably refuse. How was he living? Surely he couldn't exist on food like that. She caught sight of the shape he'd carved in the tree again. She needed to know.

"But what does it mean? That marker?"

He stared at her. The wind blew his hair into his eyes.

"It means ... you are being watched."

She didn't know what she expected, but it wasn't this. A cold sweat beaded on the back of her neck. She had to know. "Watched?"

He shook his head. "Don't worry. It's too early."

"Too early for what?"

"We have plenty of time, Eyas." There was the name again, and she wanted to ask, but she couldn't trust her voice. He picked up his coat and walked away. She sat on a bed of pine needles, watching the woods swallow him.

THE FIRE WENT OUT AND there was still no sign of Gideon. She felt ridiculous for having stayed and waited for him. By the angle of the sun, it was nearing four; shift change came and went. She stood, brushed the pine needles from her skirt and edged down the slope to the beach. The wet sand was firm and smooth now, and the beach was the most direct route back.

She climbed back up the slope to the Bay Road and had a sudden vision of herself returning from the uninhabited side of the island in the late afternoon. Anyone who worked the early shift could be outside now. She took the longer route back, across the island toward the main dock. Returning from that direction would make more sense, if anyone was watching.

The tents that lined the southeast shore behind St. Thomas's, lit by the setting sun, glowed like a chain of paper lanterns. Smoke

rose from stovepipes in tent roofs, and it carried the rich, sweetish tang of roasting moose meat. At the bend in the road a Cree
mother sat on an upturned wash basin in front of her tent, her
baby on her lap, and sang as she rocked, "*may may may may.*" The
baby leaned toward her, eyelids heavy. Behind them, pots and axes
and basins and blocks of wood were scattered on the ground. A
recent litter of husky pups, fuzzy as baby chicks, bit and chased
and rolled around on the ground with each other. Adorable, but
their teeth were tiny razors. She'd treated enough bite wounds by
now to know. Cowboy songs wailed from radios and carried across
the water, the lonely strains of their melodies mingling compatibly
with the howling huskies. Mosquitoes were legion in the soft July
air at this hour; it was probably the reason she'd met no one so far.
The road that led to the hospital was deserted, but she recognized
a broad-shouldered silhouette loping across the lawn between the
mechanical building and the flagpole entrance. Joseph didn't notice her.

She cut through the grove of cedars to the nurses' residence
and paid for it with a dozen blackfly bites. At the front door, she
waved away a cloud of flies and pulled it open. There was a perva-
sive silence inside, unusual at this hour. The big kitchen typically
hummed with activity in the early evening. Odd, but the chief's
death might account for it. She could smell toast, which wasn't a
good sign. They ate it for dinner when they were too tired to make
anything else.

Her first glimpse of the kitchen was confusing. Many more
women sat at the table than she would have guessed. No one spoke.
A few flipped idly through magazines; some stared into space and
lifted mugs to their lips. She was there a minute or two when a
freckled hand grabbed her arm and steered her toward the stairs.
Ruth's fingers were a vice and she didn't say a word until they'd
reached the landing.

"Keep going. Everyone wonders where you were." She finally released Hazel's arm. A maddening heat rose from Hazel's collar to the roots of her hair. "When they couldn't find you they started talking. The umbrella mender was mentioned." Her eyes narrowed. "Possibly by Davies."

"It was no one's business where I was. Not even his." An impossible expectation, of course, in a place this small. She'd crossed the island on her way back to avoid such speculation, hadn't she? "I was up all night doing the chief's autopsy with Doctor Davies, as I'm sure you and everyone else knows. Before that I put in a full shift. I could hardly think straight once we were done."

"We didn't need you to think." Hazel thought she'd known Ruth long enough to have seen the full range of her expressions, but the severe line of her mouth was unusual. "You knew we were expecting another large group from Cape Smith. Three boats came in shortly after noon. Babies, children, adults, elders. Some so far gone they could barely walk." Her green eyes glittered with fury. "We had to walk them or carry them from the dock, one by one."

"You know I'd have been there." She was all the more irritated because she had forgotten. She saw herself sitting under the tamarack at Gideon's camp for an hour, more than that. Why had she waited? If only she'd gone when he had. "I should have been sleeping. Anyone would have been after the all-nighter I'd just pulled, no questions asked. You know I wouldn't have stayed away to avoid work."

"I've been telling them that, Hazel, but they're out for blood." Ruth's tone softened and she sighed. "I guess we're all on edge today. Where were you, anyway?"

"Just out walking." She couldn't look Ruth in the eye. "I was too keyed up to sleep."

Ruth studied her. "Well." She rubbed the back of her neck. "Have they made arrangements for the chief's body?"

"It'll be flown out to family in Toronto tomorrow. We'll have our own memorial service at St. Thomas's on Sunday."

She nodded. "Stay in your room awhile, let them cool off. Are you hungry?"

"No. But thanks."

She climbed the stairs to her room and closed the door. The latch clicked coldly in the silence. Her explanation was evasive and patently incomplete. She owed Ruth more than that, and it was a mark of her loyalty that she trusted Hazel enough to let it go. By anyone's math, a walk around the island couldn't have taken four hours.

Her shoes were still caked with sand. She slipped them off and lay on the bed. The early evening light coming in the small window made shifting lace shadows of leaves and branches. Her body thrummed with exhaustion. The room faded with each breath.

IT WAS THE HOLLOW OF the night, no sound, no light. She understood two things immediately: she was fully dressed in her bed and she was not alone in her room. The light, measured breathing wasn't her own but she wasn't afraid. This wasn't the first time. No one locked doors up here because it wasn't necessary.

"Who's there?"

"Joseph, from the hospital." As if she could forget. He yawned. "Sorry to wake you. Nurse Ames asks you to come."

"She sent you to find me?"

"Yes, ma'am. She says hurry. She sees a foot."

Hazel changed as Joseph left the room, shimmying into her uniform, pulling her stockings up, shoving her feet into shoes. She gathered her hair with an elastic and made a fast coil, jabbed a few clips into it and splashed water from the basin on her face, all of this in the dark. It would have to do. Ruth was never dramatic. But the only hope for a breech birth was skill and speed and an extra pair of hands. She knew of only two others since she'd arrived, and one had died. Ruth was disciplined and calm in the delivery room, but Hazel knew her well enough to know that the spectre of the other breech would haunt her tonight. Her focus would be intense.

Hazel fell into step with Joseph, who waited outside the door. The July sky was inky and studded with stars. "How far apart?"

He held up five fingers. She started to jog to keep up with the big man's long strides.

"How many hours has she been in labour?"

He shrugged. "I heard screaming, I came."

"Where is everyone else?"

"Busy. Sleeping. Big day yesterday, many new patients."

Hazel nodded. Yes. She should be the one to go. Leave it to Ruth to have the presence of mind, even in an emergency, to smooth ruffled feathers and help Hazel repair the damage she'd done yesterday.

Once she'd opened the door at the main entrance, she didn't need directions. She could hear the mother's anguished cries on the first floor. She took the stairs to the second floor two at a time. The double doors to the obstetrics ward were wide open and there was a cluster of young Inuit women standing in the hallway. Hazel nodded to them as she went into the delivery room and pulled the doors closed behind her.

Frizzy sprigs of Ruth's red hair appeared and disappeared from behind the aqua linen tent. She went straight to the sink to scrub in.

"Hazel. Thank God. Finally."

"I came as fast as I could."

"Don't apologize. Just get over here. Damn it. We're almost out of time. She arrived at midnight in full labour. Everything was going swimmingly until I saw a toe." She pushed her hair out of the way with her forearm. Her hand was bloodied. "Joseph, stay. We need an interpreter."

Hazel moved to her side. The tiny foot was mottled and swollen. Worse, the woman's screams were diminishing. There was surrender in the sounds she was making now. Ruth turned to Hazel.

"She's been pushing more than an hour now. I'm afraid she'll give up soon. She's getting that look about her. Go stand at her side. Put your hands on her belly. Yes, there. When she's ready, you push too. Got it?"

Ruth was speaking at triple speed and there was nothing for Hazel to add. She laid her hand on the woman's distended belly and felt it gather itself into a hard mass that travelled upward from her pelvis. Her face was deep red-brown and shiny tight like an overripe tomato, and her eyes were bloodshot. She was not crying but she took startled gulps of air. Her beseeching stare was the shot of adrenaline Hazel needed to fully rouse herself. No one would die tonight, not on her watch. She stood up straight.

"Is this her first baby?"

"No chit-chat. Didn't you feel that contraction? Ready, mama? Ready, Hazel? Now! Push!"

Joseph stood behind the woman's head, said a single word to her and lifted her shoulders from the table. The mother squeezed her eyes shut, bore down and exhaled a string of syllables that needed no translation.

"Good. Good. One more should do it." Ruth's body was torqued, one broad shoulder angled toward the woman, her arm hidden almost to the elbow. "Breathe. Joseph, tell her to breathe into the contraction. You breathe too, Hazel."

Ruth was right. This wasn't the first birth she'd assisted, but Hazel was tense. She hooked a foot around a stool under the bed, pulled it out and stepped up. This was better. Her hands hovered over the woman's belly.

"Here comes another one. Now. Push! Push!"

Hazel pressed down on the woman's belly. Like a thing possessed, the skin under her hands rose and shifted, an aqueous, sinuous movement. Since she'd begun training as a nurse, she'd been subjected to a great many sensations, but nothing matched this one: grotesque and miraculous, two lives inside one skin, two hearts beating.

The woman inhaled sharply as Ruth's freckled arm slid out of her, and with it, the baby. His skin was mauve and velvety.

"Over here. Now." Ruth's words were edged in icy fear. Her bloodied hands held the baby out to Hazel. "Suction his mouth."

The babe had a shock of black hair and his eyes were swollen shut. In the instant before taking the baby from Ruth, she had a flash of irrational fear that he'd wriggle from her hands to the floor, but she needn't have worried. He was warm but still. Hazel laid him on soft flannel in the cot Ruth had readied, slipped her fingers into his mouth and gently opened his lips wide enough for a suction tube. Within seconds his colour changed and he began to squirm.

The mother was moaning and sobbing, calling out in jagged words Hazel didn't understand. Joseph was a hulking presence at the far end of the bed. He leaned over the woman and murmured a steady stream of rounded, single syllables. She turned her head in his direction, gratitude in her exhausted glance.

Ruth wasn't speaking, not to comfort the woman nor to give further direction, and Hazel wondered what she was contending with. It was the roughest birth she'd seen. The mother was quiet now, and Hazel hoped her silence was a tranquil one; she had the babe to worry about. He had still not taken a breath. Cry, little one, cry, she thought furiously, holding her breath as if by doing so she could make room for his. She pinched his nose and blew into his mouth. Her lips brushed against his waxy skin. His tiny mouth opened and he bawled, a lusty, phlegmy cry that rattled in his throat. He was finally breathing. She massaged his tiny arms and legs and wrapped a blue flannel blanket around him, lifted him and carried him to his mother's side. Her hair was soaked with sweat and she'd broken a few blood vessels in her left eye. Her face was still swollen and her breath came in uneven gulps. Her arms dropped back to the bed when she tried to lift them. Hazel laid the baby at her side, tucked her limp arms around him and held a cup of water to her lips. Ruth sighed and shook her head.

"That ought to do it. Fifteen stitches. That's a record for me. She'll be sore. We'll keep her as long as she'll stay."

"She'll be okay?"

"Yes. But there were some moments there." Ruth stood and pulled the sheet over the woman's knees. "Neither of them would have made it if she hadn't come to the hospital." She glanced at Joseph, who stood in silence in the corner of the room. "She doesn't need to know that right now."

"No, ma'am." He yawned. "I will go now."

"By all means." Ruth's round face was still a rigid mask. She shut her eyes and took a deep breath. The tight lock on her forehead released. Joseph walked toward the door.

"Joseph," Ruth said. "Thank you."

He nodded once and pulled the door shut behind him. Hazel wanted to go to Ruth and hug her hard, but instead tidied the cot she'd laid the babe in, cleared and replaced the bloody linen, and cleaned the suction machine.

"They'll both need a long sleep after she nurses him." Ruth was standing behind her now. "There's an empty room at the end of the hall. We'll let them sleep until … What is it now, five-thirty. We'll let them sleep until ten and after that make sure they wake every three hours until he's feeding properly." She had the mother's bed by the rails and steered it toward the door. "Follow me."

Hazel pushed the baby's cot, following Ruth's steady, slow steps along the dim hallway. The wheels rolled along the buffed linoleum floor in the quiet ward. Though they almost hadn't, this mother and baby had made it, and she'd been part of that. She was not euphoric, she was humbled. Any doubts she'd entertained, any yearnings she'd felt for more than nursing could bring seemed indulgent now, even arrogant. This was enough. She steered the cot into the room, pushed it tight against the mother's bed and set the brake.

"Thanks, Captain." Ruth's voice was uncharacteristically quiet. "Couldn't have done it without you." She reached for a crank under the bed. "She should feed him a bit before sleeping and I'm going to help her. Stay if you want, but I can take it from here. You could still catch a few winks before your shift starts, get some breakfast."

Hazel had no intention of returning to the residence now, but Ruth was right. Two nurses in the room now was one too many. She laid her hand on the mother's leg a moment before leaving the room, her mind alight.

HAZEL SIPPED BITTER CAFETERIA COFFEE from a paper cup and stood at the railing of the back-door ramp, watching the water eddy around the southern tip of the island. The early morning sunlight caught the tips of surface ripples and flashed points of white light. The poplar and tamarack trees on Sawpit Island shifted in the light wind. The back door opened.

"Thought I might find you here."

"Why?"

"Call it a hunch." Ruth took a bite of sandwich and set her foot on the lower railing. "Ugh. Bologna. Should have paid more attention, but I was famished. Grabbed the first sandwich I saw." She peeled slices of pink meat from the bread and flung them over the railing. Hazel raised an eyebrow and Ruth shrugged. "The dogs'll get it. Have you eaten?"

Hazel nodded. "You were up all night, then."

"I came back after everyone had gone to bed to check on someone else and was just leaving around eleven when she came in, screaming loud enough to wake the dead. She'd been in labour a couple of days. This is her fourth, birthed the rest perfectly well in her own tupiq, but never a breech. Her man was scared. He told Joseph he'd never heard her scream this way." She pushed the last piece of bread into her mouth and brushed her hands on her uniform. "It took them two hours by boat to get here."

Two hours of heavy labour in a boat. No wonder she was in distress. "They were lucky."

"They'd both be dead if they hadn't made the journey. I reckon they had a sense of that. Death tends to forewarn."

Hazel took another sip of coffee, waiting for the caffeine rush. "How many have you lost?"

"A few. Wouldn't be a midwife if I hadn't. It's better not to keep count."

"Ever think of doing something else?"

"Of course." Ruth untied her hair and shook her head. A mass of red curls showered her shoulders. "But not seriously. This is the only thing for me."

"You were good in there today."

"You weren't so bad yourself." She closed her eyes and massaged her temples. "We could use another midwife up here. Ever thought about training?"

"Up here? How?"

"I know a little bit about the subject."

Hazel had never seriously considered it, but a TB nurse with midwifery could write her own ticket. When Ruth walked through the doors of the new hospital, Lachlan had asked her to name her price.

"Thanks, Ruth. Truly." She drained the last silty dregs from the cup. "I'll think about it."

"As you wish." She squeezed Hazel's arm and pulled the door open. "The offer stands."

TWELVE

RAMBLING ALONG THE ROCKY NORTH beach in the grey morning, Gideon almost missed it. The wings were untouched and splayed out on the rocks, a broken supplication to the clouds. The light wind lifted and dropped a froth of white and grey down feathers, detritus of a falcon's meal: all that remained was roughage, indigestible and left to sink into the sand or be carried away on the breeze. A marvel of economy.

The bones were picked smooth and gave off a pearly gleam. Gideon crouched. The falcon had made a surgical job of the breast, stripping the flesh neatly from the bones. The gull's head was gone. It was a recent kill; how disappointing to have just missed the falcon at her meal. What remained, flesh that once connected the breast with the wings, smelled fresh, even appealing, an organic sweetness. His stomach rumbled. It might have made a good stew if she'd left a little more meat.

Other gulls circled and cried overhead. Was she nearby still, watching him examine what she'd left behind? He picked up his binoculars. Nothing obvious, but the trunk of a tree would be ideal camouflage if she huddled against it, head tucked into her back for sleep after the meal and one foot pulled up under her feathers.

The image of the falcon resting, concealed in the tree, pulsed white-hot in his carver's mind. He'd spend the rest of the afternoon giving it form on the coin he'd cadged from the nurse. He slipped his hand into his pocket. Profile of a king, the lettering said, but the face was fresh and smooth like a boy's, thick hair side-parted and combed in neat rows. The detail in the hair was good, useful. It would be easy to transform. But he must capture the image while it still burned.

He stood and began to pace, head down. He stopped every few paces, examined a patch of ground and then moved on again. The river rushed past the tip of the island with steady purpose, singing the promise of coolness in James Bay, but the day was already warm. He'd need shade. Here was a good tree, leaves turning in the breeze, branches held out to gather up the sky. He ran his hand along the bark and sat against it.

Gideon took in the rushing cobalt river, the wide sky, the searing pressure of the clouds. He'd spent months imagining himself here, but the mental pictures he'd conjured had been imperfect by a long stretch, tacking toward barren Arctic landscapes even though he doubted that would be true. But no matter. He didn't mind being wrong if the surprise leaned in the right direction.

He reached into his pack and felt for the soft cloth that protected his tools, a small green hand towel he'd liberated from a shop in a small mining town, and set the bundle on his lap while he swept leaves and pine needles from the ground beside him. The bone-handled knife was new to his collection, got in trade with an island native for his razor. He used his straightedge now, and he could use his knife if it came to that.

But first he had to coax it away from its original casting. He filed it in gentle clockwise revolutions and watched the river. Beyond the tip of the island and across the channel the water travelled north, soon to swirl into the wide expanse of James Bay. The sensation of freshwater meeting salt, the slowing of its incessant rush as it met the wider basin, the slight vertigo as the bottom dropped out from under it: if he could be an atom of water for a day, the distance he could cover!

The aristocratic face on the coin started to lift, its edges less distinct. The new shape was emerging, but the bird wasn't sleeping, not at all. This was her head, pulled into her body and looking straight at him. She was intelligent, steady, unflinching. He secured the coin in a cardboard tube he'd made to hold it steady, reached for the awl and began to shorten the strands of hair, capping them in small arcs at intervals. Each feather brought her closer. She'd been there all along, waiting to show herself.

Next was the eye. Gideon's hand hovered over one tool, then another. Which was best to render it? A falcon's eye was the centre of her being; she received all intelligence visually, or nearly all, and based her existence on what she could see from the sky. It could not be faked, glossed over or hurried in any way. A mistake here could be fatal. Initially he deferred the eye and put his tools to the feathers, but these would not be coaxed away from the king. He put his tools down and stared at the coin awhile. It came to him: he wouldn't see the rest of her body properly if her eye wasn't clear.

It was for this reason he carved, the solving of unsolvables that he was allowed only this way. That truth curled around him like a cat. He would need two tools, one for freeing it from the coin in broad strokes and the other for polishing it to a cool marble smoothness. He reached for the broken screwdriver he'd found on the road one day and had filed to a perfect flat point. He dug the edge in to make the dip where the eye met the socket, then slipped it backward, up the same path toward the centre of the eye and back down again, in this way working the convex shape from the centre outward. After the first complete circuit, the shape was good, if rough, but he could fix that. What mattered was that it held for sharp sight. He closed his eyes and saw himself through the eye he'd just carved, every pore, every hair, every molecule of oil on his skin.

Relief rode through his body like a wave. He opened his eyes and stretched. The sun, having recently appeared from behind the clouds, had passed the midpoint of the sky. He marked the time and glanced back to the coin. The falcon was emerging, but she was still a shadowy presence waiting to be drawn into sharper focus. This was not a problem. Some of them just needed more coaxing.

As he carved, his mind lit on the nurse. This coin would be hers again when he was finished with it, as they'd agreed. Would she understand? She wasn't like the others he'd known over the years. Three- or four-month *hospital rests*, as his father had put it, were long enough to get to know a ward nurse. Even the young ones had been ruined, painted over with a veneer of fortitude and grim determination, by the time they'd reached her age. It was their lack of innocence that spoiled them. But not this one.

She had beguiled him. He'd meant to be long gone by now, well on his way further north, but she'd given him her name like a gift. Hazel. In calling her Eyas he'd been deliberate, though how long it would take her to fledge was unclear. She hadn't taken anything from him, not once, and she'd given him this coin without understanding why.

It had grown heavier in his hand. The falcon was making her presence known, becoming substantial, corporeal. Gideon closed his eyes and let the tree cradle his head. The morning's work had been true. The rest was refining, but it would be a mistake to put it aside until he'd finished with it. His own meal was many hours off, and only after the hovering of her wings had faded to silence.

THIRTEEN

SOMETIMES I'D FIND HIM WAITING near the hospital for me to finish my work. There must have been times he'd wait without reason but it wasn't the same as the waiting that you're doing, Jude. I wasn't captive to a brain incident then and locked in with my thoughts like I am now. One day I'd stayed on past the end of my shift to help Ruth and when I came out I saw him hunched over his work under a tall pine. His body was like a question mark. I wonder how long he'd been there and if he even understood the flow of the shifts. It was late but the long light of midsummer in the north was only starting to fade. Children were awake past their bedtimes, zigzagging on the road in front of me and chasing each other in the last of the light. Their mothers' voices called to them on the humid air.

He spotted me and the smile on his face was nothing I'd seen before or since. It was the purest manifestation of joy. He put down what he'd been working on, fished a pouch from under his shirt and plucked something out. Then he held his hand out and said, "I think it's my best one yet," as though he was continuing a conversation we'd been having all day. I stood my ground at first but he offered the coin in his open palm and coaxed me to him in stages, first leaning in for a closer look at the coin and then sitting down on the ground beside him in full view of the cluster of orderlies smoking on the hospital lawn. Then he dropped it into my hand. The metal was still warm.

It was the nickel I'd given him. After the most cursory study I knew it had to be and said the same to him. "Yes and no," he said. The trick in his answer pleased him. His smile stretched across his face like an elastic band.

He watched me while I struggled to understand. I was reaching for my purse when he took my hand. "Closer. You have to look closer." And gently he turned the coin over in my palm.

The king's head was gone. In its place a falcon's was rendered in heartbreaking detail. The plumage on its head was smooth and it had a large glinting eye and waxy beak. As the question formed in my mind I noticed the towel on the ground beside him was laid with a curiosity shop of miniature tools that he had obviously fashioned for himself from other things. A railway nail, an ice pick, a metal nail file, an awl, a screwdriver whose broken shaft had been filed to a flat point and a bone-handled hunting knife.

The coin he gave me might have been the most beautiful of the ones he'd carved and I've kept it all these years. Later I found that he'd charmed others into making the trade because occasionally I'd get one in change from the HBC store but we never discussed it. I didn't think it was wise to point them out to anyone on the island and I think it's possible that most of the population never noticed.

At first I wouldn't let him give it to me. I sensed that I would be entering into a contract I couldn't fulfill. Even though I urged him to consider the price this might fetch on the open market he understood the real reason for my refusal intuitively and responded as though I'd slapped him. He said he was releasing his art into the wild. No one could take something away from him that he'd given of his own free will. He said it like an accusation of something we both knew I was guilty of.

FOURTEEN

RISING EARLY WASN'T A CHORE in August. That far north, morning filtered milkily through Hazel's window before five-thirty. She was waiting at the hospital dock by six, long before the rest of the crew. She'd lain awake long enough.

In spite of the fact that she'd tried to talk herself out of it for a variety of reasons, daydreams about a trip on the survey boat had continued to surface. Lachlan's comment was not so much insincere as unthinking, she'd decided; he hadn't mentioned it since and so neither had she. It would have to stay that way. She couldn't risk the humiliation of being wrong about this.

But then the flu struck two days before a scheduled trip to Rupert's House. Not one of the x-ray assistants was well enough to go. She was a natural choice, Lachlan said, given the interest she'd demonstrated in the subject. The educational opportunity would be unparalleled. It was close enough to do as a day trip, and it would make her more adept at explanations for patients, a skill few nurses possessed. Besides, Indian Health Services expected frequent reports at this time of the year, so delaying the trip wasn't an option. The ice would be back before the end of October. Lachlan said all of this in such a matter-of-fact tone that it was impossible to know whether he'd remembered suggesting a trip and had waited for an opportunity, or if she was simply a logical choice in the immediate situation. But it didn't matter. Whatever his motivations, she was going.

The hospital would get by without her. They'd closed the clinic for the day, as they always did when Lachlan was away. The fact that Charlie and Lachlan were both going was unusual, given the size of the group to be examined. But with the hospital over capacity, Lachlan had not been on a single trip so far this year and she knew that his desire to be out in the field was long past an itch. He and Charlie had danced around the subject for a couple of days. They finally settled on a series of justifications that made it not only possible but necessary for both to go, Charlie because he knew the routine and Lachlan because he was obliged to stay in touch with how they were being received in the northern communities. Neither man was willing to assist the other. That was Hazel's job.

She borrowed Ruth's down vest to wear over her wool sweater and trousers for the trip and braided her hair and wrapped it in a kerchief. Out in the open water of James Bay, the wind from the north sliced across the water and through clothing, even in summer. She'd heard the stories. She was ready.

The day was clear enough that she could make out the scrub brush of Hayes Island just downriver beyond the end of the channel. James Bay was only twelve nautical miles north but she'd never seen it. Neither had Ruth. Word that Hazel was going infiltrated the hospital gossip mill, and she noticed an increase in whispers and sidelong glances, but none of that could have dissuaded her from taking this trip. *Risky*, Ruth said, when Hazel told her she was going, but when she asked Ruth whether she'd go if asked, she looked at Hazel as if she had two heads. Of course Ruth would go, chattering classes be damned. Ruth pointed out that Lachlan was chief of staff. Gossip might be social currency, but that's all it was. Hazel wished Ruth were coming too. She'd have liked to share the trip with her.

The dock shifted and creaked behind her, alive with adult weight. She turned, expecting Lachlan or one of the crew. Gideon smiled broadly and put the pipe he'd been holding in his teeth into his hip pocket.

"Taking to the water, Hazel?"

She forgot, for a moment, that she'd told him her name. "Just a day trip to Rupert's House. Chest x-rays all around."

She scanned the shore behind him. There was a knot of figures on the road between the hospital outbuildings, probably crew. She hoped so. This was the second time in two weeks that Gideon had come to her on the hospital dock.

"Ah yes, Rupert's House." He cocked his head to one side. "I know it well. I'll be going that way myself."

This she hadn't expected. The casual words took on a darker shading. "You will?"

"Yes, ma'am, on my way to the Northwest Passage." He reached inside his jacket and pulled out a slim volume. "Captain Henry Larsen took the *St. Roch* across it twice between '40 and '44, first vessel to ever cross it both ways." By the end of the sentence, the rate of his speech had doubled. "Claimed it for Canada's own, the top of the world. The top of the world, Hazel! Think about that. It's all right here, see?" He bent over the book and paged through it until he found what he wanted, then grinned as he held it out to her. The pages were smudged with dirt and the corners were bent. "Oh, we'll meet someday, he and I, I can feel it! We're cut from the same cloth. I'll see it with my own eyes or die trying."

The men were at the top of the bank now, and she recognized Lachlan's loping stride. She handed the book back, willing herself to appear disinterested. "That's quite a distance from here."

He gave her a pitying glance. "I'll just follow the water's lead."

"You have a boat?"

"No. But they go north from here all the time. Such as this one." He set the pipe between his teeth again and smiled.

She'd seen it coming. The temperature had already risen since she'd come out here and he was dressed in everything he owned. Lachlan would be watching her closely if Gideon was still here when he arrived. How would Lachlan react if Gideon asked to travel with them? How would Gideon react if Lachlan refused? He couldn't possibly allow it. She scanned the dock. Surely Gideon would have brought his belongings if he meant to leave today, and he hadn't.

"It's not so hard, you know, hopping a boat." It was uncanny, the way he seemed to read her thoughts. "Easier than flipping a freight."

"I wouldn't know."

"Like my road brothers did a decade ago. Oh, they were pure, Hazel. Lived on their wits alone some days. Never needed a penny to travel east or west or points between! Best of the bunch rode on the rods under the train. What's slipping aboard a ship compared to that? What sense of heroics, I ask you?"

She was down the rabbit hole again, like that day at his camp. He'd moved closer to her and his breath smelled fusty. When had he last eaten? He had a faraway gaze, as if he'd already made a decision about his proximity to the world. The men were almost at the dock. She took a step backward.

"We'll see when I get to the passage, then we'll see." He stepped toward her. His blue eyes burned like twin flames. "And you, Hazel? Where does the water lead you?"

"I'm a nurse, as you know. I'm here to work."

He folded his arms. "Tell me something true."

He was familiar with her in the most infuriating way. Her cheeks burned. Her answer was incomplete but it was true enough. This was not the kind of conversation you had in polite company. She didn't answer.

"I will see the Northwest Passage in all of its frozen glory, Hazel." He had turned toward the water again and the quality of his voice had changed. It was deeper and more distant, like he was speaking from the bottom of a well, and it had a rhythm almost like music. "And one day, when the lifeblood is leaving me, colouring the ground red ..." He swung back to face her. "Whether at sea or on land, I'll know that I have lived."

He held her in his gaze and this time she didn't look away. The wind picked up her braid and lifted it over her shoulder. She couldn't have said how long they stood that way. It was unfamiliar and uncomfortable and thrilling to look at another human being with such frank curiosity. She wasn't sure she ever had.

"Everything okay here, Nurse MacPherson?"

Lachlan strode toward her. His smile was tight and his eyes were hard, flat stones. How ridiculous to be caught up in this odd man's reverie, they said. She swallowed. "Everything is fine, Doctor Davies. Gideon was just telling me about his plans to sail to the Northwest Passage."

"Ah yes. Mushfaker, wasn't it? Still here, I see. I take it you've been reading Larsen. Cracking good account. I read the *Geographical Journal* myself. But it's quite a stretch to think you're going to get up there, my good man. You will of course realize that Captain Larsen sailed her in an RCMP vessel with a crew of twenty-five."

He shaded his eyes and scanned the horizon. "And he didn't go at it from this direction."

"A trivial matter," Gideon murmured, shaking his head, and Hazel's scalp prickled.

The *Mercer* pulled up behind him. Lachlan raised his eyebrows. "Well then, we'll leave you to it. We're away in a few minutes, and I'm afraid we have no room for others. Here's the rest of the crew now, in fact. Unless there's something else you need, medical attention perhaps?"

"Not one thing." Gideon nodded to Lachlan, then turned to Hazel. He held her in his gaze a moment too long.

FIFTEEN

GIDEON IGNORED THE DOCTOR'S BROAD hint and sauntered to the end of the dock. This was a test. He could ignore the entreaties of lesser minds. It wasn't even difficult for him. He'd been practicing that discipline for over a decade now. There was no real irritation left in those exchanges anymore. If he felt anything, it was pity. They were trapped in their own flightless realities. He hung his legs over the edge of the dock. How easy it would be to launch himself when the time came.

When the *Mercer* finally pulled away, he lifted his hand and waved to the nurse. Before she turned, he saw the expression she was trying to hide. This one was different from the rest. "Soon," he whispered.

Shuffling crablike to a corner of the dock, he settled against the post, closed his eyes and slipped his hand into his breast pocket. He'd brought the journal with him this morning to share with her. It was a beautiful document, the ornate black type embossed in heavy vanilla paper. The *Geographical Journal.* Royal Geographical Society, July–September 1947. He ran his hand across the cover and let his fingertips linger in the impressions the letters made. He'd sensed its presence even while it was still buried in a pile of other magazines on the asylum reading trolley. It was meant for him. He took a few others as well, never intending to read them, and returned only those. The nearsighted volunteer hadn't noticed. When he was discharged, he took it home with him under his shirt.

He opened it to the first page now. "The Conquest of the North West Passage: The Arctic Voyages of the *St. Roch*, 1940–1944." His lips moved as he read the author's name, Inspector Henry A. Larsen, RCMP, though he had by now committed all of the text to memory.

The nurse didn't know anything about being a real voyager, but her innocent questions were a reminder that he hadn't yet compiled a list of supplies he needed to buy before leaving the island. It would be foolish to be unprepared, especially when it was all right there in the book for him like a personal invitation. The words Larsen used were a code left behind for Gideon alone to uncover. He patted his pockets for his pencil and flipped to the last page of the journal. He made two columns, Supplies and Sites. His eyes darted through the pages. He had a pot for melting ice, but he dashed the word in the Supplies column and crossed it out for the sake of completeness. He would need a stove; Larsen's was a Swedish Primus. He wrote that down, too, and paraffin wax below it.

One sentence seemed to lift off the next page and float up to him. Some nights he'd turn to it just before sleep. "This raw frozen

fish gives one a warm feeling of well-being after a few minutes."
All would be taken care of; the sea would provide. He'd only need
a jigging string and a hook and he'd be able to feed himself. He
wrote these items in the Supplies column and then, after a few
minutes of deliberation, wrote ice axe below them. Thick slabs
were best, Larsen wrote.

On the next page was a picture of Pasley Bay, Boothia Pen-
insula. A sublime and wild landscape, the very embodiment of
possibility. The *St. Roch* was anchored just offshore in the middle
ground of the photograph. He ran his hand over the glossy paper
and saw himself there, surrounded by a silent chorus of icebergs.
The method of conveyance hadn't yet come to him, but he was
content to wait. There would be a sign when the time was right.

However he travelled, he knew about the growlers, baby icebergs lying just below the swell that weren't babies at all. "Gigan-
tic sea-monsters," Larsen called them. But Gideon was small and
fleet and that was his advantage; he was unencumbered by a ship
large enough for twenty-six men. He wrote Pasley Bay in the Sites
column, and then laughed. As if he'd forget.

The pages of the journal were supple like skin, softer now than
they'd once been. He'd learned to turn them without haste; the
tear down the centre of the next page had taught that lesson. He
skimmed through the text. The place names of the north were
like smooth stones in his mouth. Resolution Island. Frobisher Bay.
Clyde River. Lancaster Sound. Cape Warrender. Pond Inlet. Dev-
on Island. He wrote this last on his list in the Sites column. Inside
the cairn Larsen and his men had built was a brass cylinder they'd
left with a record of their visit. Gideon saw himself slipping the
pages from it, uncovering the secrets they held.

The best was last, and he turned the page slowly. King's Island.
Larsen had saved the telling of it for last, and Gideon would have
done the same. He let himself come to the phrase by degree,

consuming each word more slowly than the last. A village there on the south side of the island was "built almost like a bird's nest." It was a place to alight.

He closed his eyes and laid on the dock. His arms were perpendicular to his body, poised and ready for the next thermal. He felt the marrow drain from his bones until they were hollow and ready for flight.

SIXTEEN

HAZEL WAS GLAD FOR RUTH'S vest. Once they reached the open water of James Bay, even the August sun was no match for the winds that bore down the channel out of the north, stirring waves a foot high. The bow of the boat lifted up and out of the water at the crest of each wave, crashing back down on the other side. Lachlan suggested that she go into the hold for safety, but she refused. He would not, she was certain, have given the same advice to any man on board. Besides, though she was not prone to seasickness like Charlie was, the surest way to bring it on was to go below deck in waves like these. The summers she'd spent with cousins in Nova Scotia taught her that much. She stood at the railing and pulled the knitted cap Lachlan gave her over her kerchief. Water to the horizon in every direction. Out here it would be easy to lose one's bearings.

They made the inlet to Rupert Bay by noon. The *Mercer* rounded the tip of land into the bay and set a course just south of a small island, a sleeping form of grey and green that rose in serene undulations out of the frantic motion of the bay. She could pick out the frothing mouth of the river now and the clearing that was the community of Rupert's House. It would be a job to anchor there, Lachlan had told her, the way the mighty Rupert River blasted out into the bay.

She made her way to the opposite railing where Lachlan stood with his movie camera held to one eye. He'd ordered it months ago, unwilling to let his journeys further north go unrecorded, and was finally able to use it. Late last night, when she passed his office on her way out, he was still there, camera in one hand and instruction booklet in the other.

The village of Rupert's House was smaller than Moose Factory and home to roughly five hundred Cree, most of whom had been x-rayed during last year's survey. There was also a nursing station, an RCMP base and an HBC trading post. Near the dock, a group of black-haired figures edged down the slope toward shore. This must be the group Nurse Walker radioed about. They'd somehow been missed last year. Behind them, a flash of red, then another, an unnatural flowering on the barren coast. RCMP. They'd been notified of the *Mercer's* arrival and had assembled the villagers to await x-ray. This was new, an efficiency Charlie praised. The survey boats were otherwise at the mercy of the tides and sometimes forced to work into the night.

The villagers followed the boat's progress along the beach and then stood at the end of the dock as the *Mercer* dropped anchor some distance from shore. A few broke away from the cluster and climbed in a canoe.

"Aren't we going in?"

"I thought we might try but the current is too strong. We'll anchor here and they'll row out to us."

"How do they get back?"

"Not our concern." Then, more gently, "Don't worry, Hazel. They know this river far better than we do. They'll be fine." Lachlan fiddled with the switches on the camera. "Funny that the umbrella mender was on the dock this morning."

This she hadn't expected. What had he heard about the time she'd spent with Gideon? She needed to be careful. "It is, yes."

"Those ideas of his about the Northwest Passage ..."

"Crazy. I know."

"Do you think he wanted to come with us?"

"No idea." The lie came easily. "I hadn't thought about it."

She watched the canoe approach. The bow was consumed and reborn on the navy peaks of the waves. *Tell me something true.* Curse you, Lachlan. Until that point she'd left Gideon and the undertow of his presence back on the dock in Moose Factory, and it wasn't so difficult. She was in the survey boat approaching a Cree community in far-north Quebec. From the minute she'd decided to go north, she'd wanted this, and only recently dared to think it possible. No other nurses had been given this chance. One mention of Gideon and it was all undone. She ricocheted back to what he'd said, the way it reached into her.

The first canoe carried four men and a woman with a baby on her back, and it was close enough to the *Mercer* now that Hazel could read the apprehension on their faces. She wondered what they'd been told. The barest wisp of shadow on their lungs would consign them to the hospital for so long that the families they'd left behind might think them dead. Until now, Hazel had never been part of this decision. By the time she met them, the boat was pulling up behind the hospital. It was done. There, her role was well-defined and uncomplicated: she would work to help them heal.

Lachlan had a lighter touch than Charlie but the result was the same, had to be the same. There was no alternative. First, do no harm. How else to cure the north of the disease that was ravaging it? It had cut a merciless path and had no prejudice. Young, old, weak, strong. They could offer a cure and a northern hospital for convalescence. They could help these people, and the imperative to do that went beyond professional obligation. It was the only moral choice. Wasn't it?

The woman was the first to board the *Mercer*. She was younger than Hazel. She slid the baby from the pack on her back with practiced ease, and let Hazel take him from her. With a flannel blanket she had waiting, Hazel wrapped him and tucked him tight against her chest. The mother wore layers of clothing under her coat, several cotton dresses probably traded for beaver pelts. The thin fabric whipped against her bare legs.

"You must remove your shirts for the x-ray." Henry was still translating when Lachlan unbuttoned his own shirt and dropped it to the deck. He stood – his hair a swirl of pale fire in the wind, goosebumps rising on his skin – until the five Cree patients began to work the buttons of their own clothing. The woman removed her coat and the first of her dresses. Her head was down.

"Doctor Davies." Hazel nodded toward the woman. Lachlan was absorbed in adjustments to the portable x-ray now. "Give us a minute. I'll bring her right back."

Hazel held the baby on her hip and led the woman below deck, gave her a pair of old trousers and a length of rope as a belt. By the time they were back on deck, the men were waiting for their turn to be examined, bare-chested and stoic in the sharp wind. Lachlan had mounted the machine on a tripod near the mast. She laid her free hand on the woman's bare shoulder and guided her to it. By the tremor under her skin Hazel knew that the young mother had touched the cold metal of the lens, but she didn't complain. Hazel caught her eye, took a deep and obvious breath, and held it. The woman did the same. Hazel signalled to Lachlan, who moved his finger to the switch and then shook his head.

"Again. She moved. Henry, tell her to be still or the picture of her lungs won't turn out."

Henry, slouched against the railing with his cap pulled low on his forehead, flexed his back. "*Ni pah we.*" His tone was harsh. He crossed his muscled arms and let his chin settle back on his chest. The nervous smile slipped from the woman's face and her spine became rigid. Lachlan picked up the x-ray switch again.

"Rough night, Henry?"

"Just a little tired."

"Catch up on your sleep later. Tell her we're done now, without the attitude. Even without you snapping at everybody, it's going to be a long day." He turned to Charlie. "Doctor Wilcox, can I borrow you for a minute?" He held the x-ray switch out to him. Charlie rose unsteadily, shut his eyes and swallowed. His free arm reached for a post as the boat listed. "Hazel, undress that baby for me."

She unwrapped the child and handed him to Lachlan. He slipped his hands under the baby's armpits and held him in front of the x-ray lens. The baby kicked and cried in the cool wind.

"Need another set of hands here, Hazel. Come around the other side."

She caught the baby's ankles and held them still. The muscles inside the plump flesh strained and flexed into her palms. "Just a few minutes now, sweetie, and you'll be all done." The baby turned at the sound of her voice and his body relaxed.

"Now, Charlie. Good. I think we got it that time." He turned to her, smiling broadly. "You're a natural."

He crossed the deck and handed the baby to Charlie for the physical exam. The mother stood beside Hazel, her arms crossed over her bare chest. "Henry, tell her she can get dressed. Next, Hazel. Keep them moving. I'm expecting the plane around two."

AT THE HARSH BUZZ OF the float plane, Hazel saw a second canoe leave the shore carrying four more patients and an RCMP officer. She assumed he'd come to be examined with the others, but when the canoe pulled up alongside the *Mercer*, he hoisted himself aboard and strode directly to Lachlan, leaving the others to exit the boat on their own.

"You're the doctor in charge?"

Charlie and Lachlan exchanged a glance. "We are, yes." Lachlan held his hand out over the shoulder of the man he was examining. "Lachlan Davies."

"Nick Broadfoot." He was a huge man, broad-shouldered and as tall as Lachlan. In his red wool jacket and tall hat, he was an imposing figure. Behind him, Charlie made a motion to extend his hand, then sat down again when Broadfoot didn't turn. "We have a small . . . problem."

Lachlan frowned and moved the stethoscope closer to the man's heart and closed his eyes. "Just a minute." He let the chestpiece fall and made a note in his file. "Okay. Go ahead."

"This isn't the whole group. There are more to be examined."

The float plane made several circles above them and finally skidded to a landing twenty feet away. "Fine, sir. That's what we're here for. Please bring them aboard. The sooner the better, as you see. The plane will be kept waiting and we don't want that. These films have to go back to the hospital as soon as possible so they can radio the results. We plan to be back in Moose Factory with the new patients tonight." He paused and glanced at the group in the boat. "Assure them that the exams don't take long."

Broadfoot hesitated. "It's not quite that simple."

"Why is that?" Lachlan finished with the man he was examining and motioned for him to dress. "Out with it."

"They, ah, left the coast early this morning. We think they were headed for the woods."

Lachlan flicked the eartips from his ears and stood. "Damn." He dropped the stethoscope into his bag. "I suppose you told them we were coming last night."

The Mountie lifted his chin. "We were preparing them for your visit, as we were instructed. If I'd had any idea they'd leave I'd have waited until morning."

"Do you know why they left?"

Broadfoot pulled himself up to his full height. "With all due respect, Doctor, it's about what happens when people get on that boat of yours."

"What have they heard, Officer . . ." He squinted to read the name engraved on the man's nametag as if they hadn't just been introduced. ". . . Broadfoot, about what happens in this boat of ours?"

"It's what they haven't heard, sir." His voice was quieter now. "Their people don't come back."

Lachlan sighed. "Not immediately, no. But we have better medicines now." He lifted his glasses to the top of his head and massaged the bridge of his nose between finger and thumb. "But I guess they don't know that." He walked to the railing and delivered a stack of film into the pilot's outstretched hands. "More to come. Please wait." He turned to face Broadfoot. "We'll have to go ashore after we finish with this group, obviously. We can't just leave them. Any idea where they might be?"

THE RIVER'S BLIND FORCE WAS ceaseless and mesmerizing. Henry told her that it housed a mighty spirit, and docking the

Mercer was the ordeal Lachlan predicted. They edged along the shore where the current was weaker but the engine still laboured, and then there was the gradual slope of the riverbed. The boat's deep hull hit sand well before they could dock. They reversed course and anchored offshore.

Lachlan radioed the trading post. They couldn't make it back to Moose Factory tonight. It was well past four. When the search party returned, Hazel would stay with Factor Wilson and his wife and the men would pitch tents near the shore. He'd made arrangements for Nurse Walker to stay in her station overnight. Everything about the way he described the search was coloured with his certainty that the group would be found and he'd be able to persuade them to be examined.

"We leave no stone unturned, Nurse MacPherson. They can't have gone far."

Hazel was not optimistic. The fleeing families had an instinctive knowledge of the area and a head start fuelled by mortal, adrenal fear. The search parties might as well be wearing blindfolds. "I wonder if they're still in the woods at all."

"Broadfoot said there were about a dozen in their group. Even using the most optimistic figures, that's at least four sick to slow them down. It's just that they don't understand. We have so much more to offer them now. We can help them, and we have to try."

Lachlan formulated a plan before anyone left the *Mercer*. They would fan out and search the woods in parties of two. Each of the medics would have an interpreter. Hazel would go with Henry, Lachlan with Broadfoot and Charlie with the other constable. Success or twilight would bring them back to the beach.

Since Broadfoot had come aboard, Charlie had said very little. From his paper-pale complexion, Hazel assumed that carrying on with exams while remaining upright was the extent of his power. He refused the lunch Henry prepared. As the second of the two canoes left for the shore, he called to Lachlan and gestured toward the group on board. "Someone ought to stay with them."

Lachlan put down the file he'd been reading. "I suppose you're right. We don't want to lose them, too." He radioed Nurse Walker, who agreed to set up a temporary camp.

Hazel went below deck to stow her vest and pick up a day pack. It was audacious, even arrogant, to think that white medics would find a group of Cree locals who didn't want to be found. If it had been her decision, she'd have sent the plane back hours ago. They might have even heard from the hospital already and been able to make Moose Factory by nightfall. But there was no arguing with Lachlan on this point. She'd known him long enough to understand this.

He came down the stairs and started to pack a small medical bag. Hazel set a canteen of water and some hardtack biscuits beside his bag.

"Hours yet." He was muttering, and she wasn't sure he was talking to her. He hadn't acknowledged her presence in any way. "The light will be good until at least ten."

"And then?"

He seemed startled, as if she'd been eavesdropping. "By then, we'll have found them."

Broadfoot said he'd heard that they'd gone east. He suspected that they were headed to their winter camp inland, upstream and near the source of the river. They were likely to stay close to shore. It was their usual route to the winter camps. Further inland was a bog that ran nearly to the road coming into the settlement. He kneeled on the shore and sketched out a map in the sand.

"They're on foot, gone less than six hours and some of their party are sick. They can't have made it further than here." He circled a spot on his sand map. "We'll get just ahead of them and then fan downstream." He gestured toward three aluminum boats pulled up on shore, well out of reach of the churn and boil of the river. "Two to a boat. Better get a move on. The river's in fine form today."

HAZEL AND HENRY WALKED BACK along the beach toward the dock in silence. By the time weak flashlight beams bobbed through the trees – first Charlie and the constable, then Lachlan and Broadfoot – Henry had built a fire against the full dark. Hazel stared into it, still grappling with a response for Lachlan's inevitable question. He would have convinced himself that the missing families would be waiting at the shore.

"Where are they?" He was barely within hearing range, but the pain in his voice was unmistakable. When they'd set out that afternoon, the outcome to this odyssey seemed certain to him. Hazel had expected this, but it was rare for him to be without a contingency plan. In the past few hours, his mental energy must have been consumed with an arrangement of arguments aimed at convincing the reluctant party to come back to the *Mercer* for the exam. Their absence would be a statistical outlier, an irritant.

"Nurse MacPherson?"

She shook her head. His raw vulnerability was unnerving. Until then, she hadn't realized how much she relied on his equanimity.

"Wilcox?"

"If we had, don't you think –" He stopped himself. "No."

"Nothing? How could we have missed them? There were a dozen, weren't there?"

"That was the report I received, sir, yes." Broadfoot was a hulking shadow behind Lachlan. He shifted his weight from one foot to the other and set his jaw. "I'm sorry to have led you good people on a wild goose chase."

"Don't apologize. It won't help us. We'll just have to try harder. They're out there. With sickness in their party, they have to be. We'll go again at daybreak."

"No." Charlie hadn't moved from where he'd been sitting beside the fire, his legs pulled up under him. His face was in shadow. "We won't catch them, Lachlan. They're a full day ahead of us now. Send the plane back with the x-rays we've got and tell them it's a rush order. We should leave at first light so we don't get caught with the tides."

THE BED AT THE FACTOR's house was comfortable enough, but when Mrs. Wilson knocked at her door to offer tea, Hazel felt she'd only just drifted off. She'd lain awake for hours after the trading post was quiet, watching the play of the wind in the branches of the tree outside her window once the moon rose. She reached for her watch and hurried into her clothes. Eight a.m. She should have been at the dock an hour ago.

The men had already broken camp and were carrying tents back to the boat. A small knot of Cree waited at the shore. Lachlan must have already heard from the hospital. She counted heads. Ten. They'd examined eighteen. It was a statistic that Lachlan couldn't be happy about, likely to strengthen his resolve to go back for the others. She braced herself for another argument, but it seemed that she'd missed it.

"Good morning, Nurse MacPherson." Charlie lifted his head as she walked past him, his tone buoyant and peppered with notes of triumph. "I trust you slept well?"

She bit her tongue. Everyone knew what time it was without Charlie pointing it out; there could be no other reason for this unusually friendly greeting. "Just fine, Doctor Wilcox." She smiled at him and hoped for rolling seas on the journey back to Moose Factory. She swung her pack into a canoe that was loaded and ready to go.

She reached for Lachlan's hand and climbed into the *Mercer*. There were dark circles under his eyes. She wondered if he'd persuaded someone to go back out with him.

"Ten."

"I saw."

He shook his head. "We shouldn't be leaving without the other group. He's a stubborn ..."

"You both are." She knew she'd overstepped, but she couldn't pull back from this, even if she was aware that she'd allied herself with Charlie by doing so. "How long should we have made the others wait? These people could be anywhere. They might be hiding in the woods near here, right under our noses. We're medics, not trackers."

"They can't have gone far. If we could just ..."

"But we can't." She'd interrupted him again. She needed to guard against these hasty impulses. However vulnerable he was right now, he was perceptive. She took a breath. "We have a duty to the people we've already examined and found to be sick, don't we?"

"Feels incomplete." He was muttering again. He handed her the clipboard. "Check their names off the list as they come aboard. We pull up anchor in an hour."

Of course it's incomplete, she thought.

IT WAS A GOOD DAY for sailing. With the full force of the Rupert River behind them, they'd shot out into the wide blue of James Bay. Henry hoisted the sails. The two children on the boat leaned over the railing, sobbing, and stretched their arms in an impossible reach for their village. Hazel couldn't watch. She kept her distance and turned away from them, grateful for the admission forms to fill.

Until they began to angle south toward the Moose River inlet, they hadn't once needed to engage the motor. Once it started, the ceaseless, droning grind was a wall of noise that, coupled with the steady motion of the boat, magnified her fatigue. She sat down against a case of x-ray film and couldn't keep her eyes open.

She woke to the flap of a sail with a kink in her neck. Across from where she was sitting, below the starboard railing, the new patients propped themselves up against each other. The children were asleep in the arms of the two women. Snatches of Charlie's impatient, taut patter carried along the wind. Henry, for his part, was nodding. Lachlan wasn't on deck.

She stood and leaned against the railing. Land on two sides now. They were back on the Moose River already, and it was only three. They'd made good time. It was another half-hour before the houses along the shore of Moose Factory came into view. They approached the dock and she saw figures standing there. Could Gideon still be there? She'd seen the beginnings of Lachlan's irritation when they left. If he was there again today, so much about their relationship would be implied, and most of it would be wrong. But no one else understood that. She scanned the dock. One of the figures raised a hand. Her heart raced until she could make out who it was.

"Finally." Ruth stepped aside as Henry leaped from the prow and wound the docking line around a corner post. "We thought you'd be back last night."

"Long story." Lachlan picked up his bags and waited for Henry to tie off the stern. "Let's meet in the cafeteria in an hour. I'll let Hazel tell you about it."

The last thing she wanted to do was to replay any version of it. She told herself she'd feel better after a hot bath and a night's rest. "If you don't mind, I'm going to let you tell this one, Doctor Davies. I'm bushed. I'll show these people to their beds and see you in the morning."

"Fine, good. You do that." It was anything but fine, and there was nothing she could do about it.

SEVENTEEN

FROM AN EAGLE-EYED VIEW IT would have been comical: three tin fish tossed around like so much driftwood and battling the current of the mighty Rupert. You should have seen us, Jude. If I hadn't been so nauseated I might have laughed but as it was I was merely thankful for having eaten nothing since morning. Vomiting over the side would have been a humiliation. Queasiness I could hide.

We were two to a boat and Henry was in mine. That we'd form a search party for the missing group of Cree was to me a foregone conclusion from the minute the Mountie came aboard with the news. I'd known Lachlan long enough to understand that their absence would be as palpable as a tumour and equally impossible to ignore. He'd spend the night searching if he had to and he'd

expect no less of the rest of us. I knew this as surely as I knew I'd
help him.

We'd been searching for almost an hour when I heard the snap
of a twig that was amplified in that quiet wood. Henry was several
arms' lengths away in the direction opposite the sound and occupied
with something else. I wondered if it was possible that he hadn't
heard it or if my desire to please Lachlan had manufactured it for
my eager imagination. I scanned the woods tree by tree trying to
spot the smallest movement or the slightest shift in colour. I took
care to be soundless and to channel my entire energy through my
eyes and ears. In a feat of incredible hubris I decided that I'd made
myself undetectable. I was young. Like you.

None of this worked. How much time had elapsed since I'd
heard the sound I wasn't sure but in spite of monumental desire
and what I thought to be almost inhuman stillness I heard nothing more. Whoever or whatever had made the sound had vanished
or had never existed. My disappointment was eclipsed only by the
appetite that had been building steadily since we rowed ashore.

I had shrugged my pack from my back and was digging for
a biscuit when there was the barest brush of black against rug-
ged grey bark at the edge of my peripheral vision. If I'd managed
stillness before I now withdrew my hand from the pack as though
it was encased in wet sand and prayed I would go undetected by
whatever I'd seen. Black bears prowled these woods. Taking food
out was enormously unwise. What could I have been thinking?
My urgency to locate Henry was swift and shaming. Until this
point, I'd thought of myself as independent and invincible.

Henry crouched low and scanned the wood. As soon as I turned
toward him he saw me. I tipped my head in the direction of the
movement I'd seen and relief washed over me. I was certain that
Henry could save us both from my naive blunder. The small form
of a girl emerged into the space I indicated. A dark eye followed

black hair and both disappeared behind the tree in the next instant. As my racing pulse slowed I saw her hair and her eye and her mouth again. She wanted to be seen.

Assuming that sudden movement would startle I came to my feet by degree and took a tentative step toward her. I held my breath and half-expected to watch her back as she fled on known paths that I couldn't navigate. What would Henry do in that case? He must have been watching all of this but as much as I sensed that I might embarrass myself with my clumsy and inexperienced methods I couldn't risk breaking eye contact with the girl. Surely I'd lose her if I did. I tried another step. The girl slid behind the tree but didn't run.

Henry's hoarse whisper came like wind rustling through leaves. "Wait." He closed the distance between us with practiced stealth and I took another step toward the girl. The late-afternoon sun made columns of shifting light in the cathedral of that poplar wood. The forest floor was a sprung bed of moss and loam that muffled sound and the tree the girl had chosen was deeply lined and vast enough to hide her body. As I drew nearer she rolled slowly from behind it. "*Ni ka wiy*," she said. My mother. Then she lifted her hand to her chest.

She'd come willingly and now moved through the wood ahead of us. She seemed confident that we'd follow. Until she'd held her hand to her chest I'd entertained the possibility that this was another group entirely whose attention had been aroused by the medic who'd materialized in their wood. I'd grown accustomed to being a curiosity in Moose Factory. Maybe this was nothing more than a coincidence.

But as we made our way toward a clearing I knew it was not so. A curl of smoke rose from a small fire and I could make out a recumbent form beside it. The pallor of the woman's skin was a stark contrast with the forest green surrounding her and her skin hung from the bones of her face. Even without hearing the death-rattle cough I knew that this was the disease in its final stages.

An older woman sat beside her, stroking her arm, murmuring rhythmically and rocking with her eyes closed. I felt an immediate sense of intrusion. This family had fled knowing what we were and why we came. If the youngest of them was scared was that a reason to intervene?

Making arguments and counter-arguments in my head I ran through the possibilities. Charlie would insist that we take her back to Moose Factory in spite of the disease's imminent victory as he had done with the old woman from Great Whale and on that point he and Lachlan would be aligned. Both would inhabit the certainty I'd just lost and I couldn't decide whether their attitude would reassure or rankle. They would run tests and x-ray her lungs and probe her body in intimate places to create a sense of busyness that passed for optimism. They would slip tablets between her lips to make the passage to Moose Factory bearable. When she died before they reached the hospital they would feel that they had failed to solve the medical puzzle set for them. Her death in the windowless hold of a ship would be graceless.

The girl turned to me and her eyes gleamed with hope. "*Astum.*" Come. "*Ni ka wiy.*" That nothing could be done was incontestable but my presence suggested otherwise and created an expectation that I knew I couldn't fill. I was accustomed to being a player in the intimate drama of near-death. It had never become trivial but it was expected and I had always been able to locate myself within it to take up familiar routines and assume my role. But here in this place I felt dwarfed by the trees and the sky and the water. Whatever I had to offer was manifestly inadequate. I felt a keen disparity between the scope of our powers and the endless parade of the dead rolling on and on throughout millennia, walking these woods and along these shores.

Henry had already begun to approach the group when I called to him. He stopped and lifted his chin. He was daring me. His dark eyes were fiery and furious but there was something else there too. I heard Gideon's voice. *Ask yourself, nurse. Does this injury need the hospital's water?*

I said nothing. I only shook my head and Henry turned to the girl and said a few words. His tone was clipped and final. I wanted to believe that the speed of his response signalled agreement but he gave me no more than that. In the rest of the time I knew him neither of us discussed it again.

All expression dropped from the girl's face as though gravity had redoubled its force. She fell to the forest floor like a rag doll but when she finally spoke her voice was fierce. There was a moment of silence. A shaft of sunlight picked up the needle-short ends of Henry's hair. "She asks why you will not help her mother," he said, though the fact that he knew the answer implied another question.

Only youth can produce the kind of certainty I summoned that afternoon. There can be no other explanation for the duplicity I was rehearsing. "Broadfoot said there were at least a dozen," I said, feeling if not truth then something that superseded it. "How many do you count here?"

EIGHTEEN

FROM THE UNEVEN SHORE BEHIND the hospital, Sawpit Island was a mere suggestion of land on the horizon. The inky new-moon sky showed it as an absence of light, not more. Hazel lifted her end of the canoe into the water and tried to piece together the chain of conversations that ended here, in this late-September, late-night trip to Sawpit with Gideon, and couldn't. She wouldn't have considered herself passive, and anyone who knew her would have thought the idea laughable, but there it was, the bald fact of her inaction. She'd allowed herself to be carried along to this point, canoe in the water, an eccentric drifter she'd met only a few months earlier seating himself at the other end. The canoe was Ruth's, a gift of gratitude for the safe delivery of a fourth son, the early morning breech Hazel had attended. The baby's family had returned for a visit a few months later, their eldest son paddling this canoe behind his father. Ruth would have agreed to loan it, Hazel was certain of that, had she been asked. But she hadn't.

An hour earlier Hazel was watching the fire collapse with Gideon. She'd slipped from her bed after midnight, unable to endure another night of the insomnia that had begun in earnest a week after the return from Rupert's House. She told herself that a walk would help and found herself at his camp. He'd seemed unsurprised to see her.

"A place can't hold me long, Eyas." He unfolded his long legs and stood.

She'd grown accustomed to the name. Once she finally understood what it meant, she began to think of herself in those terms. "And yet you're still here, and it's September."

He paced beside the dying fire. "Time is a construct for manipulating the masses. It has no hold on me."

Hazel sighed. What had she hoped to find here? He was resolute, and she could admire that, but it didn't change certain intractable facts. "Seasons change with or without calendars, Gideon. It's getting colder. You won't get there before freeze-up. You'll have to stay the winter now." She felt a chill at the base of her spine as the words left her mouth. He could not winter at his camp and she couldn't imagine any other home for him on this island. A decision of some kind would be forced. "No boat will get through."

He smiled with half his mouth, indulging her. "I won't be needing one."

Hazel pushed herself to standing. There was no logic that could meet his on solid ground. It was late. She shouldn't have been there anyway. She said goodnight and started down the path to the Bay Road.

"Hazel." He stood in front of the fire. His face was in shadow. "That island across the water from the hospital."

"Sawpit Island?"

"Aha. Is it settled?"

She hesitated. The insinuation seemed unmistakable, but could he know it by reputation? "I don't think so." Mostly true. "Why?"

"They must be there. No nests on this island as far as I know. And that makes sense. Too much activity. But they're living here. They have to be." He walked toward her. "I need to go find them."

The falcons. Of course. He couldn't have meant anything else.

She was exhausted. It was unlikely that she'd sleep much of the night and she was scheduled to be in the clinic alone in the morning. Lachlan would be out on the survey boat on a day trip to Old Factory at the mouth of the Moose River. It was the *Mercer's* final journey of the season. Since the trip to Rupert's House, which she knew he considered a failure in spite of the ten patients who were steadily improving in the hospital, Lachlan made it his business to be on every survey trip that left Moose Factory while keeping up with his hospital duties. The angles on his face had become sharper and the hollows below his eyes deeper. After she'd left the boat that night he had neither mentioned the trip nor invited her on one again, a fact that Ruth interpreted as evidence that he'd finally awakened to the risk he'd taken in favouring her. Hazel knew otherwise and wondered how much he suspected. She worked double shifts whenever he was gone. It wasn't recompense, precisely. Though she'd revisited the scene in the woods repeatedly in the sleepless nights that followed the trip, she'd never felt pure regret, only a nagging uncertainty that coloured every patient interaction after it.

"I've decided." Hazel wondered if she'd missed something. "I'll walk with you." The air around Gideon had changed, the waves of his agitation smoothed to a surface ripple. His steps beside her were light but unhurried.

"You can't be thinking of going there now."

THE UMBRELLA MENDER ∽ 173

"Sometimes they hunt at night." He tipped his hat forward and then pressed it snug to his crown, grinning. "I've the sense they will tonight. Even if I don't find them I want to be there when they wake up. To hear their morning sounds."

He had a way of asking for things that made them seem inconsequential until she examined them from a cool distance. Take him across the channel in her friend's canoe, without permission, in the deep black of a northern night? But he hadn't asked, now that she thought of it. He hadn't said a word. He just started to drag Ruth's canoe down the stony slope.

"That . . . belongs to a friend of mine. You can't just take it."

Her voice was a skipping stone over the bass notes of the canoe scraping the ground. Gideon was pulling it into the water. "She's not using it now, and she won't even know it was gone."

She found herself setting one end of the canoe in the water and paddling across the narrow channel between Moose Factory and Sawpit. If he could not be dissuaded, she should go with him to make sure that nothing happened to the canoe. This is what she told herself, and she almost believed it.

The air was still. The water was black as oil, the bulk of the island a density of air with the light drained from it. The stars arced over the water, an endless chasm in the night sky. She had the impression that she was floating between heaven and earth, suspended in this place with Gideon alone.

He didn't speak. His presence in the canoe was both anchor and storm. She knew they'd reached the other shore by the soft vibration of stone on the wood under her feet. She stood to pull it up on shore and lost her balance; the weight of it had shifted without warning. Gideon stepped out and walked toward the trees, leaving the canoe where it ran aground. There was the soft flatness of his vowels on the night air and the crunch of his footsteps on the beach stones.

"It'd have to be the tallest thing they could find. No cliffs here, so they must be up in the trees. I can feel it. They're here. When they leave the nest we'll know. Ah, I'm digging this. I'm really digging this."

She stood on the shore behind him and brushed the sand from her trousers. A wind picked up and carried the music of poplar leaves rustling against one another. The river polished the shore in a ceaseless rhythm. He seemed so far unaware that she wasn't behind him. In a minute she'd lose him to the dense forest. Would he notice if she didn't follow? The bulk of the cabin just behind the trees, the risky potential of it, was a pulse between her legs and a cold sweat on the back of her neck.

Gideon was headed in the other direction. He edged up a low but steep slope, lost his footing and, in a feat of agility that surprised her, rolled himself back to standing. Then he moved further along the beach. The cabin, behind them now, wasn't remotely what he was after. He'd passed it without pausing, and the realization exposed her own thoughts in a sober light.

Across the channel, the hospital sat sentinel, constant and unblinking. This was insane. She wasn't so far from civilization that just being here with him at this hour wouldn't be considered the gravest of errors in judgment by anyone's estimation, no matter what she could say about falcon nests, stolen canoes or the vagaries of life in an isolated community. The lights of the hospital would guide her back.

She pushed the canoe back in the water and lifted a leg into it. A hand was suddenly on her shoulder and she cried out. Could anyone on the opposite shore have heard? She stepped back out of the canoe.

"Gideon, what on earth . . ."

"Where are you going?"

"Back. I'm going back. This is crazy. I have clinic in the morning. I shouldn't be here now. Even if there were falcon nests here, it's the middle of the night. It's too dark to see. We've stolen Ruth's canoe. It's all wrong."

He tilted his head to one side. "You would leave me here?"

She started to shake. There was pressure behind her eyes. "I don't even know you." She fought to keep the tremor from her voice. Hearing it would undo her completely. She wiped her eyes with the back of her hand. "You left me standing on the shore. You didn't even notice that I wasn't with you."

"Not so." He took a step toward her and raised his hand to her face, touched it lightly and let it rest there. He studied her. "You are one gone chick, Hazel. I wish I could draw you right now." He paused, then held her face in both hands. "I knew you had it in you."

She twisted away from him. "No. I'm going back. Come with me if you want, but I'm going back. Now." She started pushing the canoe into the water again. His footsteps plashed in the water beside her. She felt the sudden weight of his body in the boat, the dip of his paddle. When they reached the other shore he stepped out and pulled the boat up on the bank before she could get out.

"This night doesn't want to end. Can't you feel it?"

"No. I'm going to my room. It's late and I have to work tomorrow. Goodnight."

She started walking up the path. He caught her arm. "There's something you should see. It can't wait."

She squared her shoulders and faced him. He was washed in the thin overnight light cast by the hospital windows. "Why should I?"

The flash of his teeth in the night. His voice like a song she was trying to remember. "Because you want to. Because I want you to. Because we're here and there's never been a day like this one and there won't be again!" He held up his arms as though conducting an orchestra. "This, now, here – it's everything. Don't you see?

It's a flood of sky elaborate enough to please the sea. It's all there is. Let's dig this moonless night, not sleep it away." He held out his hand. "Come with me. Come dig the wild endless black of this night."

He said nothing more. She noticed the rise and fall of his breath, the abrupt motionlessness in his limbs, the frank vulnerability in his posture. He shifted into neutral, waiting for her.

Yes. She wanted to. She didn't take his hand but she fell in step beside him on the dirt road that led north past the hospital outbuildings and the staff housing, toward the west shore. They didn't speak. A tangle of low bush and a stand of trees separated them from the nurses' residence on the north side and from the shore on the other. When she'd last walked this way it had been an uninhabited stretch of road, but now a solitary tipi rose palely from the darkness on the shore side, close to the trees.

She became aware of the crunch of gravel under their feet and the rising and falling of the grey-white mound near the door. The adult husky came to its feet and growled. She leaned toward Gideon. "Shhhhh. Just keep walking." The dog crouched with the coiled energy of a spring and showed its teeth. Its chain clanked. Hazel's heart hammered. "Run," she whispered. "Run!"

The dog was a dark snarl behind them until it reached the end of its chain, at times so close that she could hear the hollow clash of its teeth. They ran to the end of the road and down to the water. The low tide left an ashy ribbon of sand and they ran along it to the bend in the land and stopped, breathing hard. She could just distinguish the dim outline of Gideon's tent from the forest above them. The dog was a distant threat now, furious but tethered.

Gideon stopped in the shadow of his camp and stood facing the water. The beach was wide at low tide and yet he stood at the edge of the river. If he'd taken another step, his toe would have been wet. His arms were at his sides. And then there was a line from the shrug of his shoulders to the tips of his fingers that demarcated his body from the night sky, and the line rose until it was a personal horizon, Gideon from fingertip to fingertip. The line undulated once, twice, three times, slowly at first, his arms rising and falling in harmony, building in intensity and frequency until they climbed the air, lifting the thread of his body from the ground. He moved between shore and camp unencumbered by gravity, legs in motion or still she couldn't have said, wings gouging the sky around him, propelling himself toward and away from her. He grazed the air near her and it washed over her in waves.

First, she felt a compelling stillness to her core. As if frozen to the spot, she could only watch. Gradually sensation returned and along with it an adrenal quickening through the nerve centres of her body, the sly, irresistible undertow of an ocean tide, kinetic in her shoulders, arms, wrists, hands. She began to move her arms and they were startlingly fledged; the sudden drag of them on the air was a shock. She lifted them and let them fall again, tentatively at first and then with increasing force until there was a deep surge in her belly and her feet left the ground. Her toes stuttered against the earth once, twice and then not again.

When she found him she was gliding on the upcurrents and downdrafts. She chased him from shore to treeline and her voice sounded unfamiliar phrases that carried across the water.

SHE SAT ON A SOFT bed of spruce needles, breathless and spent. Gideon dropped down beside her. She turned her head and they began to laugh, a weak bubble of laughter that came to a rolling boil in seconds, and she collapsed against him.

"What's so funny?"

"Everything." His face was close now, so close. The corkscrew spiral of his laugh had a melody she hadn't heard before. "Absolutely everything in this world is the best laugh I've ever had." He pulled a silver flask from his jacket, unscrewed the lid and took a sip. He held it out to her and she accepted without hesitation, the metal smooth in her hands and the liquor a slow burn that warmed her lips, her tongue, her throat, her belly. She leaned against the tree and drank again, deep and long, like she'd been thirsty a long while. She rarely drank with the other nurses; she told them she didn't like the taste of it, but that wasn't the reason. This drink tasted like honey on fire, thick and slow and easy. His fingers touched hers as he took it back. The clouds skidded across the night sky.

"I know a song about this."

"I bet you do."

A light wind tripped across the surface of the water. She felt cut free from the fabric of her life. "Blue lake and rocky shore, I will return once more. Boom diddy boom boom, boom diddy boom boom boooooom."

He sat straighter against the tree. "Ah, this night. This wild endless moment, this perfect unfurling cosmic accident. This night is the one I want to forget last."

She moved toward him, spinning herself into his gravity. "You were going to show me something," she said, when she finally spoke. "I came, I'm here."

He smiled and stood unsteadily. He reached for her hand and pulled her to standing. "That." He pointed to the carved symbol on the tree they'd been sitting under, a quarter moon sheltering an orb.

"I saw that before. You said it meant watcher."

"No." He frowned and took her chin in his hand. "Try harder. Listen to me. It means, *you are being watched.*"

She remembered. His expression was solemn. "Yes. You are ready now, I do think so." He let his hand fall to his side. "It's a charm. Protection."

The last word seemed to intensify the effect of the liquor she'd drunk. She felt herself sway as though she'd been pushed. She tried to focus. "Protection? Why would you need protection? Who needs watching?" He narrowed his eyes, as if evaluating the risk in telling her. Her mouth was bold with liquor. "It's okay," she whispered. "Your secret's safe with me."

When he relaxed she saw that he'd been holding himself rigid. "Of course it is. You can be trusted. You have proven that." He paused and ran his hand through his hair. She wanted to touch it. "It's under us." He kneeled and motioned for her to do the same, then swept the clusters of pine needles from under the tree. He dug with his hands and brushed the dirt from the top of a wooden box that she recognized. The pepper sauce box. She hadn't seen it since that first day.

He waved her closer and lifted the lid. Her breath caught in her throat. The bone-handled hunting knife. Below this, two rows of American bills, twenties and fifties, almost level with the top of the box. Her mouth opened and closed and again. Thousands. Tens of thousands, maybe. She'd expected an odd assortment of objects, the kind he'd asked for at the clinic door these past few months. She blinked, jolted from her drowsy contentment, and thought she must have hallucinated. Surely the drink was to blame.

He faced her, his smile crooked, almost shy. "My father doesn't need this. I'm doing this for him, helping him away from what he's become, see?"

She couldn't think of a single thing to say. The bright expectation on his face fell away in the silence. "Aw. I shouldn't have expected this of you. The universe may never forgive me. I should have known!" He shoved the lid closed. "See, this is what it does to people. It's filth, it's nothing. But I'll set it free. The waters of the passage will receive it and none of us will ever be troubled by it again." He swept earth and pine needles over the lid. "You know I'm not what's in that box, don't you?" He laid his hands on her shoulders and his fingers dug into her skin. "It's dead to me, all of it, dead, you hear me? It has nothing to do with me."

She didn't know whether she was trembling or being shaken. His face was inches from hers. She felt the heat of his skin. The earth spun away from the stars. And then her knees were giving out and she was falling against him, with him, and there was no resistance. He was beside her on the ground. Pine needles were soft under her head. A cricket bleated nearby. She closed her eyes. "You lost yourself there, Eyas." His voice was just above a whisper. "Too much from my flask, maybe."

She rolled to face him. He seemed smaller, diminished somehow. She couldn't reconcile the magnitude of his character with the insignificant ripple of flesh his body made on the land. They were side by side but not touching. The sky bore down. His gaze was doe-soft and open, reading her. Her heart was beating too fast, the blood a deafening rush in her ears and a dark thudding between her legs. His fingers brushed her face and sent a charge through her body. She brought her lips to his hand and kissed it. Her hand slid under his shirt easy, slipping between the buttons like she'd done it a thousand times. She closed her eyes and let her fingers find the downy hair around his nipple. She laid her hand there and felt a frantic fluttering just under her fingers, as though it really was that close to the surface. His hand on her breast was clumsy, grasping, like he was drowning. She moved closer, pushed herself up on her elbows, and hovered over him. She wanted to touch him all over everywhere.

Her hand found his belly and then inched down to where his body was hard and straining. She tugged his belt buckle. The leather creaked as it gave way. His trousers slid easily over his narrow hips. Hers pooled at her ankles. She brought her face nearer to his; the well of his pupils was wide and black and bottomless. She touched her nose against his, felt the bump where it had been broken. Her fingers threaded themselves into his hair and rimmed his ears. His skin smelled of the river, of algae and fish oil and damp. A cold, nervy sweat beaded on the back of her neck. When she swung her leg over him, there was no resistance and she moved without the complication of thought. Everything around her looked as though it was underwater, and then it dropped away completely, all of it, everything but the universe of skin and breath and hair that was Gideon. She shrunk herself around the soft warmth of a singular purpose until she could no longer distinguish her body from his.

The light from the sun's stain on the horizon woke her. The firepit was black and still. Her body ached and her head felt brittle. The ground was cold and damp and she was shivering in spite of the rough wool blanket covering her. Her clothes were piled on top of her shoes where she'd left them. She stood on shaky legs and dressed, called his name. No reply.

She knew the way back through the forest by now and she followed the path easily by the livid pink of the morning sky. She took the Bay Road across the island, the long way around. If she hadn't been missed yet, she could say she'd been out for an early morning walk.

She reached the east shore and turned south, past the summer tents. The clinic was her responsibility today and she needed a shower. What time was it? The Cree women were preparing the morning meal. Some of the cookfires had already been lit and the rich tang of roasting meat filled the air. Men unloaded two freight canoes, swinging canvas mailbags and wooden boxes of fruit to the main dock. It was important to walk with a measured pace, she knew that, but she moved past them as quickly as she could and didn't make eye contact.

Someone called after her and she realized that she must be a sight. How could she get past Ruth and the other nurses to her room? As she neared the factor's house, she slowed her pace. She lifted her head and pushed her shoulders back. It was a morning like any other, she told herself. She was known for her early morning walks. Nothing unusual.

Snatches of country music drifted from an open window at the nurses' residence. She listened at the door a few minutes before easing it open. She stopped and listened again. Nothing. It couldn't be much after seven, but she'd missed the morning-shift exodus. For this small mercy, she was grateful, but she knew she'd only delayed the inevitable. In the kitchen, a few cups rested upside down in the sink and a jar of jam stood open on the table. She left her shoes in the hall and started up the stairs, heard the shower running. After a few panicked moments she remembered that Ruth had been on overnight duty. She went to her room and waited.

The shower stopped. She heard the door open and Ruth's heavy footsteps receded in the direction of her room. She waited until she heard the door close and then undressed and wrapped herself in her towel. The hall was empty. She locked the bathroom door and rehearsed explanations and justifications. In her eight months on Moose Factory she'd never once been late for shift, and no matter how tired Ruth was, she wouldn't miss something like this. Before she'd even turned the water on, there was a sharp knock on the bathroom door.

"Who's there?"

It was a fight to keep her voice neutral and steady. "Just me, Ruth. Slept in."

There was a pause. "I wondered. You were missed at breakfast. Better get a move on. You're already late."

"I know it. Thanks."

She started the shower. The absence of the obvious question was curious, and unusual for Ruth. It was a small mercy but Hazel doubted that she'd dodged anything. Before the day was over, she'd hear about it. She could count on that.

The warm water ran down her body and washed the whorls and smudges of dried blood from her inner thighs. She scrubbed herself with careful, medical precision, as though she was washing a patient's body, using carbolic soap and rubbing her skin dry until it was pink. She coiled her wet hair, pinned it, dressed and made her way to the clinic, still woozy, she assumed, from the drink in Gideon's flask. For breakfast she took an apple from the bowl in the kitchen, but it was still whole when she reached the hospital.

It was almost eight-thirty. The air in the clinic was suffocating. She opened a window and straightened the pile of magazines in the waiting room.

"Making up for lost time?"

"Ruth. You startled me." Hazel was not at all surprised.

"You were out all night."

"I'm here now." There was little to be gained by denial. Ruth's fury was an unconvincing mask for the hurt that was her due. Hazel had shut her out again. She hadn't alerted her to the midnight walk and couldn't discuss it now for the same reason. It seemed essential to distance herself from the event, let it exist in isolation, unacknowledged and disconnected from the rest of her life.

"I'm expecting patients any minute, and I'm on my own today. Lachlan has gone out on the boat, as I'm sure you're aware. Do you need something?"

Ruth's lips were a hard, thin slash across her face. "This is how you want it?"

"I don't know what you mean. I overslept and I'm just getting to work." She turned away from Ruth and closed her eyes. Ruth must have already guessed. Was she hoping for a different answer?

"You're playing with fire, mate."

Hazel swallowed. "I can't talk about this right now." It was the most she could manage. However Ruth thought she could help, she wouldn't understand this. Hazel wasn't sure she herself did. How could she have let this happen? It certainly wouldn't again. "I'm sorry. I really can't." She crossed her arms. "Shouldn't you be sleeping?"

Ruth sighed and raised her eyebrows. "I was. There was a radio call from the *Mercer*. I'm surprised you haven't heard. They intercepted a freight canoe at the mouth of the river carrying five from East Point in need of medical attention. Didn't say whether it was TB. They'll bring them to the clinic to assess. Three children, two adults. I knew you were alone here."

"Fine. Thanks." She knew she ought to feel grateful but she couldn't. She handed the supply closet keys to Ruth. "You can restock the exam rooms."

THE NEW PATIENTS ARRIVED SHORTLY after ten. Ruth stayed with a handful of children from the school who needed the new antibiotic salve, due that morning, so Hazel could go meet the boat.

Each section of the dock floated on four oil drums that had been lashed to its underside so it could rise and fall with the tide. Hazel watched the canoe arrive and then bob on the river beside the dock. By the time the new patients started to climb out of the canoe, she was off the dock and vomiting in a clump of bushes. She wiped her mouth with a square of paper handkerchief from her pocket, took a few deep breaths and started back up the riverbank. Joseph stood near the dock, his thick arms crossed.

"Are you sick, Nurse MacPherson?"

"I'm absolutely fine, Joseph." She avoided his solemn, searching stare. "Must have eaten something that didn't agree. I feel much better now. Who do we have here?"

She crouched and reached for the youngest child in the boat, a little Cree boy who couldn't have been more than two. She lifted him from his seat and his legs remained frozen at a right angle to his body. The TB must have gone into the bones. His dark eyes roamed where his legs couldn't take him.

"I've read about this but I don't think we've seen it in the clinic yet." Maybe the challenge in this case would draw her thoughts from Gideon like a leech drew poison. "Doctor Davies will want to see him when he gets back."

She tucked the boy into the crook of her arm and carried him against her chest, one hand on his dark hair. He was thin and light, his breathing shallow and rattling; if he hadn't come to the hospital, the disease would have claimed him before his third birthday. But he was here now. They'd be able to help him. Joseph carried the other two, a pair of little girls, against his broad shoulders. The adults followed, well enough to walk on their own, and Hazel hung back with them as they made their slow progress up the slope from the dock, all the while expecting Gideon to appear. Where had he gone?

Ruth was waiting at the clinic door, hands on her hips. "Plane from Cochrane in yet? I don't think I can keep this lot a moment longer." The schoolchildren sat against the wall of the waiting room, picking at scabs and elbowing each other. "We'll have to send for them when the salve gets here." She corralled them out the door. Hazel carried the boy into the clinic and set him on a table in one of the exam rooms.

"Come watch him a minute, Ruth? He needs to be admitted to the TB ward immediately. I'm going to get an aide." The words came fast, one on the heels of the last as though she couldn't quite get enough air, but there was nothing for it but this. The work and the work and the work. It would guide her back. It would have to.

NINETEEN

YOU'LL DRAW YOUR OWN CONCLUSIONS. You always have. I couldn't have tolerated you this long if you hadn't. From the day I met you I knew you had the capacity for something more than your family could give you and I was right.

You must understand, Jude, what I had with Gideon was more than it wasn't. On some level I was aware of the chasm that separated us and still I was far enough gone to waylay if not discharge my sense of decorum entirely and behave as though we two were the only ones left in the world. This is the only explanation I can offer for the fact that I allowed myself long private conversations with a stranger not once but repeatedly and in 1951 when I knew women who needed their father's permission to marry. Being closer to the wild meant being further removed from social rules I couldn't abide and I won't deny that the north was attractive to me for precisely this reason but it wasn't that I'd gone there planning for something like this to happen. It was true that we one hundred or so from the south were less concerned with social etiquette or perhaps preoccupied enough with the fight against tuberculosis to allow transgressions of this kind to go unnoticed or at least be considered unworthy of sustained attention. But to suggest that my response to the situation was premeditated in any way would be to have me all wrong.

Gideon was a curiosity but there was no pretense to his eccentricity. I honestly believe that he could have entertained no other way of being. If he wasn't carried away with some gorgeous idea or fixing on the movement of falcons he was in a general state of bemusement that seemed to prevent him from entering polite conversation. That handicap was difficult to disguise in a small community like Moose Factory and he did stand out whenever he made his way across the island to the main settlement. I'm sure everyone knew where he'd set up camp but in spite of growing curiosity about him and an active gossip mill they didn't seek him out. Gideon might have chosen the unpopulated west shore for that reason. It would have been only one of several clear indications that he desired the company of no one. Almost no one.

Lachlan made oblique and occasional references to Gideon that would have manifested as warnings or admonishments from other men. For him to say as much as he did indicated an emotional disturbance that he could neither manage nor ignore, a set of questions whose outcomes he couldn't work out. It would be untrue to say that I sought my superior's approval in this matter, nor was this a bid for Lachlan's attention but I did feel his agitation like a low and constant hum. I chose to see it as something I could neither affect nor change but that I was sure wouldn't develop into anything more than it already was. The fact that it didn't diminish ought to have signalled his distress and acted as the strongest alarm but I was deaf to it. I sensed that Lachlan wouldn't act and he didn't.

Gideon called me Eyas. I doubt that even now I could convey the full effect of this endearment. A nestling will fledge. I lied to myself about my motives and convinced myself that my interest toward him was platonic but he was the purest morphine and my veins sang for more. Any restraint I might have possessed was gone a month into his stay on Moose Factory and so was my awareness of how our companionship might have appeared to others.

We needed no pre-arranged plan. It was rare for me to get as far as his camp before finding him and sometimes he would be waiting near the hospital. When he was there I felt I was hovering between laughter and tears. How could I know so little about the man and yet so fiercely crave his company? This is not to suggest that I was without moments of cool neutrality. Once in a while I'd catch a glimpse of him and it was like someone had lifted a sheet of gauze from my eyes, the way you can see someone you love with the sharpest objectivity for the briefest moment and wonder what you could have been thinking. I'd have a clear view of the wild unbeauty of his tangled hair and shabby clothes. I saw the harsh angles of his cheekbones and his broken nose and the abject naïveté of his life plan. But only for a moment.

Once we drank bitter coffee from chipped tin mugs that he'd hung like Christmas ornaments on the tree branches near his camp. He would tell me about the movement of the falcons or his theories on Arctic exploration with no gaps for my voice to make it a conversation. To be honest I didn't mind. It was a relief in comparison with the long hours of silence that would occasionally fall like dusk around us before he'd read to me from his list of items for the trip. I was not alarmed when it became obvious that his plans included me and not because I didn't think he'd follow through. I would even add items to the list when handed a pencil and notebook. To my knowledge no one recovered it. Before I left the island I scoured his camp myself but I never found it.

There was a low bluff near his camp where we spent most of what few hours we had together. You'd know it by its proximity to the creek that leads inland from the shore. He had finally discovered a falcon nest in the woods near there and liked to watch the way they emerged for the hunt. The fact that they seemed shot from the trees pleased him. He would insist on silence as the birds hunted and I obliged not only without argument but with a sense that the quality of his rapture was a fragile and fleeting thing that I would be unlikely to witness again and I was right. He watched the birds and I watched him.

Each time, expecting it would be the last, I tried to memorize the exact slope of the crease in his forehead and the texture of his mouth. Sometimes when a hunt would conclude he'd rise unblinkingly and his arms would become weightless until they were perpendicular to his body. The start of it was slow and mesmerizing so that when he was finally careening to the bluff's edge I believed he would try to lift off in the direction of the river. He interpreted the sight of me running toward him as threatening and the ecstasy that had softened his features would vanish. It did occur to me that what I was doing was breaking a trance and, like a sleepwalker wakened, he would be antagonized and disoriented. But even in the knowledge that I might vex him I could not risk losing him to the river.

Once he came to an abrupt stop a couple of feet from where I was standing and asked what the hell I thought I was doing. Did I think he couldn't take care of himself and hadn't he done so perfectly well these nine months since he left St. Paul's? I did feel fear in those moments. What did I know about him at all? Here with this man who was as determined to fly as I was to catch him, what did I know about myself?

And then he'd laugh as if it had been a great joke and hold his arms out again so the wind showed me the bony angles of his arms through the sleeves. "When I reach the Northwest Passage I'll fly. I'll be ready."

Me too, I wanted to say. Me too.

TWENTY

IN SLEEP SHE WAS ALWAYS there. Even the pressure of Gideon's eyelids was no barrier. She came every night since then, five now. First came the snow, the white obliterating nothingness of it, whirling, blinding, driven into his eyes and skin, the thousand icy punctures that one by one inoculated or poisoned him. He could never be sure.

From this maelstrom, the small, sinuous curve of her body came into focus. In the dream she always wore a parka, eggshell white and fur-trimmed, the hood a tunnel that drew him to her. She pushed the hood back, her hair unbound and snaking in the cold wind, her red mouth laughing. The wind bawled in his ears and he strained to hear what she was saying but it seemed she was only mouthing the words. He watched her lips and she said it again. She wanted him to understand. *It's okay, your secret is safe with me.* He began to shiver. She unzipped the parka, drew it back from her swollen, naked belly. It was round like a melon and the skin was stretched taut, shiny. She smiled at him, a beatific vision, held her hand out, palm up, and laid the other along the lower curve of her belly. Gideon trusted her. He felt warm, washed over with love.

He laid his hand in hers and she guided it to her belly. He felt a slow, supple shift under her skin and then a flutter of panic — how could this be? — but focused on the pale ivory of her face, the soft tendrils of her hair, the inviting tenderness of her breasts. He breathed her serenity into his chest, his own belly, his skin.

Her smile became a frown and she gasped in pain as her belly split like it was overripe. His mind raced to understand and the baby's head emerged. Its eyes were swollen closed at first, but only for a moment, and then they blinked open wide and wild. He couldn't see her anymore. The baby crowded her out of his field of vision. Gideon watched, unable to do anything else. His limbs were immobilized. The baby's hand appeared from the depths of her belly, clutching something. There was a flash of metal, a slash of blinding force and speed, and Gideon knew he'd been cut, fast and deep and final. There was the metallic tang of his own blood at the back of his throat and the soft, steady rhythm as it exited his body. Then he was falling, falling, falling.

He woke in a sweat, heart pounding. Every time.

It could not be allowed.

TWENTY-ONE

HAZEL WONDERED WHERE HE'D BEEN. A week had passed since she'd awakened cold and alone at his camp, and she still hadn't seen him. This fact would have been unremarkable in most of the places she'd lived, but she could walk the length of Moose Factory in under an hour and Gideon didn't blend easily. She couldn't ask anyone; the talk would only get worse. It was telling that no one mentioned his name when she was around.

Had he gone? Foolish, even insane. He would never make the Northwest Passage this late, wherever he thought that was, neither alone nor with a guide, not that any island native would take him. It was late September. They knew better. Boats could negotiate the waters north of there for only a brief window of time in August, and for the remainder of the year it was the kind of frozen that no vessel, not even an icebreaker, could breach. Would he try it alone, convinced that where the boat could go no further he could finish the journey under his own steam, somehow? Hypothermia would set in quickly, unless he had a stash of warmer clothing she'd never seen. She saw him laid out on the ice, the insignificant ripple of his flesh on the frozen tundra, his eyes open and unseeing. She shook her head to displace the image. He was thin, frail even. How would he feed himself? What had he ever eaten besides the thin broths he cooked over his fire, spoonfuls of beans from a can? She'd brought him bread, an occasional tin of beans or fish, sandwiches sometimes, and he'd accepted these with distracted gratitude, but he seemed to ration them. Several were still unopened since she was last at his camp.

The residence was still and quiet. It was a little past seven and she had the place to herself; the other night-duty RNs were already in bed. She carried her mug to the sink, almost dizzy with fatigue. The night shift was the second of a double. There was a loud knock on the screen door at the back of the kitchen. She knew who it was, who it must be, but she lacked the courage to feel surprise.

"You can come in."

The hinge complained as the door opened. When she finally turned he was standing inside the kitchen, the shock of his blue eyes intent on her. He was both familiar and an extraordinary apparition in the kitchen she shared with the other nurses, in this place of tea and gossip, potato peelings and toast, dish towels and canned soup. The air around him seemed charged. In another kitchen, in another life, this could have been a room she shared with him, where they fed the children and pushed the table aside to dance, but she knew it couldn't be, not here, not now, not with this man. She willed him to speak, to break the spell, and then she couldn't wait any longer.

"Gideon –"

"Hazel –"

She shook her head and laughed, a nervous, twittering eruption. She tried to calm her breathing. This was not how she wanted it to go.

"Where have you been? I haven't seen you."

"I'm not seen if I don't choose to be." His tone was mild, unthreatening. "But I could say the same about you. You haven't been walking."

This was not strictly true, but he would have had to be waiting at all hours to catch her on the road between the hospital and the nurses' residence. Things were busy but not so busy that she couldn't have walked the island in her usual way, but she'd dug herself a snug shelter of work, offering to help with extra shifts, surgeries, the dispensary. Anything. She'd created an unassailable schedule that anyone could check. There were no hours that couldn't be accounted for by sleep or work.

"Well, you found me." The offhand tone she managed betrayed nothing of the heart palpitations that began in earnest at the sound of his voice. When had she become such a good actress?

"Come with me. There's something I need to tell you."

"Yes. We should talk. The other night ..."

"Not here. We'll take a walk."

"I've just worked the night shift. Can't it wait until I've slept?"

"No, no, no, it really cannot."

He had begun to shake his head before she finished speaking and was pacing now. Something in his tone warned her from further appeal, a taut and barely controlled urgency she'd never heard before. It left no room for discussion.

"Let me change, at least."

He reached for her hand, clasped it and started for the door. "Just a short walk. This won't take long."

She was still wearing her uniform. The fact that he released her hand as soon as they stepped outside allayed her growing unease. He knew enough to do that, at least. They walked in silence along the hospital road on the west side of the island in the direction of his camp. Was this another unwise decision? The prospect of being found with him in the residence seemed the greater risk.

The light in the forest was still feeble, enough so that she didn't immediately notice the changes at his camp. His tent was folded up and the firepit was dismantled. She drew a sharp breath. She'd been expecting this, dreading it, wanting it.

"You're going? Now?"

He started to pace, wringing his hands. "It's the dreams." He took a step toward her and laid a hand on her face. His eyes searched hers. Her breath fluttered. "They don't lie."

"Gideon, it was the drink." She knew in that moment that it wasn't true, and her next words were another lie. "I don't think we should –"

"Oh, you are one gone chick." His voice was just above a whisper. "The universe will unite us again." There was regret in his eyes, a sadness that seemed old and known to him. He turned away and started to pace again. "But this cannot be allowed. My dreams showed me."

His bone-handled knife lay on the ground near his pack. He picked it up and held it in an awkward grip.

"What, Gideon? What cannot be allowed?" His hand was shaking. Could he hurt her? "Please. I don't know what you mean."

"What you're carrying! You must know." The sudden volume in his voice seemed to surprise him. He closed his eyes and drew a ragged breath. "We can't let it happen." His face froze. "I keep seeing him! I can't shut him out!" He dropped to the base of the tree and blinked rapidly.

The words were an icy finger in her gut, pulling at what she'd been trying to ignore. *What you're carrying.* She was shaking her head. No, no, no, no. Her head swam. She couldn't follow where his mind had led him. Should she run? Try to take the knife? But it didn't matter. The flood of adrenaline made her knees weak. "Who, Gideon? Who?"

He was calmer now. "The child. He won't let me live. He can't. That's how it always ends. Even though I try to stop him, even when all of the other children die because of this one." Something occurred to him; he lifted his head, catching a distant tune that only he could hear. She felt him slipping away. In a few minutes she might not reach him. "But if he isn't forced ..." he said, slowly, "if there is no reason ..." He stared at the knife. "I can unmake this."

She watched him lift the knife to his throat. The shock kicked hard and she started to tremble. What was unfolding here?

"It's okay, Eyas," he murmured, slower still, a drugged pace. "It's the sign I've been waiting for. I understand now. I can go. I'm ready."

She couldn't see for the tears. There was no way to relate to this moment, no precedent to guide her. She couldn't connect the fact of the knife to anything that had gone before. She saw herself rushing him and snatching it from his fingers, hurling it into the river. And in the same instant, she knew she couldn't risk it. She might push him to act or force the blade toward him. He was holding it a quarter-inch from the carotid artery.

A crow cawed in the tree above them. Her legs almost gave out; his hand dropped into his lap and the knife to the ground. She bent toward it slowly, no sudden movements, and picked it up. She tried to locate the young drifter that had charmed her, as if doing so might transform him for them both and help him step away from this. If she could muster a laugh, maybe he would too, and the whole thing be declared a bizarre ruse. But no. She couldn't get him to focus, couldn't reach him. What lodestar could she fix him to?

The sun was starting to rise, glinting on the water behind him. It must have been close to eight by then. She should have been asleep in the residence. No one would come looking for her. No one knew she was here.

"The falcons." She fought to keep the tremor from her voice. "Tell me about the falcons." He was so vulnerable, so young. She resisted the urge to touch his face. "Did you find more nests?"

A flash of recognition passed across his face. Fixed on a point of safety, he relaxed, but he was still wary. "High in the trees. You know that, Eyas. Digging the altitude. Not so far from here." He motioned vaguely toward the trees behind them, and for a minute she thought he might start walking in that direction and forget why he'd brought her here. Her exhalation was uneven, juddering. His head jerked backwards and his eyes widened. The moment drifted open and became unstable.

"No! It cannot be allowed, don't you see?" He leapt to his feet. "Don't say you don't understand!"

She was trying so hard to stay calm, but it wasn't working. The air around her seemed viscous and it clung to the walls of her throat. The knife was a weight in her hand. "I don't know anything about anything!"

He tilted his head to one side. "I believe you. I do. But I know." His breathing had slowed again. "I know what's growing there. I've seen it. My dreams never lie."

There was only one thing left. "What if you're right, Gideon? What if there was a . . ." She could barely say the word. "What if there was a . . . baby, Gideon?" She tossed the words to him lightly, desperately, a life raft for a drowning man. In a different time, in another place, they might have been a source of joy. "A baby that could ..." She cast about for his turn of phrase, his words. "A baby that could dig the wild endless nights with us. A baby we could love."

He blinked rapidly, trying to catch a glimpse of the future she'd described. There was a clouding over, an occlusion of the vision. "No!" His knuckles were white. "You're trying to trick me! No, Eyas. It can't go that way." He shook his head. "It's okay," he said, with a sudden and eerie calm. "You don't understand. That's not how it ends."

TWENTY-TWO

A BABY, SHE SAID. A baby to love. The idea was quaint in the face of what the child meant, and the way it always ended.

Gideon saw her not as she was, standing on the packed soil in the wan late-September morning light, but in the swirling blizzard that would claim them both if he failed to act. She was beautiful, she seemed to believe what she was saying, but she didn't know what he knew. She couldn't. He shivered as the image from his nightly terror appeared before him now, the baby's arm outstretched in a deadly, gleaming reach.

Hope in the human creature was risky and left you alone eventually; as a species, they were fallible. Everyone he loved had failed him. His mother was the first, vanishing as he slept in his crib. What mother would abandon a child? He'd stared at her photo for hours on the train, but her eyes never gave up the answer to that question. His father covered her lie with one of his own, sin upon sin. He insisted that she'd died in the night and then buried himself alive in his ill-gotten gains. A succession of others drifted in and out of his life after that, promising love but only taking. Now the nurse, this beacon of purity in her medical whites and her oath to do no harm, germinating the seed that spelled his end.

He knew what needed to be done. Break the cycle. Subvert the story, render it impotent. It was obvious. His child could not kill him if he was already dead.

The nurse's small fingers were curled around the bone hilt of his knife. When had she taken it? He stepped toward her, dodging the blade just as she pulled out of reach. She was serpentine. He'd need to be quicker, knock it out of her hand. Her lips were moving but there was no time, no time. Now that he knew what he had to do, he must act. He couldn't let her keep it. She whirled away from him. Surely she didn't understand. He wanted that to be true. Was it possible that she'd intended this all along? His head felt weightless. It didn't matter. Nothing mattered. Only the knife.

He reached again and was stung. Somehow she'd pushed the blade into his hand. Why? He couldn't stop the words: "I'm cut, you've cut me!" Blood ran down his hand, into his sleeve.

Hazel dropped the knife and it lay on the ground beside her. She would want it back. She would stop him from doing what needed to be done. This fact lodged itself painfully in his chest. He stepped toward the knife and she did something he didn't expect. She lifted the hem of her uniform and began to tear it.

A moment passed as he considered this development. In the absence of a weapon she'd . . . restrain him? She was resourceful, this one. He'd already spun away from her when he realized that she'd manoeuvred herself so that her body stood between his and the knife. Coming toward him now, she reached for his injured hand. The strip of torn fabric dangled loosely from her other hand.

"Gideon." His eyes met hers and for an instant he thought he saw a spasm of pain there. "Let me bandage your hand." He felt himself bend toward her purpose. Her touch was gentle. She'd wrapped the cloth around his hand before he understood what she was doing. She was rendering it useless. He'd be clumsier with his left. He'd have to block out her voice. It was the only way.

He had the knife now. She parried with her body, left, right, back, left, reaching for it. She had intended this all along. He knew it now. She was fast, she was resolved, but he could outmatch her in this. He would have to. She didn't understand. And then somehow she was behind him, her small fingers digging into his forearms, pulling his arms away from his body. He pulled against her, a short, sharp tug. Thump. There was icy searing in his chest.

He felt a ripple of sinew along her arm, the animal strength of her. Fledgling no longer. The thought unwound itself until it was gone and he was adrift, not a spar of reason left to cling to.

THERE WAS A SCARLET FLOWER on his shirt. His knees sank to the ground. A muscle twitched in his chest, just above the place he'd sent the knife in. Breath gathered itself and he coughed, once, twice. Her face hovered into view. She was talking too fast.

"Stay here. Stay still. I have to get help. You need surgery. You need surgery but you'll be okay, you will." She wobbled as she stood to go.

"Don't." The word was thick, slow, luscious. "No doctors."

He reached for the handle of the knife. The pressure was intense. If he could just release some of it. "Don't pull it out. You'll only bleed faster. The blood has started to clot around it already. Please leave it, let me get help." She was whispering now, her hand on his arm. "Please."

He couldn't allow it. He shut his eyes and pulled the knife from his belly, straight up into the clouds. He breathed a sharp, ragged breath and laid his head back down.

"Ah." He felt the slow transit of nectar from the corner of his mouth and along his cheek. "This feels…different." He wondered at the crease above her eyes. She seemed less threatening now. A warm, immobilizing blanket of pain radiated from his abdomen. It had the medicating edge of drink to it, a fuzzy, slow arterial ooze that sapped his forward motion, left him idling. He was free. It was so beautiful, so radiant. He felt light, untethered. There was nothing left to do.

She disappeared and then she was back. Look at me, Eyas. Be a witness to this ascending moment, my grand departure. He heard the words inside his head but she didn't react. A looping tendril of her pretty dark hair swung into her face. He wanted to touch it but he couldn't lift his arm. Her knee had it pinned against him. Just as his brain groped toward a question she leaned over him, covered his wound with her hands, settled her weight on it. A column of pain sliced through him and his mouth filled with a salty, warm broth. Her eyelids lifted and her forehead creased. She moved a bloodied hand to her mouth. There was stillness. He felt the world fix itself, and was gone.

TWENTY-THREE

HERE YOU ARE AGAIN AND it seems you only just left. What brings you here with such regularity? I don't know what I could possibly offer but I'll admit I've entertained the idea that some of what I say gets through. You seem to respond from time to time and I don't know whether to credit the quality or intensity of my expression or the occasional escape of a word. It would be like the sound of Pavlov's bell for you, enough to keep you coming back.

In spite of all you've been through you have good bones. I see a resilience in you that will hold you steady if you let it. Do you fly in your dreams? Something in the way you move makes me think that you do. You unfold yourself from a chair as from the cramped corner of your life. Night must offer respite. Your fingernails and hair are clean and there are no dark circles under your eyes.

You've brought a book again. It's a good idea. I have no doubt that it improves on the tedium of one-sided conversations with an old woman that you've only begun to know and truly you have no idea who I am. You think you do: that's how you began to rely on me. From the start I knew that you don't come to trust easily. At first you couldn't look me in the eye for more than a few seconds. There has been improvement in that area in the last couple of weeks. The stroke had an equalizing effect on our relationship as far as you're concerned. That you have something over me now gives you confidence. You think I have been diminished and so you fear me less. I have not. You do not know me.

Look at me. What do you see? How am I around the eyes, the mouth? They haven't held a mirror to my face and I can only assume that there is a reason. Has the ordeal laid me bare and if so, what shape does betrayal give the eyes? What design does self-preservation impose on the mouth? Where is the locus of the instinct to allow a lover to slip away? Can you pick out the path of retreat that leads away from it? You must know. It's in the way you keep coming here. What is it you want? What is it you think I have left to give?

I am being unfair. You didn't ask to be part of my life. I brought you into mine. I'm made ridiculous by this fury and my inability to give it air. I haven't yet become accustomed to this non-verbal state, nor was I able to foresee the ramifications of the choice I made. I allowed thought and have become its prisoner. This bed and my hobbled brain confine me. The colours have gone.

It's a cruel irony that the stroke brought clarity and captivity in equal measures but you might say so what. So what? That's one of the oldest stories. It's testament to my incredible hubris that I even entertain the thought that I might be exempt though I did long ago set aside the idea that I would be punished for what I did or failed to do. It became impossible for me to believe in any kind of system of cosmic checks and balances. That kind of thinking assumes that the universe is benign.

It is not. I can find no other way to interpret his abrupt presence and absence in my life or the fact that the day he died the sun just shone and shone. The birds sang while he bled for God's sake! And the man – he was only a boy. I saw that he was younger than I was too late. He lay on the cold ground like it was a sweet-smelling bower and the scene was the fulfillment of some off-kilter romantic ideal he'd held for some time. That much seems clear to me in the unfussy and prepared way he met his end. He must have spent his life rehearsing it.

But that came later. The day he turned up I knew he was there in the same way that I knew my hand was at the end of my arm. It wasn't that I'd been waiting or even hoping for him to visit. There were days that I wondered whether he'd been the invention of my famished imagination and I had every expectation that he would vanish as inexplicably as he had appeared.

I can't accurately describe the complex set of signals that compelled me to follow him. If he had seemed deranged or suicidal I would have called for help but I didn't so I can only assume that his demeanour was as odd but unthreatening as it had always been and that some element of trust remained between us. To say that I had no anxiety about his sudden appearance or sense of urgency would be untrue but it would be equally insincere to claim that I didn't desire his company in a place away from prying eyes.

The walk to his camp was tense. Even though the morning shift had begun others were still around. I kept expecting to be accosted at some point and was somewhat preoccupied with inventing an excuse for our being together. I came up with two or three that I felt would serve. Once we'd stepped through the door he dropped my hand and he didn't incline his body toward mine as lovers do. I don't remember if he ever did.

We walked in silence but I was accustomed to that. He had never observed social niceties in the past. It seemed that his receptors for social signals had either been switched off or had stopped functioning altogether. I had the impression that he had once been as vulnerable to public opinion as I was but that it no longer mattered. His landscape was free of those concerns now. Mine was not.

I lost precious time once we'd arrived at the camp as my brain tried to assimilate the new information it was receiving. It was as though he'd suddenly begun speaking in a foreign language but I kept expecting the shapes his lips made to produce sounds I recognized. The appearance of the hunting knife disabused me of that notion with some haste. It was long and very sharp and the sort that could slice open a deer's abdomen in a single swift tear. But even during the first few moments that he held it against his throat I couldn't react.

We didn't fight. I wasn't awkward or grunting or clumsy and I might have used the word elegant if I'd ever described it to anyone. The air shrunk around us until we had each been whittled down to the slim and unbreakable sum of our wills. I sought only the knife. I desired only the knife. It was a purity of motive that I'd felt on only one other occasion. There was no sun no trees no water no earth no past no future. There was only the knife guarding the border between the living and the dead.

And then it was over. Our strange engagement collapsed. Only a moment earlier we had been matched in intention and will and released from mortal duties. Now he was prone and bleeding and susceptible to gravity.

I recognized it and I didn't. I felt the click-whirr of my automatic response to imminent death but an equally strong imperative to watch the slow leak of a life. For years afterward I tried to tease out whether that was my impulse alone because when I did find my voice he defied my instructions and demanded that I ignore every medical impulse. There was nowhere to hide. As he was exposed I was stripped of the audacious and constant argument against death I'd been practicing for years. I was raw and open to his every demand. "Pay attention," he said. "Watch."

His face was smooth in the absence of struggle. The sun caught the soft dark stubble on his chin. The slight clouding in his irises could be medically explained but I lacked the desire and couldn't remember why I'd ever had it. When I did respond to an impulse that drifted into my mind uncensored I felt I was moving as though underwater and against the current. His eyes sprang open as if a latch had been released and then the blood. Oh the blood. I wanted to collect it from the sand and pour it back into the frail house of his body. I wanted to follow every rogue bead of it and claw it back into him. Regret isn't strong enough a sentiment. It wasn't a mistake or an error. It was a transgression of inexcusable proportions.

I'd seen men die before but only as bit players in the flurry of medical drama amid lights and gleaming surfaces and complex instruments. Gideon lay on the sand. Blood pooled in the fold of his ear. His eyes were hot ice, a final flaring before going to coal. He did not fight it. We were alone. A gull cried and small birds twittered and waves lapped against the shore in an endless loop of advance and retreat, advance and retreat, advance and retreat.

He insisted that I watch. I don't know if I gave him what he wanted. I measured time with his breath, inhale one, exhale two, inhale three, exhale four, as if the number alone might revive him, as if my keeping count might arrest his brazen shuffle toward mortality.

TWENTY-FOUR

A SHARP WIND LIFTED AND dropped the edge of her skirt. Her neck was stiff and she couldn't be sure how much time had passed. A grey sky hid the sun. Bile rose to the back of her throat and she started to heave, but her stomach was empty. Her head throbbed. Her knees were crusted with blood that had already begun to darken. She sensed he was there but didn't look, couldn't.

Her legs buckled when she tried to stand and she was back on the ground again, beside him. He hadn't moved. How could this be? She wanted to shake him, bring him back from his shameless reverie. His eyes were open but unseeing. The wind ruffled his hair. The blood on his white shirt was a motionless red tide.

She pushed herself to her knees and moved mechanically, drawing his eyelids down, buttoning his jacket over the scarlet stain in his shirt, smoothing his hair. She tried her feet again and went to stand at the water's edge. She untied her shoes, peeled off her socks and stepped into the river. The water was numbing. She cupped her hand and lifted it to her bloodied knees and then waded deeper, the river stones bruising and scraping her bare feet until the torn hem of her uniform met the surface of the water and her underwear was soaked. The cold north wind brought a fine spray of rain.

As the icy water deadened sensation in her feet, it occurred to her that she could take a few more steps and let the current carry her away. She would be a pale starfish in the brackish water of James Bay. It would be so easy.

She took another step and slipped. The frigid water triggered an instinctive retreat to the shore and she stood on the sand, breathing hard, shamed by her cowardice. She picked up her shoes. The bone handle of the knife was saturated with blood. She saw no reason to clean it.

The forest was full of shadows. She passed through it without hesitation, up the slope to the intersection, and along the road directly to the hospital. Her cheeks were tight with a salt patina. Her eyeballs felt raw and her uniform was torn. If she'd met anyone on the road, not a single explanation would have served. She carried on toward the residence anyway, pulled the door open and took the stairs to her room, blind to the world.

SHE COULDN'T BE SURE HOW long the tapping at her door had been going on. The sound became part of her dream. She sculled to the surface of consciousness from a great depth, unsure where she was. The sun was starting to set.

"Hazel." A husky whisper. She sat up.

"Hazel. I've checked everywhere else. You must be in there."

"I'm . . ." She cleared her throat. "Yes, Ruth. I'm here." She sat up in bed and glanced under the covers. Her nightgown. She'd managed that, at least.

"Well, can I come in?"

The bliss of ignorance was replaced by a dull, empty ache in her chest. He was gone. She scanned the room, trying to reconstruct the moments before she'd blacked into sleep. Her uniform was a damp tangle on the turquoise carpet between the window and the bed.

"Yes. Come in."

Ruth eased the door open and took in the room with a single shrewd glance. Hazel felt her probing gaze as she stepped inside and closed the door behind her. "It's past six. Are you sick?"

"No. Yes. I don't know." Hazel put her hand to her forehead. Clammy.

"Poor dear." Ruth frowned and came around the foot of the bed. Hazel held her breath but Ruth didn't react to the mound of damp clothes. Hazel could see that she wasn't sure what to believe. Ruth raised her voice. "You're burning up. In bed all day?"

Her tone told Hazel all she needed to know. Gideon had not yet been found. She nodded, feeling the slow seep of understanding. Maybe it could go this way. "I think I'm starting to feel better." She swung her legs over the side of the bed and the sudden motion made the ground pitch and sway. She closed her eyes and reached for the table.

"Are you going to tell me what's going on?" Ruth's eyes were narrow and hard, and she was speaking in a fierce whisper. "I can't help you if you won't let me in."

Hazel sat back on the bed and dry heaved. Ruth reached for the wastebasket. "It's that umbrella mender, isn't it? Did he hurt you?"

Hazel shook her head.

"Are you compromised?"

Hazel couldn't look at Ruth. Ruth lifted Hazel's chin, still whispering. "I can help you, but you have to let me in. He's no good, Hazel. Break it off." Then she raised her voice again. "You're not going to share that all around, young lady. Back in bed. I'll let Davies know you're out of commission."

"But I'm –"

"No arguments now, Captain." She used the stern, booming voice she usually reserved for the delivery room. "You don't want to bring down the whole staff with whatever you've got. You don't want that on your conscience, do you?" Hazel swallowed, a vice grip closing around her forehead. "Stay right there, missy. I'll bring some tea and then I have to go. I have one in active labour over there." She was back a few minutes later with a tray, which she set on the bedside table. They stared at each other for a few minutes. Hazel didn't know what Ruth saw when she looked at her. Ruth left without another word.

The room swam. Ruth had chosen to be an accomplice for reasons Hazel could only guess at, but in her implied estimation of Hazel's transgression, the actual one was multiplied many times over. It became monstrous, unbearable. She'd been wrong. It couldn't go this way.

Hazel finally slept. She woke late the next afternoon, icy cold in spite of the heat in the room. She wrapped a blanket around herself, went to the green tweed couch in the living room and tried to eat the toast she'd made. It was ashes in her mouth.

The slow bleed of nightfall had begun. She saw the evergreen horizon of Sawpit Island, outlined in soft pink, beyond the poplars in the backyard. Nurses would begin to return to the residence soon. Ruth would have passed word about her illness around by now. Hazel knew three things: this bubble of ignorance could not last, he would be found and there would be questions. She had no idea how she could answer them.

The front door swung open and the newest nurse at the hospital walked past the living room door, then reappeared there a few seconds later.

"Oh! Hazel! You're here." Oda Vogel crossed the room without hesitation and sat on the couch beside Hazel, her kind eyes creased with concern. She was young and fresh off the boat from Holland. Her milky skin, wheaten hair and Delft-blue eyes stupefied most of the orderlies, as well as the hospital pilot, but as far as Hazel had been able to determine, she was unaware of her effect. She was also one of the best nurses Hazel had ever worked with. "I heard you'd fallen ill."

"I couldn't stay in bed any longer." That, at least, was true. "I must be getting better."

"Do you need anything? Can I make you a cup of tea?"

"Thank you, no. I've just had one."

Oda put her feet on the coffee table and let her head fall back. "It has been quite a day. You have not been out at all?"

"No." An icy finger of fear tugged at her gut. It had begun.

Oda faced Hazel and raised her pale eyebrows. "They found his body on the west side of the island."

"Whose?" It was the most Hazel could risk.

"That umbrella fellow's. The odd one, dressed in funny clothes. You know." She paused and frowned at Hazel. "Some of the nurses think you fancied him."

Hazel let the comment lie. Her skin was alive with pinpricks. Leaving him there had not been part of any plan; she had no plan. Her own inaction was a minute-by-minute agony. She could only shake her head.

"He had been stabbed. First murder of the year, the Mounties say. Dead almost twenty-four hours when one of the RCMP dogs found him."

Hazel shivered involuntarily. The smooth coolness of his buttons, the red red tide of his blood. The bone-handled knife.

"It is terrible, isn't it?" Oda's eyes were pale blue saucers. "There was a hunting knife. They're saying he must have got himself in trouble with an Indian, had an argument. To look at them you would not think of such violence, would you? One of theirs for certain. The handle was covered in blood. Poor man must have struggled."

Hazel's stomach lurched but she couldn't speak. She began to tremble uncontrollably. She wanted Oda to stop. Stop stop stop stop stop. Oda turned to Hazel and jumped up. "Listen to me prattling on while you are still obviously ill. Come with me now. Let me help you back to your bed."

To suppress her rising panic, Hazel coaxed her mind into what could be measured, what could be seen. The room was smaller and plainer than she'd imagined an RCMP headquarters to be, even at an outpost like this one, the unfinished wood walls decorated only with a year-old calendar and a faded photograph of King George in a cheap metal frame. On the red wool uniform of the officer sitting across from her were two gold braid chevrons. Corporal. So they hadn't sent for the sergeant. He sat down and set his hat on the desk between them.

"I'm so sorry to trouble you, ma'am." He did seem contrite, inexplicably. He cleared his throat and she recalled having examined him for a nagging cough, non-tubercular as it turned out, in the clinic not long ago, maybe the previous month. "It's just that we have to investigate every lead, as I'm sure you can appreciate, and you were a known, ah, acquaintance of Mister Pederson."

Of the scenarios she envisioned and prepared herself for during the walk here, this one was a notable omission. She had not even considered the possibility that he might be using a name that wasn't his own. "I'm sssss-orry? Mister who?"

"Pederson. Daniel Pederson." The corporal gathered the papers arrayed on his desk and frowned. "So you didn't know. We understand he went by another name, something Biblical, wasn't it?"

It would have been unwise to pretend ignorance, had she been able to manage it; he had just named her as a known acquaintance. The incredible fact of her inaction had already revealed a capacity for deceit she hadn't known she possessed. But how could she explain what had happened if she didn't understand it herself?

"Yes. Gideon." The name was an invocation she felt to the marrow of her bones. Everything depended on her ability to keep her voice steady.

"Yes, that's it. Gideon. Not the name on the driver's license we found on his ..." He stopped. "It was from Minnesota. He'd come quite a long way."

The room stunk of wet wool. It had been raining since early morning, when he'd knocked on the door of the residence and walked her here. The corporal held his chin in his hand.

"Don't you worry now, Miss MacPherson. We have no reason to suspect you. Just trying to get a few facts straight."

Just get on with it, she thought. Please.

"You were, I'm sure, engaged with medical business on the morning of October third? In the clinic with Doctor Davies?"

"No, I was –"

"Somewhere else in the hospital, then." He wrote on his ruled pad. "I've seen you there myself." His hands were thick-fingered paws, working hands that seemed ill at ease with a pen. He wrote as if a schoolteacher was standing over him. She had a memory of their conversation in the clinic: he'd grown up on a farm south of Cochrane. "Other nurses will corroborate your whereabouts." It was not a question.

"I won't keep you from your work much longer. I know how busy you are. My sister was a nurse in the war, God rest her soul." He ran his hand through neatly barbered hair, very short, and opened a drawer. He lifted out a pale pink scarf and laid it on the desk. "Have you ever seen this before?"

Her scalp tingled. "Yes," she said, making a decision in that moment. It was a relief. "It's mine."

He stopped writing. She braced herself for the onslaught, finally ready for whatever this admission might bring. It would allow a response to his death, at least. The past few days had been a fog of shock that she recognized but couldn't move past. He pressed his lips together and sighed.

"Worse than we thought, then. You should have let us know. He must have been following you, who knows how long." He shook his head and clucked his tongue. "Is anything else missing?"

She couldn't respond. There were no words for what was happening here, for what she'd become part of. But how to relate what had happened, to impress on him the blind imperative of it all? How to convey the arc of Gideon's arms and the naked fact that she sometimes believed she saw him lift off the ground? How to lay out the translucence of his skin against his ribs, or the shock of it against hers? Could she describe the ruin of his body on the sand, the gradual ebbing of his blood tide? When she closed her eyes she could see his face but she knew it wouldn't always be so, that the passing days would eventually wipe away every trace of him. It had already begun.

"Never trusted him." The constable was shaking his head again. "His kind are nothing but trouble. Sorry that you had to go through this, ma'am. I wish you'd come to us. We could have done something."

A thought surfaced. The strip of fabric she'd torn from her uniform to bandage his hand. She hadn't unwrapped it before stumbling back to the residence. Someone would recognize it as a piece of a nurse's uniform. With sudden clarity, she saw the uniform she'd worn that day, ragged-hemmed and balled up in her drawer where anyone could find it.

He made a neat pile of his papers. "That's it. That's all I need from you."

She stood, wondering whether her legs would hold.

"You take care of yourself now, Miss MacPherson, and promise me that you'll call on us if you ever have trouble again, will you? That's what we're here for."

She nodded and turned to go, then stopped in the doorway. "His . . . body." The words just appeared, a nudge from her subconscious. This was necessary and she'd known it all along. She must bring this farce to a close. The words tumbled out in a halting voice. "What happens to his body?" To her own ears, the question was an unmistakable admission of guilt.

"Autopsy at the hospital, as you know." He was frowning. "Then we notify next of kin." She started to rehearse a confession when the crease in his forehead disappeared. "I could arrange for you to view the body if you want, ma'am, but we don't need you to identify it. I wouldn't want to put you through that. I can give you my word that he is well and truly dead. He won't bother you anymore."

Hazel turned away. It was too far, the distance she'd have to cross. The heat behind her eyes was searing. She pushed the door open and hoped for pelting rain.

LACHLAN'S HEAD WAS BENT OVER his work. His hair curled over the collar of his lab coat. She was an hour late for the clinic, her hair was wet and she was wearing a uniform that was not her own.

"Rounds are done and we've only had one patient so far this morning." He reached for the light box, switched it on and turned to her. There was mild surprise in his glance – the uniform was two sizes too big, the first one she'd found to replace hers, soaked when she'd reached the hospital – but he didn't comment. She wondered if someone had mentioned that she'd been taken to police headquarters. "So I thought we should review some x-rays. We haven't had time lately."

Hazel managed to nod. Her eyeballs felt raw. Her legs were weak and she was nauseated but she forced herself to concentrate. Lachlan rummaged through manila envelopes on his desk until he found the one he wanted.

"Let's start with this one." He set it down on the light box, then took it off again. "No. I have a better idea. Let's review a normal film first. Here."

He straightened his glasses and raised an eyebrow, as playful as she'd seen him in recent memory. Since she arrived here she'd been operating on the assumption that the passion he felt would be enough to carry them both; she'd even thought she'd started to feel it herself. But today she knew she'd been wrong. She felt nothing for this work. "This one is normal, a uniform hazy grey. See? Same texture, more or less, throughout."

She didn't trust her voice. She nodded, and this seemed to satisfy him. He clipped the other one to the light box. "See that, in the upper lobe? That asymmetrical haze?" He pointed with his pen. "This is what we're looking for." In a flash of self-awareness, he added, "Or, rather, what requires our immediate response. We would prefer a healthy lung, of course." He turned back to the light box. Another man might have given this kind of fierce and devoted attention to a cherished collection of some kind, insects or rare books or antique rifles, and he was sharing it with her. There was an appropriate response to the compliment that this represented, but she couldn't think what it was.

"This one shows calcification, there, see it? And a granuloma, too, there in the apical region." He removed the film and reached for another one. "You do see it, Nurse MacPherson?"

"I think so." She broke into a cold sweat. Why answer that way? Nothing in the film he was setting back on his desk distinguished itself to her. "Could you ... could we see that one again?" He replaced the film and she leaned closer, forcing herself to concentrate. "Here? This cottony spot?"

"That's it. Yes. Good for you." A couple of weeks earlier, she would have thrilled to the unvarnished joy in his eyes. Now she felt only a flood of relief. She'd cleared a hurdle. "Now. Here's another. Tell me what you see."

He lifted a new film to the light box. The graceful curve of the ribs cradled the lungs like spectral fingers and the chest cavity seemed to pulse as though it breathed. Inhale one, exhale two, inhale three, exhale four. With each breath she took, the available oxygen in the room seemed to diminish while the image increased in size and finally lifted off the light box to float toward her. Her mouth went dry. The back of her neck tingled. The room swayed. She closed her eyes and reached for the desk.

She felt Lachlan's hand on her elbow but she steeled herself. She would not collapse against him. She took several uneven breaths and when she opened her eyes she found him staring at her. There was a prominent vertical crease in his forehead.

"Nurse MacPherson, are you still sick?"

She shook her head. "I'm fine." She blinked and tried to focus.

"Good, good." He released her arm. "Your skin is clammy. Get caught in that downpour?"

She nodded. Her ability to steady herself took on mortal significance. The shift in her state of mind must be immediate and absolute or she would be undone with no possibility for a return to anything she knew. Her body thrummed with effort. The pulse in her ears was so loud she wondered if Lachlan could hear it.

"The spots between the ribs. There and there."

"Blood vessels, most likely, dead on to the x-ray lens. The tail leads away from them, see? But there is something there. Compare the left lung to the right." His tone was almost jaunty now. For Lachlan, this was fun. "That's the nice thing about the human body. Everything comes in pairs."

She tried to smile. Was that tangled nest choking the air out, or bringing it in? What was normal and what remarkable? She had tried this before, months ago, on Sawpit. This time was no better. The sketches she'd made. Where were they? She hadn't touched her notebook in months.

"Stand back a little and let your eyes relax, let them lose focus." Lachlan laid a hand on her shoulder. His fingers were warm. She couldn't remember when he'd ever done this. "Now, tell me what stands out."

She took a step back and let the image blur. She focused on the left side and then on the right, left then right, moving methodically down through the lung space. The effort and the repetition was calming. Aha. Now she saw it, a gauzy mass in the left lung where there was nothing but a haze of grey on the right. She could still do this. The messy delirium was only temporary. She could walk away from this and return to the safe, logical haven of medicine.

"Here." Her voice sounded like her own, finally. "In the lower right corner."

"Yes, good. What do you see?"

"Clouds." She managed a smile. "Right there."

"Yes. Good. That's probably calcification." He said it tenderly. "Can you see anything else?"

The image was static now. She let her focus blur again. A crescent of dark grey, there, obscuring a portion of the cloudy mass.

"There's a shadow." He'd been standing behind her, waiting for her response. "In the middle of the white mass, there's a shadow that seems to overlay it."

"Yes, there is." She didn't have to see his face to know his pleasure at her answer. "Show me where you see it." She pointed. "Yes. What's the cause, do you think?"

Now she didn't hesitate. "An absence absorbs light. A cavity?"

"Absolutely right. It's an instance of cavitation. The body encapsulated the bacillus with calcium and the interior space liquefied. It could rupture and release the bacteria into the system. This is a mature lesion."

She felt a seductive lull that let her envision herself in this room or others like it, head bent over a light table at all hours of the day or night, charting the recession of the disease like a battle general marking captured territory with coloured flags. Work would be her anchor and Lachlan her north star. Whatever else he was incapable of providing, he was willing to guide her intellectual growth, even if only so that she could educate patients about the disease. She could fulfill his expectations this way and maybe, eventually, fall for science the way he had. The field was ripe with opportunity; all of the nursing journals said so. Good people, skilled people, were desperately needed. She could become a leader in TB nursing, maybe even go back to medical school and become a doctor. It could go this way.

The clatter of footsteps on the polished floor of the waiting room broke the spell and her thoughts ricocheted back to Gideon, motionless in the sand. She took a halting breath. Lachlan's head was cocked to one side. He had noticed the shift in her attention.

Good people were needed. She could do this. She pointed to the door.

"I suppose we should –"

"In a minute. There's just one more. You won't get away from this so easily now, Hazel!" There was an edge of disappointment in his playful tone. He didn't want this conversation to end. It was as though they'd been sitting at a cafeteria table, bantering about favourite books or music. "I need you to be able to talk to patients about this. Not nearly enough nurses can and you've shown remarkable aptitude. Come now. Don't quit on me." He picked up another film. "If you feel better about it, you can open the door and say we'll be with them in a minute, but it *is* a waiting room. They're familiar with the concept."

She smiled and meant it. She could attach herself to this. She could conduct his fervour for the work again. It was starting to come back. "Yes, of course they are. Habit. Please continue."

"Alright, then. Last one. For this session." He folded his arms across his chest. "Tell me what you see."

It seemed easier now. "There, to the right of the sternum. A mass. A large one."

"That's the heart."

Of course it was, but the embarrassment was minor. There was honour in the knowledge they pursued. She could turn away from what happened. It was over.

"But you're right to remark on it, Hazel. There is something about the heart. Here." He switched films. "Compare this one . . . to this one."

She could see it now. "The position is different. The heart is . . . larger somehow. It seems to fill half the lung space."

"Exactly. The infiltration of the disease left a vacuum in its wake, creating torque on the right side. The heart was pulled into that void. We call that retraction. You'll see it in advanced cases, as this one was."

Was. The past tense was a barb that worked its way into the memory dam she'd just constructed and pulled the stones loose. The tide was pulling her out to sea. She could only look at Lachlan. He was standing on a distant shore. He shook his head. The motion was almost imperceptible and his voice was faint. "He was too far gone. We tried to help him but we were too late."

We were too late. Another breach of the dam. She was drifting further. She heard the lapping of the water on the shore, saw the first rays of sunlight pick out the fine dark stubble on Gideon's chin. She couldn't have saved him. The red red tide of his blood. Inhale one, exhale two, inhale three, exhale four. The sky streaming. She had tried. It could not, after all, go this way. She saw Lachlan's head turn toward her in slow motion, and her legs gave out.

TWENTY-FIVE

I WAS A GOOD NURSE. Not like some of these who are in and out of my room in two minutes. I hear their coarse laughter a few minutes later at the nurses' station down the hall. You've seen them, Jude. Because I can't speak they conclude I'm blank inside too.

I would never have done that. I was good at my work. If you were to check the registry you'd find no record of my name after 1957 but it wasn't for lack of desire. I assumed that carrying on with my life was the best thing for me and didn't anticipate a problem finding work in the field. There had been strides in making the work less risky and many developed immunity but fear of infection still kept nurses away. Most of us had seen one friend off to the san so when I turned up at a TB hospital in Quebec City in late 1952 I didn't anticipate a refusal. With my experience I thought I'd be able to find a position almost any-where.

I'd been working for a few weeks when my cough attracted the attention of the matron. She realized that I hadn't yet been screened and I heard her muttering under her breath as she shep-herded me toward an empty triage room. The oversight could eas-ily have been explained by the pace of the work but she held herself responsible and visited her frustration on me. She was not gentle. The injection of the tuberculin was an abrupt stab and she tapped her toe neurotically for at least fifteen minutes and said nothing. Owing to the cough it wasn't possible for me to return to duty until the result was known but what we were waiting for I hadn't a clue. The incubation period was two days. Eventually she dis-missed me with a wave of her hand and sent me home.

The dime-sized welt on my inner arm was hard and warm but when I saw it on waking the second day I couldn't have been more unnerved. I walked to the hospital from my residence in a daze. In the eighteen months I'd worked in Moose Factory this test had been a bimonthly formality. Even when a red welt appeared on other nurses' arms and I knew it was a possibility my continuing evasion of a positive reaction gave me the understanding that I had either developed a natural immunity or had been prudent in following prevention protocol. In either case I didn't have the slightest expectation that this test would be positive.

The matron's lips were set in a hard line and she cursed qui-etly as we walked down the hall to the imaging room. I stripped from the waist up and faced the x-ray plate. The cool metal of the machine raised goosebumps on my arms and chest. I could hear her adjusting the height of the camera before she paused to ask me whether I could be pregnant. I hesitated before shaking my head. The question flickered in her eyes again but I turned back to the plate. The machine buzzed and she told me to get dressed. She

closed the door behind her and then opened it again. *Attendez ici.*
I waited.

I had twice talked myself into the notion that my cough was
a nervous manifestation of all that I had been through when she
strode back into the room with the developed film in her hand.
She clipped it to the light box and flipped the power switch on but
the resignation on her face told the story. A few moments passed
before I realized I was holding my breath. My exhalation broke the
tension in the room and she sighed. "*Vous êtes malade, mademoi-
selle.*" She drew a circle around the gauzy wisp in my left lung and
shook her head. "*Vous pouvez le voir?*"

I saw the haze that Lachlan had taught me to recognize even
before she'd circled it. They said I was lucky that it was caught early.
I had a mild case that the new drugs cleared in sixteen months.
Once I was healthy again I had an even better understanding of
the disease than when I'd left Moose Factory, which was much
more than the average TB nurse knew. This was a problem in city
hospitals.

The first time I was found unsuitable for a job in this way I was
dumbfounded. I was hired and then dismissed two months later
for forgetting to clock in once or twice, which didn't make sense. I
honestly didn't believe that any willing and skilled TB nurse would
be turned away except in the most egregious of circumstances but
when the pattern repeated itself in two more Ontario sanatoriums
I understood that my inability to conceal my knowledge and provide the level of servitude required by southern doctors was just
such a situation. In this way I was made to appreciate the fact that
I was not a doctor. I didn't feel that I was being obnoxious by act-
ing on what I knew and often I did it without thinking but when
I finally understood the source of the problem I found I couldn't
abide the lack of freedom to use my informed judgment. It would
have felt like denying that I had a right arm.

Neither could I put aside my life's work. I did think of it in those terms even at twenty-three. Lachlan had left his mark. Medical journals and course catalogues for medical school were a common fixture on my side table during that period and I was never able to part with them. You'll find them on the bookshelf if you look. I continued to learn about the disease and still thought of myself as a TB medic even long after I'd been dismissed for the third time and it was clear that I'd never work in the field again without major concessions on my part.

I don't feel bitter about this now and didn't then. I was more bemused than anything else. It seemed bizarre to me that any offer of skilled help with the disease would be refused and yet it was. Or rather I was. What I was didn't fit anywhere. This was a lesson I needed to learn over and over again until I was able to accept it. I was overqualified for nursing and underqualified for the sort of work I'd been doing with Lachlan. I began looking north again thinking that if I couldn't do interesting work I might as well work in an interesting place. There was need for good nurses in the far north and I accepted two short contracts in the mid-fifties, one on Baffin Island and the other on a ship in Hudson Bay. Each time I let the contract expire rather than renew it and each time I wondered what kind of nurse I'd become. I'd lost my taste for general nursing.

I made discreet inquiries about the head of the hospital in Moose Factory occasionally though I knew I couldn't go back. I lost track of Lachlan after he left the hospital a few years after I did and didn't know whether he still lived until a letter arrived one day. Decades had passed and I don't know how he found me but there was no preamble, just news about Charlie.

TWENTY-SIX

BY DECEMBER IT HAD BECOME possible, for hours at a time, to forget. Gideon's autopsy at the hospital had proceeded without her but she sensed it like a phantom limb, and Hazel made sure she was occupied elsewhere when the body was being loaded on the plane to St. Paul's. She knew there would have been no shortage of curious onlookers. She didn't trust herself to watch him go again.

In the early weeks she'd noticed probing and sympathetic glances, sometimes in connection with a mysterious illness that caused fainting spells, but this attention all but disappeared in the wake of excitement over a new wonder drug. Not even Ruth broached the subject any longer, though she'd tried to draw Hazel out on several occasions in the weeks following Gideon's death. Hazel refused to answer again and again, unwilling to involve her in what had happened and unable to imagine an outcome to such a conversation that either of them could stomach. But Hazel always believed that Ruth and her questions would persist. When they finally stopped, that expectation made their lack signify something greater, somehow, than the wedge Hazel knew she'd driven between them or the fact that Ruth had given up. The absence of questions made it seem as though Gideon had never existed. After the agonized passage of the previous few months, she began to wish it was true.

The weather in December, hovering around -4°F most days and milder than November by a dozen degrees, was considered balmy by Moose Factory standards. Travel by Bombardier or dogsled on the ice road between the island and the mainland was easier and so more frequent, allowing regular arrivals of holiday packages that fuelled a rotating schedule of parties in the kitchens and living rooms of staff quarters. Even Charlie made a wooden appearance at a few of them, though he ignored broad suggestions that as one of the few hospital staff members afforded the luxury of his own house, he ought to open it for gatherings.

The mood among staff was high. The orderlies organized a bonspiel on the new curling rink for Christmas Eve, and so many members of staff volunteered to wear the Santa Claus costume in the children's ward on Christmas Day that they'd held a lottery. Henry's name was drawn. Even after he'd been persuaded to add a second pillow under the red tunic, Henry was more elf than jolly old man, but his antics made everyone laugh. Until he hoisted a young Cree girl from her crib and settled her on his lap, when something in his posture recalled a gesture peculiar to Gideon, even Hazel had been able to give over to the merriment. To that point she'd been successful at concealing the flash floods of sorrow that appeared without warning, and it wasn't that she didn't recognize the image of Gideon as entertainer of children as patently absurd. But the Christmas Day episode triggered unexpectedly intense grief. She'd thought it ought to be diminishing.

January fifteenth marked her first anniversary on the island and it was less than a week away. As she pulled the last piece of Scotch tape from a length of silver garland that they'd strung across the double doorway to the children's ward, she realized that she hadn't thought of him in two days. The exhaustion and fainting spells had ebbed, too. She'd been right. The work would see her through.

She handed the garland to Sally and gestured to the waist-high stack of boxes of decorations in the hallway. "We should have these cleared by this afternoon or we'll hear from Doctor Wilcox. Where's Joseph? Let's get him to start carrying these out to storage."

"He went out with a load already." She packed the garland in a box with ornaments and brass bells. "He will be back."

The door to the stairwell opened. There was a dusting of snow on Joseph's short black hair and on the shoulders of his navy wool parka. He handed a hospital housecoat to Hazel.

"Too cold for a sick person out there, Nurse MacPherson." His expression was grave. She checked the size label. Men's small. She compiled a mental list of male patients who could fit into that coat and were likely to try a stunt like that, even though she knew who it must be. She wanted to be wrong.

"Where did you find that?"

"On the ground, outside the main doors."

"Thank you, Joseph. Take those out and come straight back." She held the door open. Sheets of blowing snow obscured the view out the stairwell window every few minutes and the temperature had plunged into the minus-thirties over the past few days. They were wearing balaclavas, fur mittens, heavy boots and parkas now, all of this for the short journeys between home and hospital. "I'll speak to Doctor Davies immediately."

THE WALLS OF LACHLAN'S OFFICE were papered with the charts he'd made of the disease's retreat, categorized by organ. She'd noticed them around the time she'd learned of his decision to exceed the recommended dosage duration for the streptomycins a few months earlier. It came as a surprise. Even in his zeal to cure the country, he'd always seemed a man who'd work within established limits.

"The native patient seems to have no natural defenses. A month off the drug and they relapse. We can only continue with it, knowing the risks." She heard this as she passed his office one day in late autumn and stopped, pretending to look through files she was carrying. "What choice do we have?"

"None." Charlie's voice had been riddled with irritation. "Which is what makes our course of action clear. I don't know why we must continue to have this conversation. You're not honestly suggesting that there's any real choice between dead and deaf?"

"Of course not," Lachlan had barked, and Hazel flinched. It was rare for him to raise his voice like this. "But I will not willingly inflict a handicap on a patient of mine, Charlie, and I would hope that you feel the same."

"That goes without saying, Lachlan. We will, of course, continue to seek the safest possible cure."

Lachlan had eventually settled on an alternating regimen of the two streptomycins they had – the plain for one month and the dihydrostreptomycin the next – on the logic that this way neither could accrue in the system to the point of deafness, nor could the disease escape the antibiotic assault for even a brief period. It was an elegant solution Hazel admired. He wasn't exceeding recommendations for each drug, strictly speaking.

Then the isoniazid arrived in early December. It was an antibacterial agent that Lachlan didn't hesitate to add to the antibiotic regimen. Together the drugs were arresting the disease in even the most stubborn cases. Trials had produced results that exceeded everyone's expectations, leading to descriptions like "miraculous" and "astonishing," even within the medical community, where this kind of imprecise evaluation was typically avoided. Lachlan had written to colleagues in Hamilton and Winnipeg and she found herself enthusing about Ulluriaq's progress to other nurses on staff. The diet change and new drug combination had brought colour to the elderly Inuit's cheeks. She was gaining weight and holding court from her bed by the window.

Now Lachlan was bent over a dosages log, scratching his head and scribbling sums in the margins. He peered at her over the tops of his lenses when she walked in. At least he had noticed.

"You haven't observed any auditory changes among the children, have you?"

"None."

"Have you checked for it?"

"If you're asking whether I've conducted formal hearing tests, the answer is no. You've never requested it."

He turned a few pages. "Then I'm doing that now. We'll give them when new patients arrive so we have a baseline, and test again with each x-ray."

She pictured the lone and antiquated audiometer in a neglected corner of a second-floor exam room. "Unless there's a new machine I don't know about, our equipment is basic, Doctor Davies. Toronto and Hamilton have much more to offer in that department."

"I'm aware of that. We can send any cases we think warrant closer attention. But we'll start testing on admission with what we've got. Rough numbers will do. Make sure it happens."

"Of course." There was an unfamiliar edge in his voice. His anxiety about dosages had flared again and she wondered what had set it off. But there were more pressing matters. She patted the flannel housecoat on her arm. "There is something else, Doctor Davies."

"Yes?"

Hazel took a deep breath. "Joseph found this robe just outside the main door on a bank of snow."

Lachlan looked up from his papers and stared out the window. "Today?"

"About fifteen minutes ago. It's a men's small. I haven't counted heads yet. They aren't all on the ward right now. Some are in the craft room, a few downstairs for x-rays. Anyone in particular come to mind?"

There was uncharacteristic definition along his jawline. "Most of the men in here couldn't get a pinky finger into a coat that size." Saying so made it real and Hazel wished he hadn't. Neither of them could say the man's name. "Get the patient list immediately, and have some aides work with you to account for everyone as quickly as possible. Ten minutes until exposed skin freezes in this wind. I refuse to lose someone to this kind of silliness."

HAZEL'S HAND WAS ON THE door to the craft room when the main doors down the hall slammed shut. Joseph stood between two sets of glass doors, stamping the snow from his boots. She caught his eye and he started down the short flight of stairs toward her.

"Find him?"

"I was going to ask you the same question."

He was silent for a few moments. The voice of one of the men in the craft room rose, loud enough to be distinct even on this side of the closed door. "He tells it too much, that one," Joseph grunted. "It was only a seal." He zipped his coat. "I will go back out."

"Wait. We don't know for certain that anyone is missing. Help me count heads."

Joseph nodded. Hazel tipped her head toward the craft room. "Find out who's in there and meet me at x-ray."

Ruth insisted on waiting with her. By the time Joseph strode through the double doors just outside x-ray, only six names remained on her list. She checked off the five he gave.

"Suujuq," he said, before she'd finished.

Goosebumps rose on her skin. She had wanted to be wrong. The moon-pale face of the Cree woman she'd left in the woods beyond Rupert's House shimmered in her mind's eye. Ni ka wiy.

Ruth inhaled sharply. "You knew?"

"No," Joseph said. "I thought maybe."

"Why?"

"No more whale." In mid-October, a beluga whale had become trapped at low tide not far downriver. Cook froze much of it and brought chunks out on Sundays as a treat. It had just run out. Suujuq's refusal of the roast beef they'd offered instead on Sunday seemed inconsequential at the time. She'd even expected it from him, and trusted that the refusal was evidence of his resilience.

"Think he's gone out to find more?"

"This man is a good hunter. He knows that there are no whales in January." Joseph's voice was shrill. "But maybe he has gone fishing."

"Why leave his coat behind, if so?"

"He did not leave his coat behind." Joseph played the words out slowly and stared out the window at the end of the hall. "He left the hospital coat."

"Joseph. You must tell us whatever you know." Hazel hadn't heard that tone from Ruth since the breech birth in June. He turned to her, his dark eyes furious.

"He is wearing his own coat."

Ruth's lips were set in a thin, hard line. She crossed her arms and pushed her broad shoulders back. "How would he have known where to find it?"

"He asked me." Joseph closed his eyes for a minute. When he opened them again there was a new, glittering hardness there. "Doctor Davies told him he was sick and could not go home yet. A man should have his own coat. It is my fault. I will find him."

"Not on your own." Lachlan turned the corner wearing a black toque and brown parka. He carried his boots under his arm. "No one goes out there alone or without proper clothing for the weather. You will lose your job if you choose to do otherwise. We go in twos or not at all and check in at the main entrance every hour. Understood?" He turned to Hazel. "We'll operate on a skeleton staff in here and send the rest out until we find him. He can't have gone far yet. You two get the staff organized and send them to the main doors. We'll be waiting for them there. Joseph, come with me."

THE TEMPERATURE DIFFERENCE BETWEEN THE hospital and the outdoors in winter often took her breath away, but on that day in January the snow blowing past the glass doors wasn't responsible for the constriction in her chest. She was protected from the weather: her new pale blue parka, made by one of the Inuit women on the ward and bought at the craft-room auction, grazed her knees and was trimmed in fox fur. The hood was up and she'd wound a scarf around it, leaving a strip wide enough to see through. She wore two pairs of long underwear over her stockings, the fur-lined leather mittens Pitsiaq had made and the heavy boots she'd been given when she arrived.

Lachlan stood a few feet from the door, an island map in hand, and assigned each pair a wedge of land that extended from the hospital dock to Sawpit Island, twenty feet along its shore, and then back again across the channel. He ordered a sharp-eyed, methodical search and reminded them that the man's coat was white, fawn and brown ptarmigan feathers, easily camouflaged in this landscape. They should pursue every movement, every shift in the horizon. She knew he was thinking about the lost group at Rupert's House.

Hazel left Sally in charge of the wards and Oda to stand inside the double doors at the entrance as a command post for the search parties. The possibility that the search might go on after nightfall was something she didn't want to consider, and Ruth agreed. In his weakened state, Ruth figured that they'd find him before dinner.

"I'll bet he hasn't gone far at all." Her strides were long and determined. "I couldn't see the channel well enough from the back window but if there hadn't been so damn much snow I reckon I'd have been able to spot him bent over a hole in the ice. Stubborn bugger can probably see the hospital lights from where he's jigging his line."

"I hope you're right." Hazel shifted a frozen patch of scarf away from her mouth. "His wife doesn't know where he is." Only last week she'd seen him crouched on the floor of the craft room, intent on his work and making conversation with the other men. He was carving another hunter and telling stories but she'd noticed a smouldering sense of regret in his eyes, as if he'd begun to assume that hunting would be available to him only in the abstract now. There was also the bittersweet fact of his children's absence. They'd been left behind in the village, untouched by disease. Every Sunday, when he went to the women's ward to visit his wife, he came back melancholy and spoke to no one. Hazel always let him be, telling herself that he would want to work it out alone and was strong enough to do so. She'd wanted to believe that what they were offering was enough.

As they rounded the south corner of the hospital the wind picked up and she tugged the scarf back over her mouth. Ruth was by then a few steps ahead and shouted something. Her words were lost in the wind. Hazel's mittens were a wall that the icy wind couldn't penetrate, and she wished for an entire outfit of the same. How could the feathers possibly protect Suujuq from the knifing cruelty of this wind? Ten minutes to frostbite in this weather. She forced her thoughts away from the idea. Sick or not, surely this man possessed survival skills that far outstripped her own.

The drifts of snow made it slow going between the hospital and the outbuildings, but she kept pace with Ruth, whose longer strides carried her toward the channel with speed. When they reached the edge of the slope that led to the frozen river, they both stopped. Ruth pushed her hood back from her face.

"Still can't see a damn thing. Wish that bloody wind would die down for a few minutes. It'll be a hell of a job to find him out here."

Hazel pushed her own hood back and scanned the shoreline, visible only for seconds between gusts of snow. The dark shapes of another pair moved further up the channel. "We'd better start across, then."

"I guess. But once we're down there on the ice we won't see more than a few feet in front of our faces." She turned to Hazel and narrowed her eyes. "And yours is fuller than it used to be, you know."

The non sequitur was shock treatment, pushing Hazel toward the reality that she'd so far evaded. She scrambled for a plausible explanation without even realizing that she'd understood Ruth's meaning implicitly.

"Yes. I seem to have put on a bit of weight." In that moment, she let herself believe that the extra winter roasts were responsible for her thicker waist.

"It's normal."

Ruth's bossy self-importance was irritating. "What is? Eating more in winter?"

The scarf Ruth had pulled over her mouth muffled her weary chuckle. "I suppose it is, but that's not what I meant, and you know it." The wind finally slowed and she turned her face back to the channel. "I mean that it's normal for early pregnancy."

Hazel didn't react immediately. She disconnected herself from the comment as if she and Ruth were discussing a patient and retreated into the safety of the cocoon she'd fashioned for herself over the course of the autumn.

"As far as I'm concerned, it's a surer bet than any pregnancy test. I can tell by the fullness of a woman's face."

"The fullness of her face." Hazel didn't feel the cold anymore.

"Yes." She swung around to face Hazel again. Her green eyes were kind but stern, and her pale eyebrows arched. "And you, my dear, are with child."

"I can't be." The denial came easily. She was practiced at it by then. October, November and December had been a fog of days she'd filled with self-imposed overwork as she waited for normalcy to reassert itself. The longer she waited, the more entrenched were her attempts to wish away what she knew to be happening.

"I assumed you knew." Ruth's voice took on a softer inflection. "I assumed you knew and weren't telling me."

"I ... no! I didn't." She eyed Ruth warily. "And I still don't."

There was a shout. Hazel strained to hear over the howling wind. Down on the ice, just to the west of the area she and Ruth were supposed to be searching. They edged down the slope, sunk to their knees in snow at times and made their way toward the figures they saw huddled there.

Joseph and Lachlan stood near a hole hacked into the thick ice. A branch lay beside it. Their heads hung and they weren't speaking. Hazel inched closer, testing the ice with her foot.

"Stay." Lachlan held his arm out so that she couldn't pass. Joseph held an axe in his left hand and the attitude of his body told Hazel everything she needed to know. The wind died down. "That water will kill you in about three minutes."

This couldn't be. It was incomprehensible that Suujuq had found the strength to break ice this thick. Even if he had, she couldn't believe he had the desire. She'd seen the difference in his outlook herself. Hadn't she?

"Maybe it was made by someone else." The words were false and grasping, even to her own ears. "Maybe one of the islanders was fishing out here."

Neither of the men responded. She saw them exchange a glance and then Lachlan gave a curt nod to Joseph, who stepped aside. Now that the wind had dropped off, the falling snow seemed benign; it fell in a drifting surrender to gravity on the black surface of the water and lingered there like a song before disappearing. On the blue-white surface of the ice, behind the place where Joseph had been standing, the brown and white feathers attached to the coat lay still and sleek like a clutch of sleeping hens, collecting snow.

Lachlan had not yet decided how news of Suujuq's disappearance should be communicated. They'd found no body and might not, even after spring breakup. She watched him closely in the days that followed, expecting the tortuous lack of resolution to manifest in indirect ways. He was not a man who tolerated uncertainty well. Once the initial shock subsided, she regarded the presence of the Inuit carver's coat beside the hole as conclusive evidence of suicide, but for Lachlan, interpretation of that scene was more complicated, reflecting on not only his skills as a medic but also his philosophy of rehabilitation. The theory that the man might have the pluck to walk away from the hospital and eventually home would be appealing, and she'd heard him advance it to one of the other doctors. She'd expected him to struggle for a few days and then come to the more rational conclusion, but days stretched into a week and still nothing was said.

Even so, an official announcement was unnecessary. She knew it when she stepped into the room he had shared with six other men. They were silent and grim-faced, dark eyes solemn with a quiet fury. She set the pail of soapy water she'd brought beside his bed and wondered what Suujuq had told them, if anything, before going.

"There you are." Ruth stopped at the door, hands on her hips, and then walked in. She faced Hazel from the other side of the bed and loosened the sheet. "I can help, you know."

"As you wish." Hazel folded the other side of the sheet toward the centre, slipped the pillow cover off and handed the bundle to Ruth, then reached into the pail for the scrub brush. "There's only the one brush, though."

"That wasn't what I meant." She hooked a finger through the handle of his sputum cup on the side table. "You should have an exam at this point."

Hazel scoured the surface of the rubber mattress cover in concentric circles. "I feel fine."

"And take vitamins."

"God, Ruth! Not now." She dropped the brush into the water, wiped the mattress with a towel and then cresol solution, and started on the pillow.

"When, then? You're impossible to find these days. I can't believe we're living in the same house."

"I don't know."

"Today. After shift."

"Fine. If it makes you feel better." She scrubbed the side table and wiped it with cresol. This kind of work usually belonged to the aides, but Hazel had told them that she'd take care of it. Ruth was still standing there, arms laden with hospital linen. "I said I'll come."

"Make sure you do." Ruth narrowed her eyes. "I'll be waiting in the prenatal exam room."

Hazel dumped the soapy water into the sink and rinsed the bucket. She combed through the days of the autumn months for the signs she'd ignored. Three months now. Her uniform, always roomy in the waist, puckered there and pulled across her chest. The change had been so gradual that it had been easy to dismiss.

She hung her ward gown on the peg, dropped her mask into the laundry bin and finished scrubbing up. Her shift was almost over but she turned down the hall toward the sunroom in the women's ward instead. She stopped outside the room and tugged her dress down, then walked in.

Ulluriaq had been facing the window but turned her head at the sound of Hazel's footsteps. Hazel nodded to her.

"Hello, Ulluriaq. Chimo."

"*Tartitartuq*," she said, without hesitation.

Hazel didn't recognize the phrase but the old woman made her meaning clear enough with her eyes. "She says, stormy sea." Pitsiaq frowned. "But she is not sick today."

TWENTY-SEVEN

THE LAUNDRY ON THE LINES outside her window undulated in the wind, finally. How many months since they'd stiffened with frost? It was April, for God's sake. She should be able to leave the thermal underwear in her drawer soon. Wearing them over her stockings for the five-minute walk to the hospital no longer represented adventure.

She didn't have to check her reflection in the mirror before leaving for the hospital. She knew how she looked, and she assumed that everyone else had become accustomed to her appearance, too. Elephantine ankles in her stockings because it was now necessary to wear the waistband at her hips. Her face was fuller, even more so than when Ruth remarked on it three months earlier; it was especially apparent when she pulled her hair off her face before every shift. Starched white uniform two sizes too big and still, just today, the bodice buckled and the waistline floated above the shelf of her belly. She dug a cardigan out of her drawer and left it unbuttoned.

Nothing had been said about her advancing pregnancy by anyone except Ruth. It was an indication, she assumed, of the sheer volume of work that needed to be done in a day. Either that or the rumour mill had managed to bypass her, which wouldn't have been difficult. In the previous six months, she'd kept to herself more than ever. In the south she'd have been dismissed as soon as she started to show. The fact that she hadn't was proof of the hospital's insatiable need for staff. She realized that she'd been counting on this fact because she couldn't go home in this condition, but thinking on it she decided that she didn't care what happened. Let them dismiss her. Let them send her home and think the disgrace would be humiliating. They'd lose a good nurse, and they'd also be wrong. Nothing anyone could say or do could touch what she'd been through.

The fact that she could talk to no one about what happened to Gideon was the shell that walled it off from the rest of her life, and it calcified with each passing week. This surprised her at first. She'd expected the story of Gideon's last hours, known only to her, to colonize her thoughts. But it hadn't. Her silence contained it the way a body encapsulated a bacillus.

Spring was coming. Another month would pass before the river was ready to accept a boat, but any day now the ice would begin to move. Lachlan had commissioned signs in Inuktitut that forbade fishing and supervised their installation at several points along the shore behind the hospital. In the months following Suujuq's disappearance, she'd dreamt of him intermittently, twitching awake in a sweat-soaked bed when his face appeared below a patch of clear ice, his mouth open and imploring. The dreams dwindled with her advancing pregnancy and resulting fatigue, but with spring breakup coming, and with it the possibility of his body resurfacing, she braced herself for their return.

Last week the Bombardier had been parked in the garage for the season. She'd never enjoyed the journey across the ice road in the odd snow crawler anyway. The round windows were drafty and it exuded an oily, metallic stink, but some days the Arctic wind whistling down the Moose River blew too cold to make a supply run to Moosonee bearable by dogsled. Everyone had been saying that the Bombardier driver had taken chances running it as long as he had this year. The sighing and cracking of the river ice, occasionally as loud as rifle shot, meant that the days of crossing the river in the tractor-wheeled bus should have been over. Ice breakup had begun.

Apart from the progress of the patients and the number of beds spilling out of the rooms into the hallways at any given time, breakup was the chief topic of conversation along the wards. They'd planted a flag in the ice mid-channel and laid bets for the day it would disappear. The pool grew to more than fifty dollars, but the money hardly mattered. Except for critical patients being evacuated by air, no one had been able to leave the island for the past two weeks. Ice breakup on any day was welcome news. Ruth refused to accept Hazel's unwillingness to participate, cajoling her for days, and Hazel finally relented. Her wager had been for yesterday, April 15.

She left her parka in the closet and took her navy wool cape instead. She heard voices in the kitchen, Ruth's and another she couldn't place. Ruth's hearty guffaw punctuated a story she was telling, something involving trousers. Hazel stopped to listen and then went out the door before Ruth finished. She could guess how it ended.

Still, the sight of a pair of men's trousers lifting and snapping in the wind at the top of the hospital flagpole made her pause.

Unmistakable trousers. She stopped and ruefully admired the spectacle: Charlie Wilcox was the only one in the hospital who wore the forest-green serge. He wouldn't take this well, nor would he find out who was responsible. She felt a little sorry for the man. Beneath his blustery contempt and impatience, she was starting to believe, lived a tender heart in need of the defenses he'd constructed around it. Yet he continued to make himself an easy target.

She headed for the far side of the property where the river bent away from the hospital and north toward James Bay. An iron-grey sky bore down. She'd come to appreciate its way of dominating all northern vistas; it had a way of putting them in their place. Man-made shelters were never more than bit players on this stage.

Although cracks had opened to wider fissures, serpentine windows on the deep blue-black silence of the water, as of yesterday the flag still stood between the hospital and Sawpit Island where they'd planted it, a brilliant red stain on the mid-channel ice.

Today the sombre grey-blue palette was uninterrupted: the river had swallowed the flag. She heard the ice chiming like broken glass before she saw it moving and stayed a safe distance from the shore. Losing her footing meant death if not by the water temperature then by the implacable, restless push of the ice that made its blind and fumbling way downstream. Some of the nurse's aides said it could heave ten-foot-high chunks of ice up on the shore and drag a body under the ice as easily.

She stood on the shore, wishing she'd brought her notebook and pencil. She'd heard about the impending breakup to the point of tedium, but seeing it was something else, even for the second time. All through the long months of winter the river had lain solemn and mute, a bridge to the mainland that someone could almost forget didn't exist in the warmer months. Now it was in motion, wide continents of ice interrupted by jagged oceans of numbing water, the whole mesmerizing parade of it moving in lockstep beside the mainland. She edged as close as she dared and picked a path on the thawing ground behind the hospital. The overnight snow was sinking into patches of dead grass that bent in the penetrating wind. Already several huge chunks of ice lay on the shore like rough gems, sent up on the land in the past few hours by the crush of restless new motion.

Further along, on the shore behind the hospital's outbuildings, there was a shift in the dull landscape. She squinted and picked out a familiar figure. Lachlan. The stiff wind picked up his hair and he held an object to his face. She lifted her hand but he didn't react until she was ten feet away.

"Oh! Hazel!" He tucked the object under his arm. His movie camera. Of course. He motioned for her to come closer. She saw his mouth move but only heard snatches of what he said.

"See ... Hazel? I ... the ... thing ..."

She shook her head. "Lachlan, I can't hear you."

He nodded and started toward her, almost losing his balance on the ice. When he reached her, she was chilled to the bone. It was still parka weather.

"Massive block of ice." He pointed. "Must be ten feet tall." This was the sort of thing that normally gave Lachlan joy; it was the reason he'd ordered the camera. Working in the north was the great adventure of his life. So why was he frowning? It came to her. He wasn't here to record the breakup. He was looking for something. Someone.

"Remarkable." The wind caught the lower edge of her cape and pushed it against her legs so that the fabric skimmed the swell of her belly. Lachlan gave no indication that he noticed anything. She'd known him for more than two years but he was still inscrutable. Could he be so wrapped up in what he was doing that he couldn't see what was plainly in front of him? "Not long now before we can get the canoes out."

He nodded. "Henry says three weeks."

She slipped her hands into her pockets and pulled the cape away from her body. "Some of the newer nurses are worrying that we won't have enough supplies to wait it out."

"Nonsense. I hope you told them so." Lachlan fiddled with the switches on the camera. "Spring breakup happens every year. We have plenty of food and medical supplies and the planes can still get in. We got some special roasts and stew beef just yesterday, in fact." His lips were mauve. He'd been out here awhile. "I'll be along shortly. You'd better go ahead."

Hazel was shivering. "Have you eaten?"

"Not yet. Wanted to get this on camera."

She started up the slope. "I'm going to the cafeteria. Can I order something for you?"

"Fried egg sandwich." He lifted the camera to his face. "White toast. Pepper. Tell them to make the eggs black with it." He turned away from the camera. "Thank you."

She picked her way up the slope, stepping between patches of polished ice that still clung to the bare earth path. Shiny aluminum pipes that carried steam between the power plant and the hospital webbed the sky. She opened the door at the back entrance, folded her cape over her arm and took the short staircase to the cafeteria.

Charlie was getting up from a table just as she reached the cashier. From the grim set of his mouth, she judged that he'd already seen the flagpole. She bit her lip to deflect the urge to smile but it was too late. He'd seen it.

"Morning, Doctor Wilcox."

"Nurse MacPherson. If you'll excuse me." He picked up his tray. He was wearing scrubs in the cafeteria. Someone must have filched the trousers from the dressing room while he was in early morning surgery. He was only ever seen wearing them outside the operating theatre very briefly, until he'd had the chance to change. Now he was stuck in them for the rest of the day.

Hazel sighed. "I didn't know anything about it. Honestly. I just saw it myself a few minutes ago. It's just a bit of fun, they don't mean..."

"I really don't have the time. There's work to be done around here, rather a lot of it in fact." He brushed past her and dropped his tray on the trolley. He was still muttering as he turned the corner to the main hall.

THE DOOR TO LACHLAN'S OFFICE was closed but she could hear his voice. He'd already begun the morning calls with posts further north. Hazel balanced the tray on one arm and eased the door open.

"Can't guarantee a flight out today, I'm afraid. The plane just left for Cochrane. I'll have to talk you through it." She caught his eye and he waved her inside, mouthed his thanks and motioned for her to set the tray down.

"Can you repeat that?" The woman's voice was coming through intermittently. Lachlan squinted and leaned closer to the radio. "It's a what?"

"An entry wound in the upper thigh. Can't find the exit."

"This is a patient you examined two days ago."

"That is correct."

"And you didn't see the wound then." Lachlan glanced at Hazel. There was a pause. "No, Doctor Davies. We were doing chest x-rays. He had the wound packed with moss and didn't mention it. But now his son has brought him back and wants me to look at it."

"Which you have done."

"Right. The skin is pink but not enflamed. It's healing well."

"Marvellous. How's his breathing?"

"Slightly accelerated, but not laboured."

Lachlan took a bite of sandwich and began moving around the room, lifting stacks of x-ray films until he found a book he wanted, red cloth with gold lettering on the spine. He picked it up and sat back down at the microphone and switched the gooseneck lamp on. She caught a glimpse of the title. *The Great White Plague*, exactly where he'd put it when she'd given it back to him.

"What's his name?"

"Abe. Tag number E5-214."

Lachlan chewed and flipped through the book. "He's lucky it didn't shatter his femur. Okay. This is what I want you to do for Abe." He gave detailed instructions and told her to expect the hospital plane to arrive in Povungnituk tomorrow, early afternoon, if she didn't call to say she'd found and extracted the bullet by tonight. Then he signed off. He flipped through the book and reached for the second half of his sandwich, and another call came across.

"Fort Albany to Moose Factory Indian Hospital."

"Go ahead, Fort Albany. This is Lachlan Davies."

There was a pause, and then the sound of a throat being cleared. "Message for Oda Vogel, sir, if you don't mind."

"Our children's ward nurse?"

"Yes, sir. From James Silverman."

"That would be you."

"Yes. Correct. Tell her . . ."

There was a pause. "Yes?" She'd heard him put James through his paces before. The Vogel-Silverman romance had been heard all along the coast since the bush pilot had left Moose Factory two weeks ago. He'd been besotted since Oda arrived from Holland and radioed several times a week with a message for her. Hazel found the whole thing irritating. She wasn't sure why she was still standing there.

"Go ahead, man, and be quick about it. These airwaves are reserved for medical calls." His voice was stern but Hazel saw the impish grin on his lips.

James cleared his throat again. "Sir, if it's not too much trouble, tell her I'll build her a house with four bedrooms. I want each of our children to have his own."

"Four bedrooms." Lachlan repeated it brusquely, and winked at Hazel. "Got it. Anything else? Quickly now."

"Sir. Tell her I'll be back in Moose by Friday. And thank you, sir."

"Pleasure. Good day."

Lachlan switched the microphone off and picked up his sandwich. Crumbs speckled his lab coat and with his free hand he lifted papers from his desk and set them back down. "You'll tell her, won't you? I'll be along in a minute."

Hazel nodded. There was an odd pressure behind her eyes. She'd never wanted the white-picket dream, not ever before and not now. The sticky-sweet thought of it was suffocating, in fact, and she wondered if Silverman knew what a fool he was, talking like that. So why did she feel so hollow?

"Ah, here it is."

She wasn't sure he was speaking to her, but it didn't matter. What she needed was air. Lachlan was studying the booklet he'd finally found, the fingers of one hand pressed to his lips while the others tapped the desk. When he stopped tapping and reached for his pen, she left his office, closed the door softly and followed the hallway out the main doors.

THE HORMONAL FLOOD THAT HAD surely been responsible for her reaction to Silverman's call subsided, leaving her damp and spent but calm and clear-minded. In eight weeks this would all be over. Until then, managing would be a matter of engaging her nurse's brain. Temporary. This was temporary. Pregnancy was responsible for this riot of emotions and it would soon be over.

There was an explosion of laughter in the hall that could only be Ruth's. Hazel left the nurses' station and made a mental note to send an aide to fetch the tray of bottles of apple juice still sitting on the counter for the little ones. They ought to have gone out already.

Just inside the heavy ward doors, the group of waiting RNs clustered around Ruth, whose head was thrown back in laughter. "What I wouldn't give to have been a fly on the wall when he came out of surgery!" Ruth was laughing so hard she had to wipe tears away with one hand and hold the handrail with the other. "You saw it when you came in, Hazel?" Some of the other nurses laughed with her, a little nervously. There were furtive glances at Hazel's belly.

Hazel was a little surprised at the risk Ruth was taking. Charlie could come around the corner at any moment. "I did. And the expression on his face in the cafeteria this morning."

"If only he wasn't such an easy target," Ruth murmured. "It's too tempting. I can't help myself."

Lachlan turned the corner at a brisk pace. Ruth brushed her eyes and cleared her throat. "Doctor Davies. Good morning."

"Good morning, Nurse Ames." He raised an eyebrow and nudged the bridge of his glasses. Even under normal circumstances, Lachlan would have been unlikely to show more than mild disapproval, but there was a breathlessness to him today. He was too preoccupied to take even a slight interest in staff discipline. "And good morning to all of you. I have good news. Some of you have noticed that we've been testing an alternating streptomycin regimen to give our most ill patients the best possible chance. And watching closely, of course." He rubbed the short hair on the back of his head. He'd finally had it cut. "Well, I reviewed six months of data this morning, and I'm pleased to report that we're winning the war. You'll have seen the improvements on the wards yourselves, and you can rest assured that we've also avoided adverse reactions." He glanced at Hazel. She'd had sole responsibility for the auditory testing. He'd demanded regular, meticulous reporting, and she'd complied, too deep in the swamp of her own turmoil to detect the undercurrent to his motivation until now. It was more than an adjusted treatment regimen; it was an attempt to compensate. "Our patients are doing exceptionally well. So good work, all of you. Thanks. That's it."

Lachlan turned and disappeared around the corner. She couldn't be sure that the rest of the nurses were thinking about Suujuq too, but there was an unusual silence. Ruth was the first to speak. "Carry on, the man says. Off you go."

TWENTY-EIGHT

IF I'D BEEN PAYING CLOSER attention I might have seen it coming. I might have sensed it in the dulling of his sharp tongue or the sudden disappearance of his chronic impatience. He'd stopped checking his watch so obsessively when we spoke. I'd assumed that this meant that he'd stopped trying to graft his Toronto template onto Moose Factory. I couldn't decide whether the peace he'd made with it signalled a willingness to yield to the pace of life on the island or was merely evidence that he could be worn down. I was wrong on both counts.

It hadn't occurred to me that I might be receiving special treatment. In my defense he hadn't shown the slightest hint of affection toward anyone in the hospital. He held the world in a kind of universal contempt to keep it at a safe distance but tolerated the other staff. I assumed that he did this to make his own life easier. Conflict has an emotional cost as you know. He'd sought the isolation of a remote community for a reason. I kept expecting him to leave for a job somewhere even further north. Which he did eventually do.

To truly make sense of the way he blindsided me you must understand how distant I had become from my own body. I'd closed the door on a basic level of honesty with myself. In the first few months I didn't yet know what had begun, but I'd been a nurse long enough to have learned that to be ruled by major or minor discomforts was to be labelled neurotic and weak. I thought I could bully into submission what I was feeling because I'd done it often enough. The morning sickness was minor enough to allow me to talk myself out of it.

I was working hard so I had a handy explanation for the amenorrhea. It had happened once before in high school when I'd been training for long-distance running and had lost too much body fat to menstruate. Of course I wasn't as lean as I'd been but I reasoned that I was also no longer the girl I was at sixteen. I knew I was tired because I'd fall asleep with my head on my arms in the cafeteria but I told myself that it was the long hours I was keeping – I'd become Lachlan's right-hand man so to speak – and the emotional load of the ordeal I could share with no one. Not even Ruth could have understood.

Of course there's a point beyond which self-deception becomes full-blown delusion and I wasn't that far gone. When Ruth called me out the day Suujuq disappeared I accepted it. However upsetting or inconvenient the reality was I would handle it and not by throwing myself off a cliff or using a coat hanger either. My moral centre was still intact even if the discovery that I was carrying a child blew the doors off my life. This was 1951, remember. In some places pregnancy was still considered an embarrassment to be kept from the public eye. Even married women routinely stopped working beyond the sixth month. Showing themselves in public in that condition was considered indecent.

I had no intention of quitting nursing. It wasn't a job. It was my life. Before all of this happened I even entertained the idea of going back to school and becoming a doctor. There was so much to be done. Money and curiosity brought a constant stream of nurses and doctors but most stayed a maximum of six months so it seemed that there were never enough hands to do the work. I stayed in the hope that the isolation of the place would mean more play in the social rules of the time than I could ever expect to find at home.

Not that I had thought beyond the pregnancy to what I'd do once the child arrived. I was as blind to the future as most first-time mothers. More so actually, because without the happy distraction of nursery planning there was little reason to see the end of the pregnancy as anything more than an end to my embarrassing predicament. That's not completely honest. It wasn't that it didn't occur to me that I was having a baby but I had become adept at exiling those thoughts to distant emotional territories.

Ruth began sharing her uniforms. She knocked on the door one morning as I was dressing and handed one to me. "Yours is going to rip if you ask much more of it and I know for a fact that your underwear is nothing to write home about." She said this after I'd refused to tell her anything when Gideon died and only barely acknowledged her accurate assessment of my condition. It was unwise of me to push away the one person who could have helped but there you have it. Why she continued to stand by me I couldn't understand and still don't. When I was finally ready to talk about it she was gone. At the time I accepted the uniform without comment and ordered more from the hospital seamstress the following day. I wore the waistband high and reasoned that the full skirt hid the swell below it. I told myself that it did. No one else said anything except the one person I least expected to hear it from.

I interpreted this lack of commentary as evidence that I'd successfully hidden the thickening of my waist. I dodged the other more obvious explanation that no one said anything because they were avoiding me in general. Conversations about anything other than medical issues had dwindled to almost nothing.

At some point I decided that standing with my back against the wall would make my profile less obvious and I avoided resting my hands on my belly. It's laughable that I had convinced myself that I was still hiding the pregnancy in the seventh month. I was a wisp of a thing and no one would notice the beach ball under my dress? You see the depths of my desperation and also the strange complicity of the staff. I assumed that they looked the other way out of sympathy or overwork or a desire to avoid conflict but there was also the matter of the baby's paternity, known only to me. At least one of the possibilities would have guaranteed the silence of the entire staff.

He caught me one day with my hands on my belly. At some point the gesture became reflex in spite of my best efforts. The baby had just turned itself I think. It was disorienting and I lost my bearings like when a swell rocks the ship and you grab something to hold onto. The expression on his face was something between terror and resignation. Now that I think of it he was probably mirroring my own.

He said nothing at that point. He just moved on once he'd found his feet again, but later that day he chanced upon me in the supply closet. I'd left the door open so I suppose he saw his chance. He walked in and closed the door behind him. Here it comes, I thought. The morality police have arrived and I'm going to have to leave the north. My mind was flailing around for a plan but hitting on nothing that was remotely logical. Adrenaline blocked my ability to think clearly. A single thought appeared on the marquee of my mind and crowded out all else: Say it and I'll scratch your eyeballs out.

He dropped to one knee, Jude. Just like that. No preamble. I can't even remember what he said but the sheer vulnerability of him in that position disarmed me. There was real need in his voice and it changed him utterly. I'd never heard it before. He was like the tin man after the heart. I imagined how someone might love him in different circumstances. Even me. He might have made a good father.

When I saw him reach into his pocket I couldn't allow it. If he'd pulled out a ring I might have fallen apart with no possibility for recovery. It could not go this way. To get himself this far he had obviously constructed an image of me that was generous beyond measure and so far removed from the truth that any life we might have built together would have balanced on a thread. He didn't know me at all. How could he? I didn't know myself.

I'd like to say that I was gentle in my refusal and I helped him see how wrong this was for the both of us and I pleaded with him for understanding and we had a tearful embrace built on a clear-eyed assessment of the situation. That might have been possible if a chorus of hormones hadn't been singing in my veins and I had not in that moment gained an honest appreciation of what I had left to do, if I had not been exhausted with the emotional effort of seven months of self-deception. This is not an excuse for my behaviour but an explanation.

I see his face in the moment after I'd finished speaking: he had the attitude of a patient with internal bleeding and the sickly smile of acquiescence. He stood stiffly and opened his mouth as if to say something but didn't. When he left the room I pulled the door closed. I don't know how long I stayed there. A minute, an hour? My disappearance in the middle of a shift might have been remarkable but nothing was said to me. I didn't cry.

The only way on or off the island was by air. This was ice breakup time. But he must have packed his bags that night because he was gone in the morning. I heard Ruth say he'd gone to the Belcher Islands. I wondered how he'd found a flight so fast. Sometimes even medical evacuations had to wait a few days. They must have been desperate for a medic up there. Better to have him gone, someone said. I can't remember who.

He's dead now, pancreatic cancer a few years back. Lachlan sent a letter with a clipping of the obituary from the *Canadian Medical Association Journal*. He never married.

Charlie Wilcox, you were a decent man. I didn't deserve you.

TWENTY-NINE

"NURSE MACPHERSON." JOSEPH PUSHED THE door to the second floor open and held it for Hazel. She had a nagging sense that she'd agreed to be somewhere that morning and was heading to the nurses' station to check. "Nurse Ames asks if you can come."

Aha. Maybe that was it. "Is she expecting me?"

Joseph shrugged. "She sent me to find you. Please come."

She fell into step with Joseph. "Where is she?"

"Women's ward. A baby is coming."

They reached the second floor. Low moans were coming from obstetrics now, and she followed them. Joseph turned in the opposite direction. His steps along the hallway were heavy. He'd accepted Suujuq's death without comment and carried on with his work, though the emotional toll was visible in his face for weeks afterward. The thought that in a couple of months she'd probably never see him again surfaced with an abrupt intensity; she didn't consider herself sentimental. It might not even be true. He might decide to wear the turquoise scrubs for the rest of his career, to stay in the place that had become his only home, and she might continue here, afterwards. Her mind branched toward a different future, one that could still include this place, this work, these people. Ruth. Lachlan. Joseph.

The surge of hope subsided. It could not go this way, no matter how she tried to blinker herself. A baby would be born between now and then, and that would change everything. She took a deep breath.

"So he found you."

"He found me." Hazel stepped into the private room with Ruth. Pitsiaq sat in a chair beside the bed, where a labouring Inuit woman was propped up, legs bent under the covers. Her dark eyes held Hazel's with the defiance she'd seen in other women giving birth, a kind of fierce confidence they might not otherwise possess. Hazel watched the woman's gaze find the swelling belly under her uniform.

"Everything okay, Captain?"

"Absolutely." Hazel stood up straighter. The work and the work and the work. It would see her through. "I'm fine."

"Good. This one's transitioning to heavy labour. Thought you should come if you were free." Hazel had never explicitly agreed to midwifery training, but Ruth had proceeded as though she had. She didn't object. Ruth was one of the few staff members who would speak with her on a regular basis. "Pitsiaq is giving me a hand with translation."

Ruth took the woman's hand in hers. "Okay now, mama. Like this." She forced air from her lips in short bursts and Pitsiaq spoke in a low voice. The woman closed her eyes and began breathing like Ruth.

"She's only five centimetres. She won't be ready to push for a few hours yet." Ruth held the woman's gaze while talking with Hazel. "But she's doing just fine."

"Anything particular you'd like me to do?"

"Pour some water for her. Her mouth will be dry."

Hazel handed the cup to the woman, who tried to accept it with a shaking hand. "Hold it for her. The adrenaline is a little much at this point."

Hazel put the cup to the woman's lips. "Oxytocin, prolactin, adrenaline. Contraction, lactation, action." Ruth chanted like it was a schoolyard rhyme. "The mighty three of labour. Her body knows what it needs to do to help this baby out, doesn't it, mama?" She stroked the woman's hand. "It could be hours yet but some walking will help. Let's get her up."

The woman's legs, swollen and dusted with fine dark hair, made a snail's progress to the edge of the bed. She sat for a moment and glanced at Pitsiaq, then pushed herself to standing. "See? Her body knows what to do. I'm just here for company."

The woman moaned. Hazel reached for her instinctively and laid a hand on her back. "Is the father here?"

"Yes. She's sick too, but pregnancy holds the disease at bay. Nature's way of protecting the vessel." She shot Hazel a wry smile. "She's been feeling well since she arrived in the fall, almost symptom-free. Once this baby comes, though, look out. Davies is thinking pneumothorax along with the drugs."

Hazel nodded. A high percentage of women with TB died within a year of delivery so they needed to be aggressive. Pitsiaq listened, turning her head toward each woman as she spoke.

"What is pneumothorax?"

Hazel glanced at Ruth. "There's a membrane around your lung called the pleura. If we fill that space with air, the lung collapses. That means it doesn't move when you breathe. With that stillness, the body can help the lung heal."

Pitsiaq nodded, but she was frowning. "Can she breathe?"

"Oh yes!" Ruth put a hand on the young woman's shoulder. "We only collapse the part of the lung that is sick. The rest functions normally. But she will have to rest."

The labouring woman moaned again and Hazel rubbed her back. "We can't let her breastfeed the baby, then."

"Nope. She won't like that, but the risk of infection is too high. Baby has no natural immunity."

Hazel's stomach lurched. "But as long as we separate them, the baby will be fine."

"No guarantees. You know that." Ruth took the woman's arm and started toward the door. "Sometimes the disease crosses the placenta. It's rare but fatal, usually within days of birth. Only one since I've been here. If she'd come to us early enough, we'd have terminated."

"Right." Hazel swallowed. It was too late to matter. "I did know."

"Alright now." Ruth fixed Hazel with a gimlet eye. "Enough of that, now. It's rare. In all likelihood, mama and baby will be just fine. We'll give them the best care. Let's walk with her. That's what she needs right now."

"Actually, I've got to get to the children's ward." She released the woman's arm. "I've just remembered they're short-staffed this morning."

"Sure. Pitsiaq will walk with us, won't she?" The young woman nodded. "You go."

"GOOD. YOU'RE HERE." LACHLAN STOOD in the doorway. Hazel was halfway through the daily doses of streptomycin and isoniazid in the children's ward. Sally was following with the PAS tablets and apple juice. "It must have been at least fifteen minutes before I realized that I was talking to myself."

"My apologies, Doctor Davies." She felt Sally's probing gaze. "You were busy and I'd promised to be up here by eight-thirty." She set the syringe on the tray and carried it to the next bed.

"Fair enough. In any case, I worked something out this morning. Meet me at the end of the hall in a couple of minutes. Bring the other nurses. I only need five minutes." He didn't wait for her response.

She pinched the skin on Eddie Kapashesit's arm and gave the injection. He grimaced but was silent. A slight, fine-boned eight-year-old, he'd arrived six months earlier speaking only Cree and was now beginning to answer in English for the other Cree children in the room. It was a status he protected with every staff interaction. He also volunteered to be the first for new treatments. Hazel wiped his arm with an alcohol swab and patted his shoulder. He frowned and pulled away.

"Pancakes with maple syrup for breakfast this morning, I hear."

"Yes, miss." His solemn gaze was fixed on a point at the other side of the room and his hair stood up at the crown where it had been pressed against the pillow. "Pancakes are good."

She finished with the injections and left Sally to do the same with the tablets. At the nurse's station she untied her mask, slipped out of her ward gown and washed her hands to the elbows. Some of the other nurses had begun to follow this protocol along with her. Ruth was not among them, though she and a number of other nurses had tested positive to the tuberculin within the past six months. Hers was a robust immune system, she insisted, able to keep the bacteria in check. She was fond of pointing out that not all positive tuberculin tests yielded symptoms. The monthly x-rays obliged by the positive test supported her claim. So far, her lungs were clean.

HAZEL FOUND SALLY FINISHING UP at the end of the hall. Sun-light streamed through the east windows of the sunroom.

"Have they all had their tablets?"

She nodded. "Once Eddie takes his, they all do." She tipped a paper cup to the lips of an Inuit toddler at her side and rubbed her back. "*Taima?*" she said to the girl. "Finished?" Hazel watched Sally's lithe movements, her slender waist. "Not so easy for the little ones to swallow."

"Yes, a chewable form would be an improvement." Outside the window, the river lurched by, alive again after six months of glacial stillness. "Breakup started this morning. Did you see?"

"Oh-uh-yeah. Happens every year."

"I suppose so." Hazel cleared her throat. "There's a tray of bot-tles in the nurses' station. Please see that it goes out."

"I will." Sally picked up her tray and started to walk out of the room. She stopped just before she entered the hall and cocked her head in response to a sound that they both heard, a nasal hiccup-honk that repeated just as she started to move again. It was familiar and alien at the same time, and it took Hazel a minute to figure out why.

"That sounds close."

"Too close."

"Do you think –"

"If there is a goose inside the hospital," Sally said, as she walked out the door and set the tray on a trolley, "we need to find it."

They strode through the hall and stopped at the doorway to each room. The beds were empty in the second room. A cluster of dark-haired boys were barefoot and jostling at the two windows, both open wide to the April chill.

"Children! Back to your beds. Immediately." Translation was unnecessary. They made their reluctant way back to their beds.

The tallest of them gave one last longing glance over his shoulder before he climbed back into his bed. Once under the covers, he sat bolt upright and craned his neck toward the window.

Hazel made her way across the room. Surely there was no novelty in ice breakup for these boys. But then she heard the nasal call again, closer. Sally went to the window and leaned out.

"*Ki shash taw*! Nurse MacPherson, come quick!"

The room had been built for three beds. Five had occupied the space since early October. Hazel rolled one away from the window and went to it. Her belly bumped the sill. She couldn't keep up with her changing dimensions. She leaned her forehead against the glass.

It was a few minutes before she could assimilate what she was seeing. She'd always been peripherally aware of migration as geese made their cacophonous way through Toronto twice a year, but this flock was in confused disarray. This was no sleek arrow of wings in the sky. It was an unbalanced spiral that looped loosely over the hospital, its rough centre point the window of Eddie's room.

Sally laid a finger to her lips and waved Hazel closer. With some difficulty, Hazel manoeuvred her body until she was leaning out of the window with her. Eddie was to their immediate left. The sound they were hearing was coming from between his clasped hands, folded in an intricate configuration that swelled and collapsed at his face. If he saw the two nurses leaning out the window next to his, he hid it well.

Eddie didn't impose his call on the flock as much as he offered it, and he waited at the completion of each call for a reply from the geese. He listened and waited, motionless. He called, the geese answered.

Hazel pulled back from the window and wiped her eyes before she turned back to the room. There was so much about these people that she didn't understand. Sally laid a hand on her arm.

"Let him," she said, misinterpreting Hazel's silence. "He won't hold them long. It is against the teachings."

The children in the ward watched Hazel with intense curiosity. She cleared her throat. "Let's get them ready for lunch. It won't be goose, but let's hope it's not bologna."

Sally gave her a wry smile. "Too bad. For goose, they would have an appetite."

Joseph pushed the lunch trolley along the hall with slow, easy strides, in deference to the tray of hot water that sloshed under the pan of meat. Chicken, by the smell of it. Hazel checked her watch. She hadn't heard a goose call in five minutes.

Sally nodded. "I heard the geese leaving."

The window in Eddie's room was still wide open and he stood motionless beside it. He was shivering. She stood beside him and put her hand on his shoulder. His toes curled.

"Eddie, you'll catch a chill." She kept her voice low and calm. "Back to your bed, now."

His eyes were glassy with fever. "My father is a great hunter, *ka ntaw hoot*. He will take me hunting when I leave this place." The other boys in the room sat taller in their beds.

"Yes." Hazel pulled the blanket to his shoulders and tucked it in around him. "You will be a great hunter. But you must get better first." She wanted to smooth his hair, stroke his back, but she caught herself. She wouldn't do that to him in full view of the other boys. "Please tell the others that lunch is coming."

THIRTY

WOULD YOU BELIEVE ME IF I told you that I toyed with the idea of staying? Maybe Ruth's broad hints as my pregnancy progressed finally wore me down or maybe I realized how much I needed her. Where would I have gone? I hadn't kept up any of my friendships in the south, so wholly had I given myself to the cause of eradicating tuberculosis in this lifetime. I had family and I'd written a couple of letters to them but I'd been unable to construct a plausible version of the conversation I'd need to have when I showed up at their door in my current state. I had painted myself into a corner.

You'll remember that I'd found that cabin, Jude. One morning in late May after I'd been forced to concede that twelve hours on my feet was no longer possible I set a basket of food into a canoe and pointed it toward Sawpit Island. There were still stars. I intended to get across before day came. I left a note for Ruth: *I'll be back when and if I desire it.*

I was alone and then I wasn't. Henry appeared wanting to row me across. I said no because my mind went leaping ahead to the scene of his departure almost before he'd finished the sentence. He'd unload everything for me and then I'd have to watch him go and that was something I knew I couldn't bear if I meant to hold myself together. And I did. I reasoned that taking myself there would be proof of my self-sufficiency. I would simply let the current carry me back across the channel when the time came. If nothing else you will understand the direction of this logic as evidence of my desperation. Henry folded his arms and stared at me. I assumed this was his version of an argument.

I held my ground but wondered if Lachlan had sent him. What I mean by wondered is hoped. Lachlan had gestured vaguely when I'd told him I had to stop working and mumbled something I couldn't decode per se but then how meaningless words are in such situations and how impossible for him. I wouldn't have expected him to finesse the conversation and might have been disappointed if he'd come up with more than that because it would have meant that I was wide of the mark in my reading of him. But he didn't and I wasn't. What had been going on under his nose was entirely out of his ken. He'd been unable to broach the subject even once. He had stopped handing me journal articles and showing me x-rays at some point and I was preoccupied enough not to notice. I suppose this was the strongest statement he could manage. At some point I registered the fact that he rarely called me by name anymore and let myself suppose that our friendship had reached another level. He hadn't gone back to using my last name either but if he'd been a stuttering man I sensed it would have given him trouble.

I took no joy in the fetal movements. When I lay on my back to watch the clouds and my belly moved of its own accord like a thing possessed I would shut my eyes and will it to be still. I told myself that if I was to get through this I'd have to hold myself at a distance this way. I couldn't give in to the onslaught of hormones if I hoped to survive the birth with my sanity intact. If I caught myself laying a hand on my belly or daydreaming about the colour of my baby's hair I would force myself to ponder names, I suppose as some kind of bizarre act of contrition since any consideration of names would invariably lead to the way Daniel had become Gideon and vice versa. You can appreciate the depths of my misery. I was stewing in my own juices.

Summer was coming. The blackflies were wolfish. I had food for roughly two weeks if I'd had an appetite. I ate mechanically and some days porridge alone. I didn't get past considering which corner of the cabin would best suit a cradle if I had one. The wood was running low. The circuits I made of the forest behind the cabin to comb the ground for fallen branches had grown increasingly time-consuming to the point that I'd spend the morning finding enough for the evening's fire. It was hard to know whether this was a factor of distance or whether it reflected the slowing of my own pace. The pinched nerve that appeared early in the eighth month ran like an electric shock down the back of my leg with each step I took. The goose step that characterized my walks might have been comical if I'd had someone to share it with.

Henry showed up one morning. He told me that I'd been out there for two weeks and it was time to come back. It was not good for me to be alone now. *Now* was obviously a relative term denoting the advanced stage of my pregnancy. Somewhat disingenuously considering the food and fuel situation I said that the only person who could decide that I should come back was me. Come back where exactly? Henry crossed his arms. The foreign sound of my own voice was a confirmation of how long I'd been alone. I held the question like a shield between us as though there was no possible rejoinder for such a well-crafted argument. Henry lifted a hand to my shoulder. "My sister will help. I have talked to her."

He caught me on the way down and came to his knees as he eased me to mine. I couldn't decide whether I wanted to hold on to him and never let go or lay open his throat. The cost of the eight-month effort of holding myself apart had been tallied in that moment and I was overdrawn. I cried without shame. I knew I would not stay with his sister but neither could I stay here. I had people of my own. Henry helped me gather my things without another word.

I couldn't look at him until we had reached the other side and I had to tell him that I would not go with him to his sister's place. I knew I could stay in my room at the nurses' residence for one more night. He didn't seem surprised. I had an immediate paranoid suspicion that he or someone else had guessed that an offer of help would expose my vulnerability, but it was a fleeting thought made irrelevant by the movement in my belly.

Ruth hugged me, hard, before I'd made it past the door. I was so beyond caring that I didn't notice whether there were other nurses in the common room, much less worry about prying eyes. She led me to my room. It was the second time in the pregnancy she'd insisted on an exam. In the past we'd spoken in strictly clinical terms as though my body was a third person in the room because I had not allowed it to go further than that. Now she forced the issue with little resistance from me. Where did I intend to have this baby? It would come when it was ready. It was obvious to me that she wanted to catch this baby and was also prepared for the fact that I wouldn't allow it. She knew me well enough by that point. I said I'd figure it out. She withdrew her hand and lowered the sheet she'd brought as if modesty was an issue. "Will you? This baby is about to drop." There was a hard brightness in her voice that I hadn't heard before. "You always say babies are born every day." My tone was harsher than I'd intended. It's curious to me now that I thought I could mask my fear that way. I knew what was coming. I'd been assisting her for months. To the rest of the staff I was apprenticing but we both knew I had no intention of becoming a midwife.

She coughed away from me and into a tissue. I'd noticed that she'd been doing that since I'd come back. "You ought to have that checked out," I said. "You have enough to deal with," she said. "It's all under control. I'm fine."

"Me too." I mimicked her tone even as I understood the full scope of this quandary. Whatever I could see or understand about the state of her health was out of my control. I could no more force the issue of her health than she, mine. She was an adult capable of making her own decisions. I could only suggest. That was the way I saw it then. I'd like to say that any helplessness I felt was mitigated by the knowledge that she was working in one of the largest sanatoriums in Canada. Surely someone would notice and take care of her. Don't we tell ourselves these kinds of half-truths?

"Please, Hazel." Ruth's tone unnerved me and my stomach lurched in the grip of the clammy fear I'd been trying to keep at bay. She had dropped the stern and bossy note that characterized her dealings with expectant mothers. I wanted to conclude that this change in behaviour proved her own illness, not underscored the gravity of my situation.

"Don't worry," I said. The words tasted like ashes. "I'm going home."

THIRTY-ONE

THE WEIGHT OF HER BELLY made it possible to sleep for only a couple of hours at a time. When she finally gave up on sleep it was five a.m., twelve hours until her train left Moosonee for the journey south. She lifted a maternity smock over her head and ran a brush through her hair. All that she intended to take with her fit into a small suitcase and she left that on the floor beside her bed. She'd be back for it later.

She approached the bottom stairs and listened for signs of life. Silence, and the kitchen was empty. Too early for even Ruth, who rose without fail to put the coffee on at six. She put a handful of saltines in her pocket and filled her canteen with water. Outside she was immediately aware of distant voices and the clunk of one object against another. Men were at the hospital dock, readying the *Mercer*, no doubt. The survey season was underway again and the boats left early to make the most of the long summer days. Would Lachlan be on it? She hadn't spoken to him since she'd left for Sawpit two weeks earlier.

Already the light below the low shelf of clouds had begun to pink the sky. Out of habit she lifted her wrist, but she'd forgotten her watch. She wasn't in a hurry but half-expected Ruth to have noticed she was gone and caught up with her by now. On the way down the stairs she thought she'd heard the familiar squeak of a hinge. It would have been odd for Ruth to let her go, considering the conversation they'd had last night. She glanced over her shoulder. No one. It didn't matter. She'd made her decision.

Between the residence and the shore, the road became a path and then disappeared completely in places, but the late June air coming off the water was soft and warm and a light breeze lifted Hazel's hair. It was a good morning for a last walk around Moose Factory. She could watch the sun light the inner reaches of the island. If the tide was low, she could walk along the shore.

She picked up a fallen branch, pulled off the spindly offshoot to make it a walking stick, and edged down the soft slope east of the hospital dock. Across the channel was the cabin on Sawpit. In the morning light it was obviously inadequate as a home, but the fact that she hadn't fashioned a crib of any description was evidence that she'd never really intended to stay until the child was born.

Henry was on the dock with a few other deckhands. He stopped mid-reach and Hazel caught his eye. She raised her hand to him and assumed that the walking stick would tell the rest of the story. He turned back to his work.

A wide ribbon of sand joined the water to the low cliffs above it, and she stayed where the ground was firm enough to walk easily. She found a rhythm that made walking bearable, even with the pinched nerve that continued to shock her left leg reliably. Wild grasses along the beach bent in the breeze and brushed her legs. Water lapped against the shore and a regatta of seabirds rested in the shallow water. The land around the hospital had been cleared of trees almost entirely but just ahead was the balsam and poplar forest that dotted the west shore almost to the northern tip. Leaves turned in the breeze and sounded like rain.

She hadn't been back to his camp in eight months. The constable had crossed her path one day after the autopsy and wanted her to know that he'd located next of kin and sent all of Gideon's belongings south to his father in Minnesota. That had been enough for the months that followed. It had been easy to stay away until now, easy like sleeping during a thunderstorm, and the longer she stayed away the deeper she slept. But she was awake now.

Even if on some level she recognized the disconnect that this line of thinking required, it appalled her that the police investigation had been so brief. How easy for them, even convenient, to be rid of him. No one missed him. No one else.

She told herself that his camp would not have changed except for his absence, which of course would transform it utterly. Without his tent and campfire, would she recognize it at all? She tried to visualize the piece of land itself. The clearing was large enough for a tent and campfire and not much more. A tamarack stood near the shore, and his tent beside that. No. That wasn't right. The tamarack was behind the tent, and the tent was at the edge of a slope that rose five feet from the river. She recalled thinking, on first seeing it, that if the water rose a few feet higher it might carry his tent away, but by the time spring breakup swelled the river, he'd already been gone six months.

She noticed a tree with split bark, an old injury that had healed but left a sliver of naked trunk between swaths of curling bark. The marker Gideon had carved into the bark would have weathered by now but the shape of it would still be distinct, wouldn't it? Less than a year had passed. She felt a nervy sweat on the back of her neck, heard the words as if he stood behind her. *Try harder. Listen.* And then: *You are being watched.* This was no casual stroll, whatever she'd told herself. Could the pepper sauce box still be there? If searchers had found it, the money inside would have guaranteed public involvement. It was not the sort of discovery that could be kept quiet.

There was a pounding in her ears and her pulse quickened with her steps. She stopped and put her hand in the pocket of her dress for the saltines. She must pace herself. There was no hurry. If the box hadn't been found by now, it would be there whether she arrived in an hour or a month.

The sun slipped up over the horizon, marking the heavy underbellies of the clouds with livid, refracted light. She made slow progress along the shore as the sun burned away the cloud cover. The dark chocolate of the river became milky as it crossed into sunlight. She could see the curve of land that marked the northern tip of Moose Factory. His camp was near.

Birdsong rose almost imperceptibly, a wall of sound that was an agitation rather than a pleasure. It felt irreverent, like laughter in a church. A harsh, grating, mechanical bleat distinguished itself from the soft arc of the morning chorus. It ended as abruptly as it began. She stopped, waiting for it to repeat. When it did, she moved closer to the water's edge and scanned the trees that stood above the shore. Could she pick out a nest on her own? Gideon pointed one out once, high in the canopy. She remembered it as a tidy bundle of twigs that was almost invisible against the trunk. Gideon had always seemed to have a visceral awareness of a falcon's presence. Not so for her.

She checked the treetops, beginning to hope that she might see one huddled there. The call stopped. Did they hunt this early in the morning? The sky was cerulean now. If the falcon swung out over the water, its dark blade of flight would be easily visible.

By the kink in her neck she knew she'd watched long enough. The train would leave Moosonee at five and there were still things to be done. She started walking again when a shape streaked from the trees and looped higher and higher above the ground. She waited for the falcon to drop from the sky and felt Gideon's breath on the back of her neck, saw his arms lifting in the half-light, felt her pulse accelerate. She closed her eyes, felt the blue burn of his gaze, the surge deep in her belly, the drag of her arms on the air. She opened her eyes and the falcon was gone.

The rising heat of the day lay on her skin like a wet cloth. She lifted her hair off her neck, twisted it and fed a twig through the coil to hold it in place. Not far now. The intervals between the rhythmic contracting and relaxing of her belly shrank as her pace increased, but there was no pain. These false contractions had been going on for weeks now. Ruth predicted another week and Hazel had watched her with other pregnant women long enough to know that her sense in these matters was unwavering and true. She would have believed Ruth if she had told the hour as well as the day.

She edged her way up the slope, planting her stick as she went, and stood in the clearing. Stones still marked the perimeter of the firepit. The white pine was just outside of her peripheral vision. Her face was wet with tears.

She opened the canteen. The water was still cool. Out of the corner of her eye she saw a flicker of white among the branches of the tamarack. A white enamel mug, spotted with rust, rocked on its perch in the branches, just out of reach. She found herself eyeing the trunk for toeholds. She'd move with care. It couldn't be more than a couple of feet up the trunk. She imagined the cool metal smoothness. She would take it home, keep it safe, have it for her own.

She found a handhold and lifted one foot to the scaly bark before she stopped herself. She took one last look at the mug and then backed away from the tree. If she was to get through this she must maintain some control, even if her hormones urged otherwise. She was a nurse. It was her job to be calm under pressure. She could do this.

The carving on the white pine had weathered but was still distinct, and the bed of needles under the tree was as she remembered. She came to her knees and swept them to one side, thinking that she could use a walking stick to dig if she needed to, but the ground was soft and came away from the lid with little effort. She tapped the wood but it rang without echo, and the fact that the box was not empty settled like a weight on her chest. He'd never had the chance to take it to the Northwest Passage. This was left undone. She wiped her eyes and pushed the dirt away from the box until her fingers found the edge of the lid. She traced the shape of it and felt for the latch at the front. There was none. The lid moved on simple hinges. She'd only have to find its lower edge to lift it.

She stopped and eased herself back on her heels. Her belly tightened and she laid a hand on it. What kind of fool's errand was this? She had neither the intention nor the ability to finish what he'd started, and she'd thought the idea peculiar in the first place. For a moment she thought she might sweep the pine needles back over the lid and return the way she came. There was grace and nobility to this idea, enough to carry her home. She could step away from this, leave it behind, untangle herself from the wild delirium of his existence. His belongings would be lost to the world.

She was brushing the dirt from her knees when she knew she couldn't leave without it. It had pulled her into its gravity just as he had pulled her into his. She saw him as he had been on that first day at the clinic, a crooked smile on his mouth. *I've come about the umbrellas.* It had been his constant companion. It had absorbed his warmth and chafed his skin. However misguided his intentions, there was beauty in his tenacity and the singularity of his vision even now. She couldn't leave this to rot in the ground.

The lid wouldn't budge the first time she tried to lift it and she had to work the edges longer than she'd expected to free it. She held her breath. It was possible that the money was gone, replaced with something else, or that it had never really been there at all. Was she prepared for anything? It hardly mattered now. She slipped her fingers under the lid and lifted it.

The rows of bills were untouched. In her heart she'd known and expected this. The effect of the knife's absence she hadn't. She saw him brushing the earth from the lid before coming to find her that day. Her chest felt tight. He opened the box, and then what? Was it easy for him, or had he laboured over the decision before letting his fingers touch the bone handle? He intended to be back, but later; this much was obvious in the fact that the lid was hidden with soil and branches. He would have had to lay the knife on the ground while he did that, one more opportunity to walk away from what he intended to do, and yet he hadn't. It all seemed so deliberate, measured. Calculated.

She struggled to remain in control. If she expected to make the journey home, she must do this. There was a child and she might never practice medicine again. No one knew the money was here and she might need it. It occurred to her that Gideon might have taken the knife out for another reason, earlier in the day, another day even, that he might not have dug it up with the intention of coming to find her. She wanted this to be true.

She came to her feet and pulled on the leather shoulder strap, an old belt that Gideon had screwed to the sides of the box. Nothing. She took a wider stance, grasped the belt with both hands and pulled again. Still nothing. The rain and the snow over the past eight months had packed the ground around the box. She picked up her walking stick, kneeled beside the box and dug a trench along each side. She stood again and pulled. This time the box shifted in its soil cocoon, but only just.

She worked the ground and pulled at the belt, worked the ground and pulled at the belt. When the soil finally released the box it came out like a cork from a bottle and she lost her balance, dropped it and took the brunt of her weight into the arm she'd flung out. She landed on one thigh hard enough to bruise. Her hair was damp against the back of her neck and she was wet under her arms. She was breathing like she'd just run up a hill. The box lay on its side, contents scattered on the ground.

When Gideon opened the lid to show her, she'd seen rows of American bills level with the top of the box. She'd assumed, with the help of his protest, that more of the same lay below. Wrong. A half-dozen packets of twenties lay in a disordered heap with a small assortment of yellowed maps and booklets. She recognized the *Geographical Journal* but hadn't seen any of the others before.

What must have once been skeins and skeins of the lichen was now, after eight months of decomposition, a wilted and musty salad at the bottom of the box. She blinked and sat back on her heels. *Tell me something true.* She closed her eyes against the vision. True? His name wasn't Gideon. His box contained only a fraction of his father's ill-gotten gains, if indeed that story had any truth to it. She had no way of knowing whether he'd ever intended a journey to the Northwest Passage. Could she trust anything he'd said? She sat with one hand on the box and the other on her belly, waiting for the slow seep of despair. It didn't come. No devastation, no outrage, no sorrow. She felt numb.

Soil clung to the sides of the box. She brushed it away and set it down beside her. The wood was damp and the words had faded but were still visible: *Pepper Sauce, Stickney and Poor.* She tipped the box to its side again and tapped the bottom, releasing the woolly plants into the hole the box had occupied. A small square of paper fluttered into the hole. She frowned and reached for it. There was writing on the back. *Jenny and Daniel, Frogtown, 1932.* In the small black and white photo was a young, pretty woman cradling a baby and smiling for the camera. Hazel stared at it until her vision blurred and then dropped it back into the box. She wiped her eyes and drank from her canteen, watched the strange, lethargic shape-shift of her belly under the fabric of her dress.

The sun had almost reached the midpoint of the sky. The off-shore breeze cooled her damp skin as she piled the bundles of cash and the booklets, guides to bushcraft and edible plants and northern fauna and birds, into the empty box. She hoisted the strap to her shoulder and stood over the hole in the ground. This gap in the soil seemed a clear admission of guilt. Henry had seen her leave; could he guess where she'd been going? She hadn't even been conscious of it herself. It was rare that anyone ventured to this part of the island, but Gideon's camp was no longer a secret when they found his body. Even if they did, even if they linked this hole in the ground to her, she'd be long gone. She laid a few branches across it and started back through the woods.

The morning chorus had subsided. A relay of stray calls, one to another, carried through the woods. Her stomach rumbled. It had to be well past noon. She let the strap slide from her shoulder, lowered the box to the ground and reached for the last saltine. The box had already started to chafe and she rubbed the sore place on her hip. Among the low foliage, the damp wooden box announced itself in no uncertain terms, its antiquated letters still visible on all sides. She would have to pack it inside something else.

She hoisted the box to the other shoulder and saw herself stepping off the train in Toronto. Then what? Who and what would greet her there? She hadn't made a single phone call since returning to Moose Factory last night. No one knew she was coming home.

AT THE SCREEN DOOR OF the residence, she listened. If any of the nurses was at home, she must be sleeping; the only sound was the constant hum of the refrigerator and the steady tock of the stove clock. She let herself in and ate a piece of buttered toast at the table. She was upstairs before she saw anyone.

"Hazel."

Sally's voice was stripped of its usual buoyancy. Hazel reached for the door to her room as Sally's door opened. "I'll be right out."

"Ruth tried to find you." Hazel turned. Sally glanced at Hazel's belly, the box, her damp hair. "She wanted to see you before she left."

"I'll find her. I'm going over to the hospital now."

"No." Sally was frowning. "She's gone. Plane left an hour ago. That cough was bad this morning. Didn't you hear it?"

Hazel shook her head. Questions seemed pointless now.

"They took her to Mountain."

Of course. She couldn't be treated here, among peers. Given the swiftness of Ruth's evacuation, Hazel assumed that Lachlan had been watching and waiting, held off only temporarily by Ruth's bullish resistance. "You're on the late shift?"

"Yes. I should go. More work with Ruth gone." She pressed her lips together. "You leave today, eh?"

"Five o'clock train."

Sally nodded and held out her small hand. Her voice was husky. "*Wachiye*. And good luck. You will need it."

"*Meegwetch*." She took Sally's hand. "I am . . . glad to have known you."

"Same here." Sally squeezed Hazel's hand and started down the stairs.

SHE DIDN'T REALLY NEED THE small exam light, but she turned it on anyway. She tried to work quickly, aware that Lachlan might be back at any moment, but she felt as plodding and cumbersome as if she'd been moving through water. When she reached for an upper shelf in the clinic room, the hard wall of her belly met the table and shortened her reach. She stepped up on a stool and opened the cabinet door, took two small glass bottles down and then took a third.

A small pile was forming in the pool of light on the table and she checked it against the list in her head: clamp, scissors, stethoscope, gauze pads and alcohol, sterilized water, glucose water and a couple of clean towels. Green soap, Dettol cream, silver nitrate, a razor and blades, a suture needle with black silk thread, sterile powder, cord tie, sanitary pads. Every item she took had to be essential. When she left Moose Factory in a half-hour for the train in Moosonee, she'd be alone, carrying everything herself. Her hands shook. In the distant reaches of her mind, she knew this was not a plan. This was lunacy. She didn't care.

She reconsidered the second towel for a few minutes and finally picked both up and dropped them into the laundry bag at her feet, which also held the pepper sauce box. Its sharp outlines were visible through the cloth bag, if anyone cared to notice. She had the sudden suspicion that she'd be allowed to leave the island carrying anything at all, so long as she left and they could be rid of her.

The rest of the supplies would have to go inside her suitcase, which was full. She opened it, took her thick sweater out, and dropped it into the dirty laundry cart. She stowed the bottles of sterile water between the flannel swaddling blankets she'd found on her bed. She wiped her eyes and wondered whether they could have been left by anyone other than Ruth. Who else would have thought to do that? She swallowed and forced her thoughts away.

Water. What she had wasn't close to being enough. She must remember to refill her canteen.

She added the rest of the supplies and closed the lid. The latches wouldn't close. For a minute she considered leaving her notebook behind, but tossed her nursing cap and uniform into the laundry cart instead. Now the suitcase lid closed easily. She fastened the latches and picked it up, pulled the drawstring on the laundry bag and looped it over her shoulder. The cord dug into her flesh. Heavy, but bearable. The walk to the dock wasn't far.

She set the case down again to open the door to the exam room and heard a familiar baritone. The door opened and Lachlan stood in the doorway with a patient behind him. He cleared his throat.

"Nurse MacPherson. Excuse me. I didn't know you were in here."

"Please come in. I'm finished." She didn't want to see him, nor could she bear to know that he could just let her leave. "I was just picking up a few things." She stood to the side to allow the patient to pass. There was no point trying to hide anything now. She'd have opened her bag to show him what she'd taken if he'd asked, though she knew he wouldn't. When the patient brushed past her, frowning, she stepped through the door, fully expecting that Lachlan would close it behind him without another word, and he did.

"Would you excuse me? I'll be right back." She heard the door open again and then felt him in the room behind her.

She stopped where she was and closed her eyes. She'd counted on his inaction and hadn't given a thought to what she might say to him. She heard his steps on the linoleum behind her, and then they stopped. Another door opened. Of course. He needed something from the other room. She took another step toward the door.

"Nurse MacPherson. Hazel."

She stopped again, but didn't turn around.

"Have you ... do you have everything you need?"

She faced him. His shoulders slumped and his head tilted to one side. His eyes were tired and his hands dug into the pockets of his lab coat. Her next breath was unsteady.

"I think so." This was no time to dissemble.

"You ... shouldn't be leaving now."

"I'm fine. I can take care of myself."

He looked at his shoes and back to her, then pulled his hand from his pocket and held out a packet of codeine. "Here," he said. "Just in case."

She took it from him and slipped it into her dress pocket. It was as much as she could expect from him, and more than she'd thought he could manage. She picked up her suitcase and walked out the door.

JUDGING BY THE LOOK ON Joseph's face, she was a sight. Before she'd left the residence she'd changed into a dry maternity smock and retied her hair, but the twist at the back of her head was slipping again and strands hung in her eyes.

He held the door for her as she left the hospital by the back entrance. When he reached for her suitcase, she gave him a warning glance. He stood slowly and let her pass. That was the last time she saw him.

The dock wasn't far but before she'd even passed the power plant she'd already needed to stop and put both bags down twice. It was four o'clock now, the time she'd arranged with Henry for the trip to Moosonee. She must keep going. She reached for the suitcase handle and met warm skin.

"Don't worry, Nurse MacPherson. I will carry it."

Henry started down the slope to the dock. The laundry bag swung and collided with his leg twice before he set it down to grasp the cloth more tightly. The wooden box would be easier to carry by the leather strap, but she couldn't bring him into this, too. He'd never mentioned what had happened in the woods at Rupert's House. She'd thrust him into a precarious place that day, not wondering or even caring how it might affect him. Never again.

At the end of the dock, the canoe waited. She held the rails as she walked the gangway. The wind had picked up since she'd gone into the hospital and the dock bucked in the waves. She noticed the crease in Henry's forehead as he lifted her two bags into the centre of the canoe. He motioned to the bow, holding his hand out for her to take. She reached for it and missed, lost her footing and landed heavily in the boat.

Henry watched her a minute. "You should stay. You should not be travelling now."

"I'm fine. Pregnancy is not an illness."

"My sister..." Henry looked at her with sad eyes. "Okay, nurse."

He reached for the docking line, untied the freight canoe and threw the rope into it. He pulled the ignition cable and they were away, skimming the south shore of Sawpit Island toward the channel to Moosonee.

She watched Moose Factory recede. As soon as they entered the channel, the hospital and the island itself would disappear behind the trees. The sun glinted on the windows of Lachlan's office, second window from the flagpole end. He would be at his desk writing, immersed in the day's work. She was sure of that.

THIRTY-TWO

IT WOULD HAVE BEEN ABSURD for me to deny it any longer: I wouldn't make Toronto and neither did I have time to return to Moose Factory. A gush of amniotic fluid woke me before the train pulled into Cochrane. I wouldn't say that I was surprised by this as much as I felt foolish for my attempts all through the pregnancy and even as I was packing medicinal supplies to deny what was so plainly about to happen. My fugitive days were over. I had been caught. For the first time in months I glimpsed the evasive and deluded woman I'd become. I was overwhelmed with a desire to apologize and beg forgiveness and explain. No more than five minutes passed between contractions.

The train smelled of stale sweat and smoked cigarettes and loneliness. I sat catching my breath and wondering how I'd conceal the mess I was in until I got myself off the train. The fact that I would give birth alone and in unfamiliar surroundings came into sharp focus. But I didn't panic. Panic is the province of those who want to preserve the status quo and have the illusion that they can. I did not. Neither did I have maternal leanings toward the child I carried. Harsh as it sounds I was less concerned about the health of the baby than I was about my own and the concern I had for my own health was miniscule. I was not distraught, I was nihilistic. I had passed into that state sometime during the previous month.

If I was grateful for anything it was for the dark smock I found in a collection of used maternity clothing Ruth had gathered from hospital remainders and donations from the Lion's Club in Toronto. It was nothing I would have selected for myself but handy in this case: the navy gabardine hid the fact that it was soaked. Nevertheless I waited for the aisles to clear before standing to collect my things. The seat was soaked too. I must have been a sight. The pinched nerve made me flinch with each step. A wooden box bumped at one hip and I carried a light blue suitcase in the other hand. Something in my demeanour must have been vaguely threatening because no one moved to help me even when I stepped off the train. The fact that I'd chosen to travel alone in my condition may have suggested mental instability. I was given a wide berth.

As much as I wanted to get up and walk away from the train, as well as from the labour itself, the physical imperative and the pool of fluid forced me to focus. If I could not decide if and when I would have this baby, I would decide how and where. I would not be a passive participant in this event and neither would I be at the mercy of the head of Lady Minto Hospital's obstetrics unit who would undoubtedly insist on conventional practices. By this point I could recite Ruth's diatribe on this inefficiency of modern hospital birthing chapter and verse and she'd never liked the man that ran obstetrics in this town. They had clashed on a few occasions. If I was to get through this I knew I could not tolerate a protracted labour. Gravity would be allowed to do its work. I would labour in my own time and in my own way. Unless I had no choice I would not go to the hospital. I knew where it was if I needed it. Cochrane was not a large town. I had been there only once to pick up supplies but I remembered its basic geography. The hospital was on the edge of town due north from the train station as the crow flies but Commando Lake stood between them. To reach it you went east and then north and then west and north. My ability to distinguish normal from abnormal labour was never in question. I'd worked with Ruth often enough. If I needed help I'd know.

I began walking away from the hospital along Railway Street with this in mind. My legs were slick but not dripping. It was June and warmer than usual. The amniotic fluid became sticky and created friction on my inner thighs. The dress was a sweaty tent and I found myself checking the position of the sun in the sky to count down the time until it set and I could be cooler. I had to stop to pin up my hair. The way it stuck to my neck felt smothering. My progress was slow but I was determined to keep walking. Each step brought me closer to the end of this. As it was my first labour I knew I didn't have to rush. Walking would be productive in more ways than one. I passed a general store and a church and a few houses. I thought that if I followed the signs toward the highway I was likely to find a cool forest to shelter in while I laboured.

All things considered this plan made sense to me. I felt I was being quite reasonable. At the hospital I'd be stuck in an airless small-windowed room and given over to the care of a doctor and a few nurses before I knew it. I'd be treated like a sick person, which I was not. What I needed was open space to pace and howl. I had refilled my canteen and bought a packet of saltines before leaving the railway station.

When I reached the junction of Railway Street and the highway I found what I wanted. Away from the shelter of the buildings in town a light breeze dried and lifted the hair off my face. On the other side of the railway tracks and across a farmer's field was a copse of trees. Water glimmered at the far end of it. As I stepped off the road I heard the crunch of tires on gravel and the slowing of a car. Someone called to me but I didn't answer. I didn't want to be engaged in conversation or to be questioned or to have to explain what I was doing. I needed a rest stop but felt I ought to wait until the car pulled away. I didn't wish to give the signal that I needed help. I watched the car until it was a pinpoint on the horizon then sat down on the box and drank from the canteen.

The field I walked across was fallow and the grass had grown to knee height. It must have rained recently because the grass was damp. It felt cool on my legs and I was thinking that it would feel good to lie down in it when I noticed the outline of a silo. It had no roof. Its walls were thick and uneven and by the size of the trees that partially obscured it I guessed that it might have been standing a hundred years or more. Its walls would hold moisture and the interior would be cool. It could draw heat from my skin.

I had found what I wanted. There would be no interference here. I could hear the soothing music of a nearby river. I had everything I needed in my bag. Ruth frequently admonished panicked birthing mothers that women had been doing this since time immemorial and I heard her voice now.

I had a flash of yearning for her infectious laughter and her opinionated diatribes and her unshakable presence. When I found myself wondering if I'd ever see her again I sent my brain to chase down the names of the hormones that pulsed through my veins and their effects on my body. Oxytocin, prolactin, adrenaline. Contraction, lactation, action. I repeated them aloud in time with my steps. It seemed important to cultivate objectivity especially as

I had begun to feel the first wavering of my resolve. That would not do. I would take what these hormones had to give but prevent them from running roughshod over me. Emotions had to be left out of it. They would only make me soft and interfere with my ability to engage my logical brain. I needed to be my own nurse. I wanted to be my own nurse.

I noticed that my pace had picked up and I forced myself to slow down. The adrenaline was kicking in. Burning it out this early in labour would be unwise. I'd need it later. I touched the wall of the silo just as the contractions reached a crescendo: they had become acute rather than merely chronic. The sound of my first cry of pain was unnerving and I tried to contain myself. I transitioned to hard labour bending myself away from the contractions. This was before I realized how counterproductive that strategy was and finally gave over to it. I didn't care if the woods echoed with my cries or if it seemed that I had lost control. I couldn't have come to that conclusion if Ruth had been at my side telling me what to do.

The silo had only a crude low opening that I had to crawl through on hands and knees. I pushed the suitcase and the pepper sauce box through first. As soon as I was on all fours the pressure on my lower back lifted as though I'd shed a heavy pack. I knew now why Ruth had counselled birthing women to do this and I knew I'd found the right place.

I stayed on all fours until the light inside the silo began to fade. I piled the suitcase on top of the box to keep nocturnal animals out, laid a blanket on the ground and found my flashlight. I called out once, a name, and not again.

I COULD LIE AND SAY that I'd forgotten what I drew, but there would be little point. I have drawn that shape with my hand and in my mind over and over again through the years. You saw the carving above my door. I'd never fancied myself an artist prior to this and still didn't, even under circumstances that could be argued were unique in every way imaginable and might give way to this sort of expression. From an artistic standpoint it doesn't offer much beyond rudimentary shapes anyway. It was nothing like the drawings in my notebooks. You might think it was a charm but if so it should have been most potent when I first drew it after she was born.

If you check the pepper sauce box for a false bottom you'll find a copy there. I was feeling sentimental when it was time to leave the silo but I couldn't find blank paper so you'll see that I drew it on the back of a menu from the train. It was ridiculous to think that I might forget the shape it took or the body memory of shaping it that night. I see the ghosted image of it when I close my eyes as though my retinas were branded with it.

It was a spontaneous gesture. I wasn't seeking to commemorate anything but the desire to draw on the silo wall was an imperative like contractions or afterbirth. By that point my emotional landscape was unrecognizable anyway so what was one more peculiar impulse? Birthing hormones had seen to it that I was not despondent but nothing could have surprised me at that point. I had been in advanced labour and felt compelled to walk away from the hospital. I had heard my own solitary voice swirl around me like smoke and lift up and out of the top of the silo. Behind me was a child that belonged to me. My child. Mine alone. Any filters that might have caught stray impulses in the past had gone missing or disappeared altogether.

I had crawled back out through the low door and tried to stand. It was too soon after my labour but the silo wall held me up. The sky was an inky blanket of stars that enveloped me. I was insignificant and I was omnipotent. I was alone and I was in the company of every single being in the universe. It turned out that Ruth was right: the female body knows what to do, and when. It does not need to be coached or cajoled or coddled. It only needs to be kept company. I felt for the cord and held it through that one last wave that rode my body.

I wasn't squeamish. I had seen my share of blood in my nursing life but never that much and never coming from my own body. Even with the warm, sticky sensation on my feet it felt like a hallucination. I could feel myself swoon. In an effort to summon the necessary logic to hold it off I attempted to recall the amount of blood that should be lost in a normal delivery. I had a fleeting impulse to gather everything up and drag myself across the field so I could wave down a car and go to the hospital but then I saw the remains of the campfire and everything came clear.

The silo wall was an ocean of cool against my overheated skin. I leaned a wrist against it first but by the time I had finished drawing my whole body bent toward it. If anyone had chanced upon me at that moment it would have been difficult to explain: I was at the edge of a small forest, alone, naked, bleeding, collapsed against an old silo. I was clutching a piece of charcoal and there was a crude drawing by my own hand on the wall behind me. No one came and I pulled myself together as we do when resources fail to appear. The baby might have made a noise just then.

My daughter. She had fair hair and milk-white skin like her father. Like you. After you were born my sister showed me the photograph she'd taken of her new granddaughter. I couldn't look at it without thinking of Gideon and my own child. Our child. I had so little time with her. I wish you could have seen her beautiful rosy pink mouth.

I put her to my breast and then wrapped her and laid her on a blanket and had just started to fall asleep when my body remembered what it had left to do. I had to go outside. She was still sleeping when I crawled back in. I collapsed into a cave of exhausted sleep beside her.

I don't know how long I slept and couldn't immediately orient myself when I woke though I did feel a generalized anxiety as though I had forgotten something. I was on my back looking at the sky through the silo's missing roof and trying to make sense of the flutter of leaves overhead and the distant sound of running water. My mouth was dry. My head felt brittle and the light sliced like razors though I didn't recognize the symptoms as dehydration.

As soon as I moved my legs and felt the aches in unfamiliar places it all came back. I turned my head and caught sight of the tiny bundle beside me on the ground. She seemed to sleep. I heard Ruth's voice counselling new mothers that babies should be allowed one long sleep and beyond that ought to be awakened for feeding every three hours. I couldn't find my watch and had a vague memory of removing it with my clothing. Judging from the angle of the sunlight it was mid-morning. I did a quick calculation and realized that we had slept at least ten hours.

Her back faced me. I had laid her on her side and she was in that position still. I lay there a moment or two willing her body to move with the rise and fall of breath and hoped that in not seeing it I was just overfocusing. She was less than an arm's length away but I was afraid to touch her in case I might consign her to earth that way. Breathe, I kept thinking. Breathe.

I finally understood after the positive test at the Quebec san. My pregnancy had masked a reaction over the previous nine months and owing to it I had also been exempt from x-rays. Once I was admitted to the hospital I couldn't avoid a complete physical exam, which of course revealed my recent pregnancy. The examining doctor filled the silence with a series of possibilities as I tried to find my voice. Was the child born healthy? I closed my eyes when he said congenital TB. How could I have given my child a disease I didn't yet know I was carrying? I saw his next question coming from a long way off but still couldn't avoid the full force of its impact. Where was the child now? Where indeed.

Is the silo still visible? A few years later I thought I might go back, but I never did. What would I have done if it was gone? But now I'm certain it remains. The progress of the town could not have been so significant.

You could go, Jude. One day what I'm saying will get through and you will hear me. You could take the train to Cochrane and follow the station road until you reach the junction of the highway. The field is a little beyond the junction and the silo just inside the woods at the far side of it. Walk closer to be sure you don't miss it. You'll know it by my drawing, an arc sheltering a sphere. I do think it's possible that out of reach of the wind and the rain all these years it has endured.

If you crawl through the low door you'll find a small mound in the ground inside. Take care you don't disturb it. This is important. She could not have come with me. It must be clear to you by now that I could not have taken her with me. I trusted the stars. That place was right for her. It was late June and the soil was warm when I laid her down.

I keep trying to reconstruct the exact expression on her face but at this point I know I can't tease out what I've laid in as insulation over the years from what I actually saw. I'm content with that. Every history is a reconstruction. But I do know that the rules of grace clearly state that infant death is the province of angels and as such can only be a thing of beauty. I don't doubt that her face was relaxed in death and wore an attitude of peace that signified her release from gravity. This last I know is true because there is no other explanation for the pale shell her body had become, the way it had the weight and frailty of a bird's and not the warm squirming density I felt when I held her after she was born. Before I even saw her face I knew she was gone. I am certain that there was no ugliness in it. She was like her father that way.

Let us live and love,
not listening to old men's talk.
Suns will rise and set
long after our little light
has gone away to darkness.
Kiss me again and again.
Let me kiss you a hundred times,
a thousand more, again a thousand,
without rest, losing count, so no
one can speak of us and say
they know the number of our kisses.

– Catullus

ACKNOWLEDGEMENTS

At the beginning of this road is Dr. Barclay McKone, MD, (1914–2006), a pioneer in the field of tuberculosis treatment in Canada, in whose story I found the seeds of my own. I am privileged to have known him. I'm also grateful for the chance to know Lorna McKone, whose intelligence and fortitude were a source of strength to him and whose grace continues to inspire me.

For their generosity of time, medical expertise and patience with my endless questions, I'm deeply grateful to northern nurses J. Karen Scott and Heather Clayton, and to TB specialists Dr. Michael Gardam and Dr. Pam Orr.

For research assistance, thank you to librarians extraordinaire Gian Medves at the University of Toronto and John Tagg at West Park Healthcare Centre (formerly the Toronto Free Hospital for Consumptive Poor). Thank you to Dr. Warren Ober for King Arthur mythology, to Mike Pezak for nickel carving expertise and to Master Falconer Matt Lieberknecht.

I am grateful to many in Moose Factory. At the hospital, Susan McLeod, Joe Cheechoo and Dr. Murray Trussler were invaluable. Former TB nurses Carol Hennessey, Aggie Corston and Daisy Turner shared their stories. For hospitality, thank you to Chief Randy Kapashesit, Greg Williams, Burt Wapachee and Clarence Trapper.

For financial and moral support, I am indebted to the Canada Council for the Arts, the Ontario Arts Council and the Toronto

Arts Council. Thank you to Chrissy and Kyle at Spark Box Studio in Picton for providing a quiet, art-filled residency.

Thank you to the good people at Wolsak and Wynn, especially my superb editor Paul Vermeersch and publisher Noelle Allen, for believing in this book. Deep gratitude to my agents Shaun Bradley and Meghan MacDonald, who had faith in this book from the beginning.

For lighting the path and for camaraderie and conversation, I'm indebted to Kathryn, Alissa, Miriam, Marcia, Jared and Guy. For reading early drafts of this novel, I'm especially grateful to Stephanie, Nate, Brian and Joanna. Thank you to all of my family and friends for moral support. Special thanks to Mary, who regularly sent useful pieces of research my way; to Kate and Zak, webmasters extraordinaire; and to Andrew, who helped choreograph a pivotal scene.

My children, Liam and Emma, thank you for respecting the sign on my study door and for giving me a reason. This book is for Drew, always and always, my tireless first reader, who shares this life with me and showed me where to watch the falcons in downtown Toronto.

NOTES

This book is a work of imagination that relied on research for historical and medical accuracy. Dr. Barclay McKone's papers "Moose Factory Indian Hospital," "Eastern Arctic Medical and X-Ray Survey 1955" and "Rehabilitation for Indians and Eskimo" were an invaluable genesis for this novel and they are housed at the Thomas Fisher Rare Book Library at the University of Toronto. Some of the other works I consulted deserve special mention. For social histories of tuberculosis, I can recommend *A Long Way from Home: The Tuberculosis Epidemic among the Inuit* by Pat Sandiford Grygier; *The Weariness, The Fever, and the Fret* by Katherine Mc-Cuaig and *Living in the Shadow of Death: Tuberculosis and the Social Experience of Illness in American History* by Sheila M. Rothman. For a fascinating study of eccentricity and madness, I appreciated *Eccentrics: A Study of Sanity and Strangeness* by David Weeks and Jamie James. For records of other northern adventurers, *Intukweensquaw of James Bay* by Irene McNulty Culver; *Into Canada's North: "Because it was There"* by Mildred Young Hubbert; *Northern Nurses* volumes 1, 2 and 3, edited by J. Karen Scott and Joan Kieser; and "The Conquest of the North West Passage: the Arctic Voyages of the *St. Roch*, 1940–1944" in *The Geographical Journal* by Henry A. Larsen, RCMP.

On northern Canadian languages, I appreciated *Arctic Languages: An Awakening* by Dirmid R. F. Collins. For assistance with the Inuktitut spoken in Nunavik, I'm grateful to Dr. Christopher

Trott in the native studies program at the University of Manitoba, Leena Evic at the Piruvik Centre in Iqaluit and Caroline Palliser in Nunavik. Thanks to Daisy Turner at the elder lodge in Moose Factory for the gift of the dictionary she wrote, *Moose Factory Cree*, and to Joseph Boyden for helping me find Greg Spence, who also lent a hand with Moose Cree spelling.

The song lyrics sung by Hazel on page 178 come from "Land of the Silver Birch," a traditional Canadian folk song based on a poem of the same name by Pauline Johnson.

Excerpts of this novel first appeared in *Descant* (Summer 2012) and *Ars Medica* (Spring 2013).

Ewan Whyte's beautiful translation of the Catullus poem I used as an epigraph appears in *Catullus* (Mosaic, 2004), and I am grateful for his permission to use it.

CHRISTINE FISCHER GUY's fiction has appeared in journals across Canada and has been nominated for the Journey Prize. She reviews for the *Globe and Mail*, contributes to Ryeberg.com and themillions.com and teaches creative writing at the School for Continuing Studies at the University of Toronto. She is also an award-winning journalist. She has lived and worked in London, England, and now lives in Toronto.